TWO WRONGS

MORGAN MANDEL

Hard Shell Word Factory

Dedication

Special thanks to my husband, Paul, who cooked his own meals and watched television alone many nights while I worked on this book. Also to my good friend, Jeanne Rybarczyk, who introduced me to Pat White. If Pat had not taken me to my first Chicago-North RWA meeting, this book would not have been possible. Lastly, thanks go out to Deb Rittle, Mary Micheff, Jennifer Stevenson, Laurie Brown and Christina Fixemer for all their help and encouragement.

Trade Paperback ISBN: 0-7599-
Published February 2006

eBook ISBN: 0-7599-4062-2
Published January 2006

Hard Shell Word Factory
PO Box 161
Amherst Jct. WI 54407
books@hardshell.com
www.hardshell.com

All characters in this book have no existence outside the imagination of the author, and have no relation whatever to anyone bearing the same name or names. These characters are not even distantly inspired by any individual known or unknown to the author, and all incidents are pure invention.

Prologue

February 12, 1996

"WHAT'S GOING ON down there?"

Danny Callaway heard the question, but couldn't answer. His brain froze in the cold February air as he stared at the broken rag doll that had once been his sister, Mary Alice.

In his sixteen years, he'd never witnessed death first-hand. Until now.

Mary Alice's still form lay sprawled against the alley's cement. Her head stuck out at a crazy angle like the girl in the *Exorcist* movie.

Hoping against hope, he checked for a pulse at her neck. Nothing. He tried her wrist, but got the same result.

His mind was all jumbled. All he could think of were stupid things, like how he'd heard guys call Mary Alice a prude because she closed the top buttons on her blouse and never wore mini-skirts.

She'd sure be embarrassed not to have anything on at all. Someone had to cover her up and make her look presentable. Maybe Mom could help.

But how could he tell her? A sob tore through his throat. He clamped his mouth shut to keep the bile from rushing out.

Through the shock and pain, one thing remained clear. Kevin would pay for this.

Chapter One
Danny

THE TRIAL BEGAN, yet it couldn't be happening. Mary Alice couldn't be dead. It had been six months since Danny had discovered his sister's still form on that cold February night, yet he still couldn't believe he'd never see her again. She was family, a part of his life. It didn't seem right being without her. If only she'd come back, but that was impossible.

Slamming home that fact was the prosecutor, Bill Rosenberg, who held up a photo. "With the court's permission, may I present Exhibit One, a picture taken at the crime scene?"

No, Danny wanted to shout, knowing firsthand what the photo contained. His heart beat fast as the picture made its rounds. He clenched his fingers to keep from snatching it away. His sister's memory was sacred, yet these people eyed her lying exposed and defenseless.

He watched helplessly. Finally, the photograph reached the end of the jury box, where a frail, bent-over lady cupped it in her palm. Her eyes filled with tears. Danny blinked rapidly, reminding himself that men don't cry. He turned his attention to his parents. Mom had no such compunctions. Her shoulders shook. Tears streamed down her face. Dad leaned over to comfort her.

Watching their anguish made matters worse, but Danny wouldn't cave in. He'd never break down in front of his sister's killer. Stone-faced, he concentrated on what the prosecutor was saying. "I'd like to call Officer Dugan."

The officer testified that he'd been first on the scene.

"Can you describe the position of the body?"

...the body. Danny swallowed hard at the image conjured up in his mind.

The prosecutor bore on relentlessly, digging for details, inquiring about the state of rigor mortis, the head wounds, the color of Mary Alice's lips. The image deepened.

That's my sister. She's a person, not a thing, Danny wanted to shout.

The subject was exhaustively pursued. The officer answered each question matter-of-factly. Easy for him. It wasn't his sister he was talking about. Each new detail drove a fresh spike into Danny's heart.

It took forever for the line of questioning to change.

"Officer Dugan, I understand you exercised a search warrant. What was it you found at the defendant's home?"

"Hair strands from the defendant's brush, a book of matches, a pair of gym shoes..."

The list was long. Dear God, let it be in there somewhere—the necessary ingredient to convict Kevin.

"The items mentioned are State's Exhibits One through Twenty. Thank you. That will be all."

For some inane reason, Danny's attention drifted to the bald spot on the prosecutor's head. The fluorescent light gleamed on it, casting an eerie glow, reminding Danny of how Otto Meyer's porch light had shone down and illuminated Mary Alice's still body.

He shivered, lost in painful remembrance. He had to be strong. His sister counted on him. He would not break down. Staring straight ahead, he pretended not to understand the dreadful implications as the officer spoke about sexual assault.

The prosecutor called up a forensic pathologist who verified his written reports about semen, torn tissue, and bruises. Did everyone have to hear this? As the questioning resumed, Danny tried to zone the man out, but couldn't.

A lab technician stepped up to the stand.

"We examined blood samples extracted from Kevin Green's shoe and found them to be O-negative," the man said.

"Is that Mr. Green's blood type?" Rosenberg asked.

"No. His blood tested B-negative."

"What about the victim's?"

"Mary Alice Callaway's was O-negative."

"Thank you."

Up to this point, slick-haired Eric Dominski, the public defender, hadn't said much. Suddenly his slim body jerked into high gear. Gesturing wildly, with arms outstretched, Dominski debated about the blood, saying Kevin could have walked by, stepped on it and not have committed the crime.

"Wasn't Mary Alice Callaway's blood on her brother's clothes? Didn't he say he'd discovered her body? Could he be the one who killed her?" Dominski shot out.

Danny glared at him. Rosenberg had warned him not to get rattled by the public defender. The guy was a grandstander, who, due to a backlog of cases, tended to ignore his homework and make up for it by trying to manipulate the jury's emotions.

Danny knew this, yet it was hard to keep calm when he was being accused of something so base.

The prosecutor ignored the theatrics and fired back, mentioning that cortex pigment granules were found on the victim's body. Danny frowned. What was he talking about?

"Could you repeat that in layman's terms?" Rosenberg asked.

The man explained that pieces of hair seemingly identical to Kevin Green's were picked up off the body.

The public defender rolled his eyes, then asked if other hair types were found.

"Yes, that of Danny Callaway, as well as Larry Murphy, the boyfriend."

With a smirk, Dominski pounced. "It could've been any of them. And since the DNA samples have conveniently disappeared out of the evidence room and the body has since been cremated, that leaves it all wide open, doesn't it? No further questions."

Dominski was a sicko. Danny's neck grew hot. His stomach churned like a runaway washing machine. He was no pervert. Mary Alice was his sister. He'd only found her, that's all.

Nosy Meyer had watched from the window when Danny had taken out the garbage. He knew. If only Meyer had been awake when the murder had taken place. Then Kevin wouldn't look so smug.

And what about Larry? Danny had never cared for the guy, but that was beside the point. Mary Alice's boyfriend didn't deserve to be fingered. He had to be ready to explode.

As if to answer Danny's questions, the prosecutor called up Larry Murphy. Larry's face was pale and bathed in sweat as he approached the witness stand. When he got there, he sat at the edge of the chair, as if ready to bolt. He licked his lips and shifted his weight. Behind black-framed glasses, his eye movements darted back and forth between the prosecutor and the doorway. From the way he acted, anyone would think he was the one on trial.

"Lawrence, can you recall what you and the victim did the day of the murder?"

Choking out the words, Larry said that he and Mary Alice had discussed getting married after graduation. On the day in question they'd gotten carried away and ended up making love in the back seat of his car. Unfortunately, there would be no wedding.

As he testified, his eyes shifted, never quite meeting the

prosecutor's, almost as if he were ashamed.

The thought of his sister having sex with Larry, even though he was her boyfriend, was a little strange. Not long before her murder, Danny had overheard Mary Alice tell Mom she'd definitely walk down the aisle as a virgin. Had she loved Larry enough to give in? It was so unlike the stubborn, old-fashioned sister he knew.

Danny glanced at his father. The vein on his forehead had grown larger. Mary Alice had been his princess. He'd shielded her from everything, even taking out the garbage. The idea of his unwed daughter doing the dirty deed obviously didn't sit well with him. Dad's hands clenched and unclenched, like he wanted to strangle Larry.

Before that could happen, Larry was excused. Danny followed him with his eyes, still trying to understand what Mary Alice had seen in him. Larry was short. His hair was stringy. He was creepy and not at all special. How could he have convinced Mary Alice to do it? Was it because he was an underdog? His sister had always had a weakness for lost causes.

There was no time to dwell on it. Danny's name was called next. It was his turn. He'd anticipated and dreaded this moment. As he brushed past his mother, she gave him a small smile of encouragement. He knew how much that gesture cost her.

Everyone's eyes were on him. On suddenly weak legs, Danny wobbled up to the wooden chair. After he was sworn in, he sank down, but immediately straightened up and planted his feet. This was important. He dare not blow it.

Rosenberg began. "Danny, can you describe the relationship between your sister and the defendant?"

"Well, Mary Alice had been going out with Larry Murphy since they were freshmen. Then this year, when they were seniors, Kevin Green started hanging around her, too. She told me she didn't want to hurt his feelings, since he was a new guy at school and all, and had this dyslexia problem."

Danny stared straight at Kevin. His green eyes looked wounded. He didn't want everyone to know about his disability. Too bad. He hadn't spared Mary Alice. There was no reason to feel sorry for him.

The prosecutor continued. "Can you tell me, did you ever witness the defendant making threats to your sister?"

"Yes."

"Please elaborate."

"On the day she was killed, I came back from school and found them shouting at each other in front of our apartment. Kevin was ordering Mary Alice to go to the Snowflake Prom with him. She told him she was going with Larry. Kevin said he'd see her dead first."

A loud gasp echoed through the courtroom. Danny hesitated.

Rosenberg prompted, "Go on."

"I told him to lay off. She could go with whoever she wanted. He told me to butt out. Then old Otto Meyer from the first floor yelled that we were too loud and he'd call the cops. Kevin left."

"Thank you, Danny. As the court can see, the defendant has displayed ample motive for committing the crimes of which he's been accused. Unfortunately, due to his infirmities, the first floor neighbor, Otto Meyer, cannot be present today to testify. I am introducing as Exhibit Number Five, the transcript of his deposition. Mr. Meyer has stated he heard the entire conversation among the now deceased, the defendant and Danny Callaway. He corroborates Danny Callaway's testimony."

The district attorney paused. Danny knew what was coming next. They'd gone over it a million times. His heart lurched in anticipation.

Rosenberg proceeded. "Now, Danny, I know this is painful, but can you please describe what happened later that evening."

Danny took a deep breath. He didn't want to remember, but he had to. He must be brave. It was his duty. He began slowly, as if by delaying the process the outcome might be different.

"Dad was still driving on his bus route. Mom and I were the only ones home. We thought Mary Alice was at her friend Donna's house. When it got late, we weren't worried, figuring they were tied up talking about prom stuff. Anyway, it was during the ten o'clock news that Mom made me take out the garbage. I took the back stairs to the alley."

The hard part was next. His throat closed up. He couldn't talk about it. He just couldn't.

Rosenberg handed him a glass of water. "When you're ready, please continue."

Danny swallowed hard. Dear God, he didn't want to think about it. He forced himself. Pain ripped through his chest and head, making him want to bellow.

He described step-by-terrible-step exactly what had happened. In a different lifetime, he'd rushed downstairs to take out the garbage, afraid he'd miss the basketball highlights.

Once again he discovered his sister's still form. He bent over to find her pulse, but there wasn't one. His body trembled from shock and cold, just as before. He couldn't think. To the accompaniment of Otto Meyer's raving on about noise in the alley, he turned and ran up the stairs.

After he'd finished the account, Danny felt as if he'd run a marathon. He was out of breath. The room spun. Vaguely he heard a murmur swell through the courtroom.

"Thank you, Danny," the prosecutor said, then sat down, abandoning Danny to the mercies of the public defender.

Danny had almost managed to pull himself together when Eric Dominski leaned over the stand.

"Danny, I sympathize with you. It had to have been devastating to find your sister like that."

The compassion in the man's voice brought a fresh spate of tears to Danny's blue eyes. He swiped them away with his hand. He had to be strong. He had to watch for tricks.

The public defender continued. "Young man, it's a terrible fact that your sister was brutally murdered. I agree that punishment must be meted to the wrongdoer. However, in achieving that end, we must exhibit caution. We must not inflict harm on an innocent party. Kevin Green is that innocent party."

Danny raised his eyebrows. Kevin deserved what he got.

"You seem startled. Well, what I'm saying is, I don't doubt that you witnessed an argument between Kevin Green and your sister. However, a spat over a prom date is no motive for raping and killing anyone. Wouldn't you agree?"

"Objection, leading the witness."

"Sustained."

"Let me rephrase that. Danny, is an argument over a prom a valid reason for killing someone?"

"Maybe not for a normal person. Only for a monster like Kevin Green."

"Please answer the question yes or no, Danny."

If only he could wipe that smart-alecky look off of Dominski's face.

"No," Danny spat out.

Glancing past Dominski, Danny fastened his attention on the true object of his hatred. Kevin balefully returned his gaze. The evilness in the sea green eyes hovered like an obscene presence. Couldn't the public defender sense it or didn't he care?

Dominski's next words showed how oblivious he was. "Danny, you're under duress. It's understandable that you're not making sense. I wouldn't think clearly either if it were my sister.

"Get to the point, counsel," the judge broke in, frowning.

"Yes, Your Honor. Let me clarify things. The fight happening the same day as the murder was just a coincidence, nothing more. Someone with a far greater motive was at work here."

Rosenberg jumped up. "Objection. Conjecture."

"Your Honor, if I may exercise some leeway to prove my point?"

"If it's germane."

"Thank you."

The prosecutor turned back to Danny. "You attribute Kevin's dyslexia as the reason your sister was kind to him. Instead, could it be that she saw past his disability and knew he had more brains than anyone gave him credit for? Also, let me add, because Kevin is intelligent, wouldn't he have known a rejection over a prom date is no reason to commit rape and murder?"

Danny couldn't contain his rage. The words spilled out. "You're wrong," he shouted. "His mind's twisted. He killed my sister."

Judge Frederick banged the gavel. "I'll have no outbursts in this court."

"No further questions."

Danny fumed in frustration.

"Counselor, would you like to redirect?" the judge asked the district attorney.

Rosenberg nodded. "Tell me, son, what's it like being without your sister?"

Danny had no time to prepare himself. The pain rushed out, filling his being. "It's hell," he gasped, before breaking into giant sobs.

Rosenberg rested the State's case.

THE NEXT MORNING it was the defense's turn. Dominski called up Kevin Green, who was so tall he dwarfed everyone in the room, except Danny. Otherwise, he appeared ordinary, with his well-groomed, straight, sandy hair, his conservative tan suit and his pale blue oxford shirt. What gave him away was the vacant look in his eyes. Didn't he have a conscience?

Dominski glanced at the paper in his hand. "According to the coroner's report, which is labeled defendant's Exhibit Number One, the crime occurred between eight and ten the evening of Friday, February 12th, 1996. Mr. Green, can you tell me exactly where you were at that time?"

"I was at home watching television. I was there all night."

"Do you have any witnesses to that effect?"

"Yes. My Dad was with me."

"Then it's obvious you couldn't have committed the crimes alleged by the prosecutor."

As he nodded, Kevin's face assumed a choirboy expression. Danny wanted to smack him in the mouth.

"Were you so upset about not going to the prom with Mary Alice Callaway that you raped and murdered her?"

"No. I didn't even like her that much. Everyone knows I can get any girl I want." He gave a short laugh. "The prom was no big deal anyway."

Liar! Kevin had been furious with Mary Alice. Danny darted a look at the jurors. Could they tell Kevin was acting? Their impassive faces gave nothing away.

Rosenberg advanced. "Come now, Mr. Green, do you really expect us to believe you were at home all evening?"

Eric Dominski jumped to his feet. "I object. Badgering the defendant."

"Objection sustained."

The prosecutor continued. "Tell me, Mr. Green, what programs did you watch?"

Kevin mumbled, "I don't remember. It was a long time ago."

"How convenient. The truth is you don't remember because you weren't there."

Dominski started to rise, but Rosenberg sped on. "Mr. Green, isn't it true that on the evening in question, you waited alongside Mary Alice Callaway's apartment building, dragged her into the alley, raped her, smashed her head into the ground and killed her?"

"Objection!"

"No!"

Dominski and Kevin both shouted at once.

Kevin's face flushed scarlet. Sweat dripped from his forehead. "I didn't do it," he said.

At that, Danny gripped the arms of his chair to keep from rising. He had to stay put. If a mistrial were called, Kevin could go free. He had to trust Rosenberg.

"Let me ask you this, Mr. Green. How did Mary Alice Callaway's blood get on your shoe? How did your hair get on her body?

"I don't know." Kevin looked wildly at Dominski, who shook his head.

"No further questions."

Danny clenched his fists as Kevin walked off the stand.

The defense attorney called Kevin's father, Derek Green. Looking a bit lost, he shuffled up. The frayed cuffs of his shirt sleeves stuck out from under his shrunken coat. He'd probably bought his clothes at a secondhand shop. Danny felt sorry for him. The man obviously didn't own much. What's worse, he had a murderer for a son. How did it feel to know that? Or did he believe Kevin was innocent?

Dominski's questioning resumed. "Mr. Green, were you at home with your son the entire evening of February 12th, 1996?"

"That's right."

"That'll be all."

Rosenberg sidled up. "So, Mr. Green, no one was there except you and your son. Is that correct?"

Derek Green nodded. A brief, sly look crossed his face. The man was hiding something. Danny's pity for him fled.

"Sir, you do realize you're under oath. If I were to prove you were lying, you could be sentenced for perjury."

"Objection. Badgering."

"Sustained."

"Now Mr. Green, you're a decent father and love your son, don't you?"

Derek blinked, then whispered, "Yes."

Bill Rosenberg withdrew a book of matches from the exhibits and placed it on the witness stand in front of Derek. "Do you love your son so much that you'd go to jail for him?"

The man shrank away from the matchbook.

"What's the matter, Mr. Green? Does Exhibit Number Three look familiar?"

Derek glanced sadly at his son, turned back again and nodded.

"That's right. It should. Officer Dugan found this matchbook in your apartment. As you're aware, it's from Big Sam's Pub. Now, what if I were to say I can produce two witnesses who swear they saw you there the night of the murder? Would you still insist you'd stayed home?

"All right, Mr. Green. Once more, I'd like to know. Were you away from home at any time that night?"

"I guess I forgot." Derek's voice came out softly. "I did leave for a few drinks."

"Now we're getting somewhere. What time were you gone?"

"I don't remember."

"How convenient. Thank you. That will be all."

Kevin's Dad stumbled off the stand, with his face set in a grimace.

Danny glanced at Kevin who frowned and bit his lip. Eric Dominski's mouth sagged. Danny smiled to himself. Rosenberg was right. Dominski had not done his homework.

The public defender shrugged his shoulders and said, "The defense rests," as if nothing had happened.

Was he bluffing, or was his ego the size of a football field?

In a solemn tone, the district attorney began his summation. "There you have it. The defendant, Kevin Green, as witnessed by the victim's brother, announced his intent to kill Mary Alice Callaway. The motive has been established. Blood stains, hair strands, and clinical evidence point to the defendant's guilt. Also, the defendant's alibi was a fabrication. He claims he was at home with his father the night of the murder, yet his father wasn't there the entire time and can't vouch for him.

"Not that it would matter because Kevin Green was not at home that night. Instead, he was wreaking vengeance on Mary Alice Callaway, a hapless young woman who'd made the mistake of saying no to him. Mary Alice was never allowed to attend the prom she'd been looking forward to. She'll never be able to do anything again because her life and her breath were snuffed out by the defendant, Kevin Green.

"Folks, look closely at the defendant. On the outside he appears normal and decent, but peel off that civilized veneer and what emerges is a dangerous and vicious animal. The jury has no alternative but to find Kevin Green guilty of aggravated criminal sexual assault and the far greater crime of first degree murder."

Wow, the prosecutor sounded convincing. He had to win. Dominski couldn't do better, could he?

The public defender stood up to give it a shot. "Ladies and gentlemen. First, don't be swayed by the heartrending photos of the victim. We all know what dastardly crimes were committed upon Mary Alice Callaway, but that doesn't mean they were done by Kevin Green. I have proven the clinical evidence is far from conclusive.

"Second, do not allow the prosecutor's persuasive words to cloud your judgment. Kevin, an understandably frightened youth, enlisted his father's services to produce a false alibi. That does not mean he committed the heinous acts of rape and murder for which he is charged. I repeat, he merely told a lie—nothing more, nothing less.

"Third, he had no motive to rape or kill the victim. He did not do so.

"Ladies and gentlemen, this young man's life is in your hands. I warn you to be absolutely certain of your verdict. If you mistakenly pronounce Kevin Green guilty, you'll turn him into a victim. He'll be convicted of rape and murder, while the actual perpetrator runs free. Kevin Green does not deserve to have his life ruined because of one small lie."

What hogwash. Of course Kevin did it. Lying was just another sin on the creep's list of crimes. Stuck-up Dominski had a lot of nerve to stand up there and pretend Kevin was innocent.

The judge reminded the jury of their instructions. Danny watched as the jurors filed out. Some frowned. Others shook their heads. Their confusion worried him. Were they gullible enough to believe Dominski's words? Did they think Kevin was guilty only of lying?

Larry Murphy watched also. His face looked sickly white, which was understandable. After all, in a few months he would have been Mary Alice's husband. Like Danny, he probably wanted to murder Kevin.

Danny looked back at his parents. Mom's eyes were red, her mascara tear-smudged. Dad rubbed her hand, then spoke to Danny. "Well, son, it'll be over soon, for good or bad."

He admired his dad, who was a giant not only in size. He was a true man, never shirking from his duties, driving for hours on end with constant back pain to provide for his family. Someone he'd sacrificed for had been brutally murdered, yet he kept his composure.

Danny could only follow his example. He sat stoically, even as the room's air conditioning weakened and the temperature climbed. His shirt stuck to his back. Time dragged on.

The suspense and heat wore at him. Had his story been convincing enough? Had the jurors believed him? They had to. It was the truth.

What would they decide? During yesterday's briefing, Rosenberg had explained the choices: assault, aggravated criminal sexual assault, first degree murder, second degree murder and manslaughter. If Kevin got first degree, he'd fry. The jury had to pick that.

By the end of the afternoon, the jury had still not returned. Court recessed, then reconvened the next morning. The waiting continued into the afternoon. Danny sat uncomplaining, thinking of his sister, hoping her killer would not escape.

Finally, he heard what he'd been listening for: the drumming sound of footsteps approaching. The door swung open. His heart thumped madly. Soon he'd know.

With inscrutable expressions, the members of the jury filed into the box. What had they decided?

Judge Frederick nodded to the man with the big nose. "Mr. Foreman, has the jury reached a verdict?"

A hand clutched Danny's windpipe as the paper moved from the judge to the court clerk. Judge Frederick said, "Would the defendant, Kevin Green, please rise."

Kevin stumbled upright. With a swagger, Dominski rose beside him.

"Please read the verdict."

Through the loud roaring in his ears, Danny could barely make out the words, "We, the jury, find the defendant guilty of aggravated criminal sexual assault."

Mom gasped. Dad put his arm around her waist. The courtroom remained deathly still. What about the murder conviction?

The clerk continued. "For the unlawful death of Mary Alice Callaway, we find the defendant guilty of second degree murder."

Danny's heart plummeted. Second degree! There must be a mistake. It should be first degree. Someone should say something.

No one did.

An acrid taste filled his mouth. His entire body felt raw and battered, as if he'd been the one assaulted. He turned toward his parents. Dad's features were etched in pain. Mom's face was gray. The nightmare hammered itself home again. Mary Alice had died. So should Kevin. Danny wanted to scream.

Larry Murphy looked relieved. The corners of his mouth were turned up, as if he were holding back a smile. Didn't he understand? Kevin had been convicted, but he wouldn't get the death penalty.

Danny frowned and focused his eyes where they belonged. Flames of hatred darted into Kevin's back.

Kevin whirled. "I didn't do it. Callaway, you motherfucker, this is your fault."

Before anyone could stop him, Kevin jumped over the railing and rushed at Danny. The bailiff dashed after him. Kevin swung his arm. Danny ducked, then stood rooted. Suddenly he couldn't move.

The sea green eyes bore into his. Kevin poked a finger into Danny's chest. "I'll get you for this, Callaway. When I'm through with you, you'll wish you were dead instead of your sister."

That did it. Rage coursed through Danny's veins. He punched his fist into Kevin's gut. The bailiff lodged himself between them.

Dad pulled Danny away. "That's enough, son. You're better than him. Don't stoop to his level."

"But he killed Mary Alice."

"Harming him won't bring her back. Remember, two wrongs don't make a right."

Danny tried to break free, but his father wouldn't let him. Danny would not strike his father, who stood like a rock, though his eyes were wet and red. His mouth held the same bitter twist as before. He suffered, yet, as usual, he didn't focus on himself.

"Son, please have consideration for your mother. Hasn't she been through enough?"

Danny glanced at Mom. Her small frame had shrunk as she slumped in her seat. The sight was his undoing.

"I'm sorry," he said, not only apologizing for himself, but for the entire nightmare over which he had no control.

Dad nodded and released him.

Danny stumbled to his mother. With a pang, Danny reached down to grasp her shaking hands. How could he help? What should he say? Whatever came out wouldn't be enough, but he had to try.

"Don't worry, Mom. We'll manage somehow. Remember what you've always said. The good go to heaven. Mary Alice is already there, waiting for us."

Mom's violet eyes were awash with tears. Her lips trembled. Danny's words could never give Mom what she wanted. Nothing could bring Mary Alice back. He smiled in reassurance as ice froze his heart.

Chapter Two
Kevin

AS HIS MANACLED body sped through the darkness to Heartland Penitentiary, Kevin's mind spun backward to the day of the murder. He was not on the bus, but in the classroom.

"Turn to page twenty-one," his English teacher, John Davis, had directed.

Kevin heaved a sigh and opened the book. The letters danced nonsensically on the page. Reading was difficult and not worth the effort. To keep awake, he doodled in the margins.

For the hundredth time, he wished his old man weren't a screwed-up drunk. Then they wouldn't have been kicked out of their apartment.

At his old high school, Kevin had had it made. His teachers couldn't deal with his dyslexia, so they'd passed him along from grade to grade. Other students were forced to study, but he'd enjoyed a free pass. The guys had envied him for that. Also for something else. He had a hot bod and had made it with every chick in class

He frowned, thinking of his new classmates. The North Siders were a different breed. They didn't say what they thought. They slunk around, whispering behind his back, making fun of him. They had no clue how smart he was.

His eyes lifted from the book. With a defiant twirl of his ballpoint, he fastened his gaze on Mary Alice Callaway, the occupant of the next desk. She was a looker. Beneath that frilly white blouse with the high-neck collar, her huge tits jutted out, almost begging his palms to envelop them. She was the only worthwhile thing in the whole school.

She had a right to be stuck-up, but instead she was nice. She never made fun of him, but acted like he really counted. Too bad she had a thing for Larry Murphy.

Kevin narrowed his eyes as he caught four-eyed Larry exchange a no-one-else-exists look with Mary Alice. Man, he'd give anything to wrench off the creep's bifocals and jam his pen straight into those pumice-colored eyeballs. Larry didn't deserve Mary Alice. It was a mystery what she saw in that short, stringy-haired dud.

The bell rang. Larry the Wonderful rushed off to his law clerk job, leaving the blonde and beautiful Mary Alice alone in the hallway. It was Kevin's chance. He had to take it. He had to convince her.

Adopting a Brad Pitt smile, he sidled up to her. "Mary Alice, honey, could I walk you home?"

She flushed, then said, "Why sure, Kevin."

He was in heaven. He knew he was moving, yet his feet barely touched the ground. She spoke to him, but he didn't know what she said. He watched in fascination as her blonde curls bounced wildly in the wind. Her glossy lips moved up, down and around, giving him a giant boner.

All too soon they reached her apartment building. Sweat broke out beneath his parka.

He looked deep into Mary Alice's shining blue eyes and popped the question. "Would you like to go to the prom with me?"

She had to say yes. She belonged to him.

"Kevin, I'm sorry, but I'm already going with Larry."

She couldn't mean that. He grasped her shoulders and looked deep into her eyes, trying to make her understand. "But you can't. Tell him you've changed your mind."

Her face flushed. She bit her lip. With a little persuasion, maybe she'd give in.

Too bad that's when her kid brother, Danny, showed up and butted in with his two cents. To top it off, Old Man Meyer shouted down at them to keep quiet. His dream was shattered.

The prison bus rocked, jerking Kevin's shackled hands and feet, forcing his mind back to the present. It was over. Mary Alice was dead. He squeezed his eyelids tight, but the tears trickled out anyway, forcing him to face the facts. He'd loved Mary Alice. He'd never see her again. He missed her. Coupled with the wrenching pain was another realization: his life was ruined. If only he could go back and erase his mistakes.

It shouldn't end this way. He shouldn't be the one to pay. Danny Callaway's words had damned him. It might take a while, but there was one thing he would do. Get even.

The jolting ride on Oganawa Drive to Heartland Penitentiary grew hot and sweaty.

As the bus approached the compound, the gates swung open, then quickly shut, trapping Kevin inside.

He wanted to scream, "I don't belong here. Let me out," but it was no use.

He was unceremoniously pushed off the bus and forced down two flights of stairs to a cold, damp room. A combination of piss and B.O.

bombarded his nostrils, making him want to vomit.

Realizing the futility of it all, he lowered himself onto the nearest bench and avoided eye contact with anyone. His thin T-shirt and ripped jeans offered scant protection against the bone chilling dampness, but he wouldn't shiver and show weakness.

Soon he was shoved into a so-called "reception" area and ordered to line-up and strip. Before an audience of inmates and guards, he underwent a humiliating body search. He stood stoically as goose bumps broke out over his arms and legs. Even when the guard stuck a gloved finger up Kevin's ass, he didn't flinch.

Next he was thrown into a chemical shower and deloused. His skin emerged red and raw, but he pretended it didn't matter. He stumbled into the standard regulation gear of cotton shirt and blue jeans. His pride remained intact, but his body had overreached its limit. He tried to stand, but instead swayed.

His eyes drifted shut. The guards shook him awake and marched him through a long corridor, up three more flights of stairs, then into a cage.

Half-asleep and disoriented, Kevin couldn't focus. All he could see were blurred bars. The nine-by-six cell closed in on him. He wanted out.

A voice said, "Take a load off, man."

Through the blackness Kevin barely made out a lanky, dark-haired guy.

"I'm Brad Sturgess. We'll spend some time together, so how about we get along? You can have the bottom bunk tonight."

No one was that nice. What was the catch? Kevin gave him a double take.

Brad patted him on the back. "Hey, I've been there, too. I'm on your side, buddy."

Kevin nodded, too washed out to speak. Gratefully he sank onto the thin mattress. Before long he fell into a nightmare-ridden sleep, dreaming he was in prison, waking up to find he was.

WITH TIME, HE managed to relegate his prior life to a tightly closed compartment. The past was a never-never land. For his own sanity, it was best forgotten. He forged new friendships, soon discovering that the queers were attracted to him because of his bod. Also, the murderers welcomed him as one of their own. He would not disillusion them. It was ironic that in this crummy hell he'd gained acceptance.

Despite that, he longed to be free. The days stretched ahead endlessly. Not a studier by nature, he attended classes just to relieve the boredom. In one he worked on the dyslexia problem he'd been cursed with. It wasn't easy, but he did make progress. Still, he'd never enjoy reading.

He always looked forward to electronics class. The others watched open-mouthed as he deftly pieced intricate components together. With practiced ease, he mastered complicated wiring. He'd known he was smart, but hadn't known how smart he was.

On top of that, he turned into an auto mechanics whiz, diagnosing and solving automotive problems.

Right now his fingers itched to touch a grease-filled motor, but that was denied him. There would be no classes while lockdown was in effect.

Kevin paced his cell.

"Sit still. You're driving me nuts," Brad Sturgess said, gazing up at Kevin from the bottom bunk.

"Gonna make me?"

"Hell, no. Why bother?"

Kevin resumed pacing, ignoring his cell mate's sigh. All around him rose the usual din of yelling and swearing, enough to burst his head. Lockdowns were the pits. He despised being stuck in one place. The combination of stinking bodies and putrid toilet smells pierced his nostrils and clung to every inch of his clothing.

Ever since Billy Holliday had stabbed a guard two weeks ago while trying to escape, privileges had been denied for everyone. Kevin had known what was coming down. He'd been the one to show Billy where the electrical connections on the fence were frayed enough to deaden the charge. With a life sentence hanging on his head, Billy had had nothing to lose by fleeing.

Kevin wished him luck and cursed him at the same time. He'd give anything not to be stuck in this shitty lockdown where he was forced to endure the rigors of thinking. Thinking was dangerous. That's when the tightly shut compartments of his mind creaked open, spilling out horrific details he'd rather forget.

It was happening again and he was powerless to stop it. The reel of events began to play. He didn't want to remember Mary Alice, especially the way he'd last seen her. For the thousandth time, he wondered why he hadn't behaved differently. His cowardly actions had cost him big time. He'd regret his mistakes forever, but it was too late to undo them.

If only he'd told the truth, maybe things would have turned out differently. The problem was he'd seen the way the judge and jury had reacted to Danny Callaway's testimony, gazing in awed fascination at the All-American traumatized brother of the rape-and-murder victim.

Kevin knew right then it didn't matter what he said because he didn't stand a chance. The jury would convict a monkey if Callaway decreed it.

Yeah, Callaway had put him here. Every torture-filled moment was the creep's fault. God, he hated him.

At the thought, Kevin banged his fist into his palm. He was sick of being a victim. It was time to strike back.

He knew of incidents where inmates had exacted revenge. Only a month ago, Anthony Edwards had ratted to a guard about Billy Holliday's hidden stash of hash.

Not long afterwards, Anthony's only son was gunned down just steps from his porch. When Anthony had learned of it, he'd sobbed like a baby. Poor Anthony had always bragged about how the kid was the best of him and his wife, Miranda. Now the poor fool was hurting and would never be the same.

Kevin felt kind of guilty about that since he was the one who'd snitched on Anthony. He should have kept mum. Anthony didn't deserve a dead son. Prison was rotten enough.

And now Billy was out there somewhere, trying to escape. If by some miracle he did succeed, Kevin would get his payback.

Chapter Three
Danny

LIFE WAS PAINFUL and different without Mary Alice, but Danny wasn't the only one hurting. A week after the verdict, he heard a rustle inside his sister's bedroom. He found his mother standing in front of Mary Alice's closet, skimming her fingers over the pink prom dress.

With a sad smile, she turned to Danny. "It's so soft and pretty. I remember when your sister bought this. She was so excited."

Danny's heart dropped. Unable to speak, he swallowed past a lump in his throat. His mother and sister had been as close as a mother and daughter could be. They'd shared a lot. Mom had to miss her.

He wished he could erase that sad lost look from his mother's face. It stabbed his heart.

He bent and placed his hand on Mom's shoulder. "Are you all right?"

"As right as I'll ever be," she said, blinking back a tear and turning toward the closet.

With a helpless feeling, he left his mother and stepped into the living room, where his father sat in front of the television. In that world, violence was make believe. As Danny joined him, Dad didn't even glance up. With a bitter feeling, Danny realized that his family existed, not lived. He wanted his parents back. He wanted his sister. Both were impossible.

Tucking the *Sun Times* under his arm, he retreated into the bedroom. He'd gotten into the habit of checking for articles about the trial. The day of Mary Alice's death, Sylvia Stewart, a wealthy socialite, had been kidnapped. With the paparazzi focusing on Sylvia, they hadn't doled out much attention to Mary Alice. Since then, only dabs of news escaped.

He lay with his head against the head rest and scanned the paper. Today there was a profile of Kevin. The reporter speculated about whether being ostracized because of dyslexia had contributed to Kevin's criminal personality. Danny didn't believe it. Other people suffered from disabilities, but didn't resort to brutality. The truth was Kevin had no soul. He was evil at heart.

The end of the column caught Danny's attention, making his head jerk back and his heart pound fast. In Illinois, prisoners' sentences were cut short by the equal number of days spent in "good time."

That wasn't right. Why should Kevin get out earlier? Why should he even be alive? Mary Alice hadn't deserved to die, yet she had.

That did it. He clenched the paper as his resolve hardened. He would not allow the person who'd killed his sister to walk the streets. Kevin must die.

After he'd made the pact with himself, Danny spent hours speculating about the best method. What should he use? A kitchen knife, or was that too messy? What about a revolver? Or maybe a brick? That should be hard enough to bash in Kevin's skull.

Those and other desperate thoughts crowded Danny's mind. Time passed in a dark blur. Happiness was a thing of the past.

He hadn't realized Labor Day had come until his buddy, Tony Vanetti, called. "How about you, me and Ritchie meet over at Chase Park for a game of horse?"

At Tony's words, a feeling of melancholy washed over Danny. His eyes stung. If only he could go back to when his major concern was basketball.

It had been a long time since he'd seen his friends. He could use some support. His secure world had crumbled and he teetered on the edge, ready to fall into an abyss. He had to do something. He couldn't go on this way.

Taking a deep breath, he said, "Sure, I'll give it a try."

A long-forgotten surge of excitement filled him as he laced up his shoes. It seemed forever since he'd played.

He set off on the five-block trek from Magnolia to Clark Street. The night breeze had a cool edge to it, reminding him that summer had fled. Breathing in the crisp air, he felt alive. Was it wrong to feel so good? As he drew near, his steps quickened.

At the basketball court, he found Tony passing to Ritchie Corcoran, their high school buddy. Ritchie lobbed the ball to Danny. Danny dribbled, enjoying the familiar knobby texture against his palm. Thunks echoed off the cement.

He threw himself into the game. Sweat bathed his body, yet he ran and played, concentrating only on the sport, blocking out everything else.

As he toweled himself afterwards, he had a revelation. Through basketball, he could work off his anger and stay in shape for Kevin's release. It would be his salvation.

IN SENIOR YEAR, the three friends gravitated to Senn High School's basketball team. After a particularly intense practice, coach said, "That's a wrap."

Danny dashed to the shower. Soon all he heard was the bacon-sizzle of water hitting tiles.

He waved to Ritchie and Tony as they left for cheeseburgers. With steely determination, he threw on his sweat suit and headed to the workout room. He pulled out the seventy-five pound weights and yanked them high. He was not like his friends, no matter how much he wished he were.

That December, Dad's arthritis grew so bad most of the time he couldn't get out of bed. Money was short. Danny hired on at Dean's Computers. When he wasn't ringing up customers, he was absorbing knowledge from the technical support team.

Mom put in for overtime at Jennings Groceries, where she was already a checker. The rent increased, as did the utilities. It was hard to get by.

Danny felt sorry for his father, who'd prided himself on being the family's provider, but now was forced to sit at home. Danny knew something of the mental torture his father experienced. He himself had to keep busy because pain and bitterness lurked deep inside of him like a cancer ready to spread at the slightest provocation.

Thank goodness he had basketball. Through will power and natural coordination, Danny excelled. The scouts noticed and hung around the games.

"Danny, you lucky son of a gun. How'd ya pull that off?" Tony asked as the three friends walked side-by-side down Clark Street after an early May practice. He was referring to the coach's announcement Danny had just won a DePaul University basketball scholarship.

Danny grinned sheepishly. "I didn't do anything special. You guys should've gotten them, too."

Ritchie jabbed him playfully on the shoulder. "Hey, lucky, while you're coasting through college, think of us poor slobs sweating over our full time jobs."

Danny took the ribbing in stride, not mentioning he had little time for loafing.

TO FINALIZE THE first semester's registration at Lincoln Park Campus, each DePaul class was designated a separate area of the Schmitt Academic Center. Not far from Danny's group stood Larry

Murphy and the sophomores.

Larry's eyes flickered briefly at Danny in recognition before he turned away. Who could blame him? Seeing Danny had to make him uncomfortable. If not for fate, Mary Alice would have been Larry's wife by now.

Danny sighed and turned his attention to picking classes. He chose a computer course. Since he'd started at Dean's, his interest in the field had intensified. Computers were more predictable than people.

That afternoon, he attended his first college basketball practice. There he encountered another form of discipline. Coach Jagierski, the crew-cut taskmaster, glared at the hopefuls. "If you're here for a good time, you may as well leave. Before you play one game, you'll do the drills. This is the tip drill. Richard, tip the ball against the basket four times. On the fifth tip, jump, grab it with both hands, come down and pass to Danny. Danny, do the same, and down the line. Okay, go."

At the next session, Coach Jagierski primed them with individual drills. Danny learned the sliding drill. He stood at the free-throw line facing the coach and slid where directed.

He knew the fundamentals would help in the long run, yet Danny itched to play a real game.

As the season progressed, a pattern seemed to develop. Danny and a few others were allowed more playing time. The players came to depend on each other and melded into a unit. Often when Danny was taken out to rest, not long afterwards the coach shouted, "Dan, get back in there."

Eager to do more than his share, Danny gave it his all. No one could suspect that deep inside him swelled an overpowering rage, which dogged him daily. When he ran, the devil nipped at his heels, prodding him on, making him move faster and faster, daring him to forget.

For two years, Danny focused on schoolwork and basketball, though in the back of his mind, his goal remained intact. He had a lot of time left for that. Too much.

A chilling reminder brought him up short a few months after the start of junior year. A crowd had gathered by the bulletin board. When Danny made it to the front, he found the picture of a missing co-ed named Dawn Neilson. His heart lurched at the sight of the blonde, wavy hair and sweet features. The resemblance to his sister was uncanny. He prayed that the girl was safe.

Three days later, as he entered study hall the normally quiet room buzzed. He spied Tony and walked over.

"Let's get out of here," Tony said, leading Danny into the hallway.

Mystified, Danny followed.

"I hate to tell you this, but you know that girl, Dawn?"

Danny nodded. His heart hammered.

"The cops found her in an alley four blocks from here. She was molested and beaten to death. They're calling it a copycat killing."

Oh, God. Danny shut his eyelids tight, but couldn't block out the image of Mary Alice's body. As the familiar helpless rage consumed him, he clenched his fists. Kevin may be imprisoned at Heartland, but he was as much responsible for Dawn's death as Mary Alice's. He'd influenced another sick soul to follow in his footsteps.

Chapter Four
Danny

ALMOST FIVE YEARS had passed since Mary Alice's rape and murder, yet Danny's resolve remained firm. One afternoon, heart pounding, he stepped into a small Milwaukee gun shop and strode across its worn linoleum floor. Behind an ancient glass and wooden counter, a wizened shopkeeper perched atop a tall stool.

Danny broached him. "Sir, I'm new at this. Can you recommend a gun for combat competition?"

Without blinking, the man tapped on the scratched glass. "Sure. You want one of these beauties. This is a Colt .45 Combat Commander. It's got speed, a steel frame to absorb the recoil and a handy short length. The gun practically shoots by itself."

"Could I handle it, please?"

The man nodded and pulled the instrument out.

The cold steel rested against Danny's palm, sending shivers up his spine. Was he cut out for this?

His thumb tightened on the trigger. He felt the firmness of the barrel. He'd make himself be.

The old man drummed his fingers on the glass.

As if it were loaded, Danny gingerly replaced the instrument onto the counter. "Okay, you've sold me."

He drew out a fake Wisconsin ID and gun permit, then handed the man cash. Before long he'd emerged outside, with the automatic hidden in a brown paper bag.

The cold February air caught Danny's giant sigh of relief and turned it into a huge gunsmoke-like ring. Either the man hadn't noticed Danny did not resemble the photo ID, or more likely, he didn't care. Also, he hadn't done a background check. It shouldn't be that simple.

Why did it matter? He'd gotten what he wanted. That's all he should care about. The automatic was a means to a bitter end.

When Danny arrived home, he wrapped it in a linen towel and placed it at the back of his closet next to his box of basketball cards.

The next morning he snuck out to the forest preserve and experimented with trigger finger pressure, kick back velocity and other elements he'd read about in the learner's manuals.

On subsequent trips, he familiarized himself with setting sights and aiming at targets. First he used bull's eyes, then cans. He threw high, low and sideways, trying to hit as many targets as possible. Each score was Kevin.

One spring afternoon Danny placed his towel-wrapped gun under the car seat and set out for practice. Within minutes the sky darkened. He could barely see the targets, yet when he inspected the decoys, he saw that he'd hit most of them. He wrapped the gun in his towel, satisfied he'd done a good job.

As he stepped into the old Buick, an unwelcome but familiar sensation stole over him. Frowning, he placed the deadly instrument under the seat. Would he always feel like a criminal?

To make matters worse, a mile after he'd exited the forest preserve, a patrol car flashed its lights and pulled up alongside the Buick. Cold sweat sprang to Danny's forehead. His fingers slipped on the wheel. By transporting a concealed weapon he'd purchased with a fake ID, he was breaking the law. For sure he'd pay. How had they found out?

What would his parents think? They'd had enough to go through.

With heart skittering, he pulled to the side of the road, rolled down the window and watched the officer approach.

"I don't know if you realize it, son, but your tail light's out. I'll give you a warning ticket this time, but you better get it fixed."

With a shaky smile, Danny thanked him then saluted a goodbye. That was close.

Later, after a cold shower, he calmed down. One near miss would not deter him. Actually, it had been good practice. He better get used to risk-taking.

Danny continued mastering his weapon in private, leading a normal life in public. He aced his classes. He continued to work at Dean's. He played basketball every chance he could get. He kept himself so occupied, before he knew it he'd reached senior year.

ON THE FIRST day of math class, Danny slipped behind the third desk by the window. Sunlight streamed through the partially open blinds. Strands of long, strawberry curls cascaded in front of him, sparkling like a kaleidoscope. Fascinated, he eyed the glitter. His fingers itched to reach out and tweak just one curl to watch it spring back.

Call it intuition, but the owner of the sparkling locks somehow sensed he was staring. She turned and smiled at him. "Hi, I'm Cathy

McGuire."

He couldn't look away. Almost in awe, he gazed into innocent azure eyes. Freckles dotted a perky nose and splashed over creamy cheeks. It was the face of an angel come to earth. He was lost.

"I'm Danny Callaway," he said, as the voice inside of him shouted, "She's the one."

His attention was sidetracked by the math professor's joke. Cathy's laugh tinkled like piano notes, squishing Danny's insides to mush.

He was hooked. Each day he looked forward to seeing Cathy. There was no harm in looking. He wanted her so badly he ached, but he'd never get this innocent involved in the dark side of his life.

Despite his resolve, when the guys swarmed all over her, alarm stabbed him. It didn't help to remind himself he had no claim on her and she had every right to date whom she pleased. The thought of her doing so tore at his guts.

Surprisingly, she didn't seem interested in the other guys. It was almost as if she was waiting for Danny to make a move. He could be conceited for thinking that, but deep inside he hoped he was right.

After a frustrating month, Cathy stopped him after class. "Danny, did the prof say chapters eight through ten or eight and nine?"

He gazed into the guileless blue eyes and noted that this time, instead of running down her shoulders, her bright strawberry locks were confined inside a tight braid. He hardened, picturing himself loosening the braid while Cathy lay beside him in bed.

"Only eight and nine," he said, turning away, determined to resist.

He had to be strong and do the right thing. He'd look and not touch. Cathy deserved better.

Then fate stepped in.

Chapter Five
Kevin

BRAD WAS LEAVING. Kevin blinked back unmacho-like tears and shook his cell mate's hand for the last time. "Hey, guy, don't forget our deal. Oh, and drop a line, okay?"

"Sure. And remember, don't give up. You'll make it, too," Brad said.

Kevin nodded, pretending he didn't have fourteen years left in the hell hole. Shit, he'd miss Brad. They'd swapped dirty jokes, out-farted each other and woven intricate revenge schemes long into the night.

From the beginning, they'd confided in one another. Only Brad knew the real truth about Mary Alice, and only Kevin knew the lowdown of how a young waitress had falsely accused Brad of restaurant theft. It was scary to experience firsthand how easy it was to get framed.

Kevin envied his buddy. Damn, he wished he could join him and work on the schemes they'd cooked up. It would be a long haul without Brad.

With a last wave, his freed cell mate disappeared. Kevin sighed. He had some other buddies here, but old Brad had been a corker. Things wouldn't be the same without him.

Then he remembered. The letdown of Brad's release had made it slip his mind, but this was important. Billy, who'd escaped months ago, had finally contacted him. He could have ignored Kevin's request, but instead was honoring it.

Things should be in place by now. Anticipation coursed through Kevin's veins.

Even before the noontime start of the DePaul homecoming game, he'd staked out a good spot in the rec room right in front of the TV, impatiently waiting. First the band played the alma mater. Then the Marquette players ran out.

After that, one by one the DePaul players were announced and ran onto the court. A single name remained to be said. Kevin sat upright, eyes glued to the set.

"Danny Callaway."

The words blasted in his ears.

"Hell!"

What had gone wrong? Callaway was not supposed to be there. With an angry scrape, Kevin pushed back his chair.

"What's the matter, Kevin sweets, do you prefer blonds?" Pedro Paratta, an inmate known to be drawn to his own sex, asked.

"Eat shit," Kevin said, turning away.

With a hopeless feeling, he trudged back to his cell. Callaway was invincible. God, he hated the jerk's guts.

Chapter Six
Danny

IT WAS HOMECOMING day. After the national anthem, Danny scanned the Allstate Arena. Almost every seat was filled, except for the two in the fourth row. He frowned. The weather was fine. The apartment wasn't far. Mom was supposed to drive Dad over after breakfast. Where were they?

He'd taken extra steps to ensure their attendance. His parent's Chevy was in the shop, so Danny had gotten a lift from Tony and left them his trusty Buick.

He hoped Dad's arthritis hadn't flared up. Maybe he couldn't move and Mom was having trouble helping him. Or, maybe they'd forgotten to bring the tickets and had turned back for them.

It wouldn't take long. They'd probably show up any minute. They knew how important it was for them to be here. At half-time, all the seniors' parents would walk out to mid-court with the players.

The first quarter began. Danny blocked everything out of his mind and focused on playing. He scored tons of points and some exciting slam dunks. The crowd was getting into the game.

Toward half-time, the two seats were still empty. Where were his parents? They needed to get here soon. He tried the phone in the locker room. No one answered. They had to be on their way. When he saw them, the mystery would be solved.

The announcements began. Each senior was called out onto the court, flanked by his parents. Danny's name was announced. Mom and Dad did not appear. Trying to hide his disappointment, he stepped out by himself and received his plaque, forcing a smile onto his face. The fans cheered and Danny waved.

His eyes caught a flash of color on the sidelines in the front row. Catherine's curls glittered beneath the gym lights. The sight warmed him, making him optimistic. He shouldn't worry. There had to be a logical reason for his parents' absence. He'd find out about it later.

DePaul emerged victorious. As Danny approached the locker room after the game, he glimpsed Cathy standing beside the door. His heart beat faster.

"Danny, you played great. You're very talented."

Her face turned a lovely shade of pink. Feeling his own cheeks grow hot, he stared at her flushed face. He wanted Catherine more than was good for either of them.

"Thanks, Cathy, I do my best. I've always liked basketball," he said, fighting a wave of longing.

Her attention still didn't take his mind from the fact his parents had not arrived. He wondered if she sensed his hurt. He'd wanted his family to share this important game with him.

He looked into Cathy's pure, sincere face. She was an angel, so much different than the evil person he was inside. What should he say next?

His problem was solved when one of the opposing players approached.

"Way to go, Danny," Rolf Stallworthy said, patting him on the back.

Cathy came out of her spell and turned to her friends. "Well, I better be going."

"It was nice to see you, Cathy," Danny said.

Watching her retreating figure, he felt a pang of regret. If only he could keep her alongside him forever. Before he could prevent it, the vision again entered his mind of Cathy stretched out beside him as he counted and kissed her freckles and tasted her fair skin. At the thought, his body strained to find release inside of her.

Tony Vanetti stopped by, bringing him down to earth.

"Danny, Tracy's waiting in the Mustang."

Tracy Santore had been Tony's constant companion since grammar school. She was so familiar she seemed like one of the guys.

Danny came to. "Oh, yeah, pizza at Tobasco's. I'll shower and be right out."

He needed to cool off bad. Cathy did strange things to him. Did Tony get that way over Tracy or did he take her for granted?

Danny turned the water on full blast, almost punishing himself with its force. He had to forget Cathy. She'd be better off without him. The demon in his soul would only do her harm. His family was cursed. He'd hate to have his bad luck extend to her.

That reminded him. What about his parents? What had happened to them? The small, niggling voice grew louder, refusing to be drowned by the gushing stream of water. Something was wrong. They'd said they'd be here. Was it Dad's back? Had the car broken down?

He had to find out. He quickly toweled himself and threw on his clothes. With the cotton shirt clinging to his damp skin, he rushed to the phone. It rang with no answer. Where were they?

Maybe a tow truck was picking them up. The next time he called they'd be home and apologizing for missing the game. Fighting a sense of urgency, he silently climbed into Tony's back seat and barely listened as his friends discussed the win.

After Tony pulled up at Tobasco's, Danny jumped out, intent on finding a phone. Ritchie blocked his way, standing outside the door with his hands clasped and lips quivering. Danny had seen that look before. His heart pounded.

"Danny," Ritchie's voice cracked. "Danny, I heard on the radio there was an accident in our neighborhood."

Accidents happened all the time, but somehow Danny knew this one was different. Ritchie put an arm around Danny's shoulders.

"I heard the description, so I called the police. I'm sorry, Danny, but I think it's your mom and dad. They hit a telephone pole. They're dead."

Tony and Tracy came up behind them. "Are you sure?" Tracy asked. "There might be a mistake."

"I hope to God I'm wrong, but it sounded like them. Danny, the police want identification. I'll take you there."

"I'll come, too," Tony said.

Danny spoke up. "No, please. You and Tracy go inside."

"I can't or I'll puke," Tony said, turning from the restaurant. "Let's get out of here. Listen, Danny, if you need anything, let me know."

Ritchie quietly opened the passenger door of his Pontiac. Danny slumped onto the passenger seat. Icy fingers of fear clutched him. This couldn't be happening. They couldn't be gone. They were all he had. When he arrived at the morgue, there would be two other bodies waiting, not theirs.

All too soon they pulled up before the weathered brownstone building.

"Good luck, Danny," Ritchie whispered, as Danny stepped inside the quiet, icy room.

The bright light hit his eyes, making them water. He shivered as an attendant pulled out the fifth drawer from the wall.

He closed his eyes and prayed, then opened them and looked.

A sinking feeling hit him at the sight. "Mom," he said in a strangled voice.

Nodding at Danny's confirmation, the man pulled out the adjoining drawer. Danny forced his smarting eyes to gaze at the shell of the man who'd struggled hard to provide for his family despite constant back pain. This shouldn't be.

Closing his eyes tight, he jammed his knuckles into them. He would not cry. He stood there for God knows how long. Time had no meaning. The sound of a throat clearing jarred Danny from his trance. "Sir..."

He was at the morgue. The attendant was waiting. No use wasting the man's time. On wobbly legs, Danny started to move.

"Sir," the man began again. Danny stopped and turned.

"If it's any consolation, it appears they died instantly."

"Thank you," Danny said, appreciating the attempt to ease his pain.

He hoped it was true. At least their faces had remained unblemished. They'd looked almost as if they were sleeping.

He sighed. Well, now they were at peace. They'd joined Mary Alice and wouldn't miss her any more. The problem was they'd left him behind. He wanted them back. He wasn't a child, yet he longed for Mom's embrace and Dad's pat on the back.

He found Ritchie waiting in the hallway, where the temperature had turned stifling. As if from a distance, his friend's voice echoed. "Are you okay, Danny? Is there anything I can do?"

He shook his head. There was nothing anyone could do.

WHEN DANNY ENTERED the empty apartment he still expected to see Mom and Dad inside. Sinking onto the couch, he stared at the pathetic reminders of his parent's existence—Mom's reading glasses beside the lamp, Dad's slippers on the floor next to his chair.

Chills raced up and down his spine. His body shook and he couldn't stop it. This was worse than Mary Alice's death, or maybe it seemed that way because the pain was so fresh. He had no family. How could he survive?

With the support of Ritchie and Tony, somehow he got through the funeral arrangements, though he was close to cracking.

A few days later, as he walked behind the coffin at Our Lady of Lourdes Church, the wind picked up, turning the air bitter cold. It was not a typical day for mid-April, but nothing was normal any more.

At the cemetery chapel, Ritchie and Tony stood guard beside him. Others were present, but his mind didn't register their identities. All he could think of was he'd never see his parents again. Like Mary Alice, they'd disappeared from his life.

When the service was done, he trudged out into the blustery, cold world. The cruel wind froze the tears to his cheeks.

As he turned toward Tony's car, his angel appeared. Cathy seemed to almost float up to him with her brilliant red hair flying in the wind. The sight made his heart ache. Mom hadn't even met her. They would have liked each other.

Her cold hand clasped his. "Danny, I was out of town. I just heard about your parents this morning. I got here as fast as I could. I'm so sorry. If there's anything I can do..." Her eyes filled.

"Thanks for coming, Cathy. It means a lot to me."

His voice sounded strange to his own his ears, but he felt totally drained and past hiding his feelings. He could only gaze at the soft vision, soak in her beauty and drown in her tranquil blue eyes. She was his one slim hope in an unpredictable world, yet a dream he dare not pursue. Resolutely he turned from her.

That evening as he lay in bed, emptiness hit him. He listened to other footsteps on the apartment building's stairway, knowing they could never be Mom's or Dad's. Other people had families. He had none.

LIFE WENT ON. Danny filled his days, doing his best to cope with his loss. He excelled at basketball. Pro scouts approached him, but he decided to graduate first. It had been his parent's wish for him to get his degree.

His obsession with Cathy grew, perhaps due to his loneliness. He knew better than to lead her on, but he couldn't deny himself a few small pleasures, such as taking her out to lunch. It felt so right to be near her. Still, that was as far as he went.

A month before graduation, Cathy approached him. "Danny, I was wondering. There's a party I've been invited to, but I've got no one to take me. Would you mind?"

He raised his eyebrows at what had to be a lie. What guy in his right mind wouldn't escort her? Not that she encouraged any of them.

Here she was, practically begging him. This was his chance, but his conscience told him not to take it. She didn't fit into his plan. Innocence and revenge were a bad combination.

The beautiful Cathy stood before him, biting her lip. He hated seeing her feel bad. Wavering, he glanced at her reddening lip. He ached to run his tongue over the spot and soothe it, then go further.

His eyes traveled down to her pert, upturned breasts, her minuscule waist, and her long, slim legs. Not for the first time, he wondered if Cathy had ever made love to anyone. The thought made him break into a sweat, almost like it was Mary Alice's rape all over again. Cathy was his, though he hadn't claimed her.

Her face flushed. His strength fled. Taking a deep breath, he plunged in. "Sure Cathy. When do you need my services?" He'd tried to sound like it didn't matter, though his mouth felt dry. A real man was always in control. That's what women wanted.

Her forehead puckered. He wondered if she regretted asking him out. Maybe he'd sounded too macho. Quickly he added, "Seriously, Cathy, it would be my pleasure."

Her forehead cleared. "The party's this Saturday at Don Grant's house."

"Oh, yeah. He asked me, but I didn't think I could make it. My work schedule got switched, so now I can."

He'd call in sick if he had to.

Now that he'd made the commitment, he looked forward to the night he'd be with her. The week dragged. Finally it was Saturday and Danny stood before the hall monitor at Cathy's dorm, waiting to be announced.

As fresh as the spring evening, Cathy glided down the stairs in a denim mini dress. Her legs stretched long and lean. Her dainty feet were tucked into smooth leather sandals, with pink polished toenails peaking out.

She was really something, a temptation too great to resist. While he strolled across the parking lot with his arm around her waist, he swore he heard the birds sing.

As they approached his much-repaired beater, his face grew warm. Someone like Cathy deserved better.

It got worse. When they arrived at Don Grant's place, Corvettes, Mustangs, even Porsches were parked out front. They made his old Buick look like a piece of junk. As if sensing his discomfiture, Cathy glanced at Danny and smiled, putting him at ease. The gesture confirmed she was beautiful inside as well as out.

At the party, another incident strengthened that notion. A buffet was set up in the basement, where Danny and Cathy waited in line. When Cathy leaned against the brick wall something moved.

"Cathy, watch out, there's a spider."

He reached for a napkin to kill it.

Her hand caught his. "No, Danny, don't. It deserves a life, too."

Had he heard right? Most women would have been only too eager to dispose of the insect, yet Cathy thought of the spider's life.

He felt the pressure of her fingertips on his arm. His pulse raced and his pants tightened. He felt like pushing her against the wall, crushing his lips into hers and prying open her teeth with his tongue.

She looked back at him innocently as an alarm rang in his mind. Was he no better than Kevin Green?

That reminded him. He had no right to lead Cathy on, not with that unfinished business to attend to. He had to let her go. Sooner or later she'd find someone better.

He wrestled with his conscience, but, for the time being, it lost. He couldn't make the break, not now. She'd become too important to him. If Cathy were gone, who would he have?

A week later, when she invited him to her parents' home, against his better judgment he accepted.

AT CATHY'S HOUSE, Ted McGuire reached out, almost crushing Danny's palm in his strong grip. "Your last game was a dandy. Great job, young man."

Danny smiled in embarrassment until Cathy's Mom, Nancy, appeared in a cool cotton dress and calmly announced that dinner was ready.

When his leg accidentally brushed against Cathy's under the table, he was grateful for the cover provided by the napkin in his lap. He looked around, wondering if anyone had noticed his reaction.

Cathy's sister, Dora, younger by a year, sat across from him. With a leather barrette firmly clasping her long, straight, dark hair away from her face, she bore scant resemblance to her sibling. Her knowing amber eyes bore into Danny's soul, threatening to expose its dark secrets. Something about her made him uneasy. It was almost as if she were a witch casting a dangerous spell. If it weren't for Cathy, he might be tempted.

Ted caught the direction of Danny's gaze. He was only too glad to fill him in. "Did you know that our Dora is entering law school?"

"Is that right?"

He'd always admired independent women. This one was a knockout to boot. Ted had a right to expand his chest.

"Dora's one smart cookie," Cathy said.

"So are you," Danny added.

Almost with relief his eyes fastened on her. Cathy was smart in ways that counted. She'd make a loving wife and a wonderful mother. She obviously took after her mom, who was in her element caring for her family. Not only that, Cathy was the type who saw the good in everyone. She was tactful, funny and sweet, with a knack for making people feel special.

He fought back a small doubt, but it escaped anyway. At times her goodness made him nervous. He was far from perfect. Cathy, who didn't notice the inner battle waging inside him, flushed at his praise.

"Well, I wouldn't dream of being a lawyer myself. Owning my own floral shop will be quite enough for me. I love being surrounded by flowers and plants. They're so beautiful. I can't wait to make my own creations and share them with my customers."

Her mother smiled. "Cathy, dear, you do a marvelous job in our garden. I remember how in San Francisco, our neighbors were always jealous. You really are very clever."

Danny glanced with renewed appreciation at Cathy. He couldn't ask for a more ideal companion. She had it all and he couldn't blame any man for wanting her. There were so many other guys she could pick—ones with looks, brains and money. Why did she want him?

Cathy leaned against Danny, saying in a soft voice, "I have enough intelligence not to let you slip away."

Once again she'd read his mind and dispelled his doubts. Danny flashed her a grateful smile. Picking up on the exchange, Dora eyed them thoughtfully.

Talk turned to the variations in climate between San Francisco and Chicago and the reason why the family had moved. Holding her husband's hand, Nancy explained they'd decided to be closer to Ted's dad, Nelson, after he'd suffered a heat attack.

They'd discovered this wonderful Georgian home in Park Ridge, which was just perfect. Unfortunately, Nelson had died shortly after their relocation. They didn't feel like facing another upheaval, so they'd stayed on.

"I like it better here. There's something about battling the elements that makes everything more real," Dora added.

She talked about the first snowfall she'd seen. Danny hardly paid attention. Something had dawned on him. Since Mary Alice's death had been a local story and had not claimed national attention, the McGuires hadn't heard about it. It was a relief not to have to discuss it with them. Some things were better left unsaid.

"I'm glad you decided to stay," Danny said, giving Cathy a special smile. "I got the best part of the deal."

The McGuires had started a new life in a new locale. He could understand how fresh habits caught on, especially pleasant ones like spending time with Cathy. He was doing way too much of that, but couldn't stop himself.

He drifted along. Soon it was graduation day. Because there were so many graduates, the ceremony was held at the McCormick Place Auditorium.

From his vantage point in the middle of the line, Danny watched proudly as Cathy marched up to the stage and was awarded her diploma. Then it was his turn. As he stepped up, his eyes filled. Through a mist he grasped the precious paper and scanned the crowd for Cathy. Their eyes met. She blew him a kiss.

Then, against reason, he sought out his parents. Of course they weren't here. Sadness pierced him. They'd wanted this diploma so bad. They'd have been proud of his degree in Computer Sciences.

Through a wet film, Danny stumbled down the aisle. He'd almost reached his seat when he caught sight of the McGuires. Ted flashed a thumbs-up sign. Nancy and Dora smiled encouragingly. His heartstrings tugged. They were his family.

Through the conclusion of the ceremony, he sat lost in thought. He cared for the McGuires too much. If he were a normal guy, he'd propose to Cathy before it was too late. With all his heart, he ached to do that.

Everyone clapped. He stumbled from his seat to join the other exiting grads. Stepping into the June sunlight, he blinked.

Out front were Tony, Tracy and Ritchie, donned in mortarboards and gowns also, beaming triumphantly. It had been a tough road for them. They hadn't earned basketball scholarships like he had, yet they'd persevered. This was an occasion to celebrate. The only bad part of it all was Danny's conscience, which kept tearing at him, reminding him that he was taking advantage of Cathy.

"Notice anything different?" Tracy asked.

What a crazy question. They all looked the same in their caps and gowns. She brought up her left hand directly in front of his eyes before he caught on. A small diamond winked. Danny groaned inside. This development would not help matters.

He tried to smile.

"Congratulations, Tracy. I wish you both the best."

Almost on cue, Cathy stepped up beside him.

Tony grinned devilishly. "It'll be your turn next, buddy."

Danny didn't answer. He'd give anything to be like his friend, but he wasn't. Not with the image of Kevin Green dogging him.

Chapter Seven
Kevin

THE PLAN HAD backfired. The parents had used the Buick and had been killed instead. Kevin knew he couldn't trust anyone to do the job right. He'd do it himself when he got out. He was not happy with the situation, but at least here he could get a good education on what to do when he was sprung.

He had much to learn and able instructors to teach him. While he scrubbed floors, he drew out Steve Summers, a black inmate who'd conned his grandmother into willing him her money before he laced her tea with rat poison.

"I'd have been home free if that motherfuckin' hardware man hadn't ratted, excuse the pun," Steven said, wringing the mop and rinsing the floor.

Kevin sympathized, but made sure to quiz Steve on the type and proportion of the poison he'd used. He wouldn't rule out any possibility, though he wasn't sure if he'd have the opportunity to use this one. Well, there were other routes.

While scrubbing a urinal, Kevin leaned on the brush and gabbed with Daryl Johnson, who was wiping down the adjoining stall.

"I hear you know something about lock picking."

Daryl filled him in on the basics, but stressed the job required finesse. "Judging from the way you handle a toilet brush, you might be in trouble, boy," Daryl jibed.

Kevin flipped the brush at him, making Daryl jump.

On kitchen duty, Kevin ran into Stone Branton, a wily munitions expert who'd been nabbed blowing up a tire factory.

"Hey, Stone, that must've been some explosion," Kevin said, flashing an admiring grin, as he guided a batch of red onions into the dicer.

Stone gripped a potato and grinned. "You're damn right. You could see the smoke and flames for blocks—a sight to behold, if I do say so myself."

"What went wrong?"

"Hell, I almost made it. It was just my luck I didn't notice the prick of a guard taking a whiz behind the bush. Wouldn't you know, he saw me leave. When the explosion happened ten minutes later, he remembered my face and picked me out of a book."

"How'd you do it anyway?"

"Oh, I rigged it up ahead of time, drove a few blocks, and then pushed my handy dandy remote. I could've used a cell phone, but those things can be traced."

"Sounds like you've got smarts."

"Damn right, Jack. It was almost worth getting caught. That explosion was somethin' else."

Enough B.S. He wanted details. "Hey, Stone could you teach me how to make a bomb?"

Stone carefully placed the potato back on the counter and looked across at Kevin. "Sure, pal. The first thing to remember is respect. Bombs are dangerous. You do everything perfect or you don't live to talk about it."

As Stone explained the makings, Kevin was amazed at how simple it was. That suited him fine, since he dare not scribble any bomb recipes and leave them around his cell. He'd keep this bit of knowledge, along with the rest of the stuff he'd learned, deep inside his brain until the exact right moment.

The following Monday afternoon, as he cut through the rec room, the place was buzzing.

"What's going on, man?" he asked Pedro.

"Wake up, sweetie. What planet are you on? The basketball draft's today."

"Oh, yeah. Thanks for the heads up."

"Glad to oblige," Pedro said with a knowing smile.

The draft. The blood rushed to Kevin's head. Ages ago he'd dreamt of being a pro. He was quick, tall and fast. He would have made it.

"Who do you think they'll pick?" Kevin asked.

"That fine lookin' Callaway's a shoe-in," Pedro said.

Kevin gnashed his teeth.

Chapter Eight
Danny

THE FIRST MONDAY in June found Danny bunched inside a small seat at the Universal Center with his buddies, Tony and Ritchie, seated beside him. Licking his lips, he glanced at the stage where the sportscaster positioned the microphone.

"Don't worry. You'll get in," Ritchie said, flashing a reassuring smile.

Danny shifted in his seat. He had to make it. Basketball was his lifeline, his avenue of escape.

The lights dimmed and the ceremony began. With envy, Danny watched as the other players' names were called and their assignments were announced by the commissioner.

On the fifth call, the moment he'd been waiting for arrived. "For the Cyclones, the first round draft player is..."

Danny held his breath and leaned forward. *It's got to be me, it's got to*, he pleaded inside.

"Dick Holmes."

He swallowed in disappointment. The scouts had acted interested. They'd insisted he be here today. He'd thought he had a chance. He slumped back in his seat.

Tony tugged his arm. "Don't let it get you down. There are more teams."

True, although Danny had set his sights on playing for the home team. That's where his friends and memories were, though his family was gone. Still, at this point, he couldn't afford to be particular.

More picks were announced. Danny's hopes waned. Somehow he'd have to cope, basketball or not. He tried to look interested as even more names were called and congratulations rang out.

"Due to a last minute trade with Los Angeles yesterday, the Cyclones are allowed an additional first round draft pick," he heard the commissioner say. "The fifteenth pick for the first round is...Danny Callaway, a graduate from DePaul University."

Had he imagined it?

"Hey, man, you're in. Get up there, Danny," Tony screamed, pummeling Danny on the back.

"Give me five," Ritchie said with a broad smile.

Danny's body felt numb as he walked up the aisle and onto the stage. The lights almost blinded him as the commissioner shook his hand and placed the coveted Cyclone hat on Danny's head. "Congratulations, son."

Through dry lips Danny croaked out, "Thanks."

He couldn't believe it. Something was right about the world after all.

After Danny had exited, one of the sportscasters, Frank Monson, cornered him in the hallway. "How does it feel to be a Cyclone, Danny?"

That was just the start. From now on he'd be grist for the media. He answered the man, but couldn't remember what he said.

As he climbed back into his seat, a sense of awe overwhelmed him. He'd worked hard, yet he still couldn't believe he'd made it.

Too bad Cathy couldn't have been here. He'd like to have shared this milestone with her. When he'd mentioned the draft to her last week, she'd given him a funny look and said, "I'm sorry, Danny. I've got the flower arrangements for the Bergdorf wedding to prepare. It's one of those society things. It's my big chance and I want to do it right."

He was tempted to ask her if half a day would make a difference, but kept silent. The shop was special to her and he respected that. Also, he had a feeling she was hinting about their own wedding plans. It wasn't fair to string her along, yet he hadn't let on why he couldn't go down that road.

"Don't look so glum," Tony said, poking him. "You made it, remember?"

Danny smiled as excitement welled up. Tony was right. Today was special and he may as well enjoy it.

"Let's celebrate someplace," Ritchie said as they filed out of the Universal Center.

"Sorry, guys. I've got a private party at Cathy's."

Amidst knowing looks and congratulations, Danny hopped into his car and headed northwest to Park Ridge. It was already past eight. She should be home.

He dashed to the front door, banged on the brass knocker and waited, shifting his feet. No answer. Maybe she was still at the shop. He'd go over there.

Just as he turned, the door swung open. There was Cathy, smelling flowery and feminine, looking angelic, in a pink chenille robe.

The sight nearly made him forget why he'd come over. She was incredible. He could only stare at the damp strawberry tendrils framing the perfect oval face, then downward to the flash of pale perfect legs. Her freshly scrubbed appearance, a contradiction of sexuality and vulnerability, made something stir deep within him. He stood awkwardly, feeling an overpowering urge to lose himself inside of her.

"Hi, Danny," she said, sounding embarrassed, as if she were ashamed of her unadorned looks.

It was amazing how unassuming she was. Cathy had no idea what effect she had on him.

He imagined what lay beneath the robe, then frowned at another thought. She shouldn't have opened the door so fast. What if it hadn't been him, but someone dangerous? The picture of his sister's prone body flashed through his mind making his blood curdle.

"Cathy, please be careful. It could've been anyone out here. We can't have anything happen to you."

She threw him a reassuring look. "Don't worry, I saw you through the peephole."

Of course she had brains enough not to do anything foolish. Cathy was not as helpless as she looked.

He stepped inside and gathered her tightly in his arms. He pulled her close, feeling the staccato beat of her heart. Its wild rhythm matched his.

That wasn't enough. He swept her off of her feet, whooped loudly and twirled her around. He gently replaced her bare feet onto the slate floor and looked straight into her eyes.

"What was that for?" she asked in an out-of-breath voice.

"Cathy, you're looking at the newest member of the Chicago Cyclones," he said, eagerly watching for her reaction.

She looked up at him, as if expecting to hear more. When it didn't come, a flicker of disappointment crossed her face. Smiling brightly, she said, "Danny, that's wonderful. Congratulations. I knew you'd make it."

Had he imagined that look?

"Cathy, you are happy for me, right?"

"Of course. Don't be silly. What makes you ask?"

"Oh, nothing."

"You've worked hard. You deserve it. Besides, you're a natural."

"Thanks, Cathy. Oh, by the way, they're sending me a contract. Is your Dad in? I wonder if he'd look it over when it comes."

"Everyone's gone to a movie. They asked me to go with them, but after I'd finished the Bergdorf's wedding bouquet plans, all I wanted was a long soak."

Pushing the picture of a bathing Cathy out of his mind, Danny said, "Sounds like you had a tough time."

Her face flushed as she described the tactics she'd employed to deal with the demanding society bride.

While the innocently naive Cathy went on about the travails of floral shop ownership, all he could think of was that they were alone on one of the most important days of his life. It should be celebrated with someone he cared for deeply. Did she guess what was going on in his mind?

Her hand fingered her open collar. She flashed him a tremulous smile.

He placed his right hand on top of hers, reaching inside with the left to trace the smooth creamy skin of her fair neck. He moved down slowly across her back, feeling a quiver run through her. If she objected, he'd stop.

Nothing resembling a protest came from those sweet lips as he inched his fingers down further to engage them at pulling open the sash of her robe. It revealed the satiny, freckled skin beneath.

He gasped at the sight of pert, round breasts and a cute, tiny belly button, followed by the thin patch of strawberry curls.

He swallowed, trying to keep from staring, as his body went rigid. Drawing her close, he plunged his tongue deep between her waiting lips, tasting her sweetness, wanting every inch of her. She melted into him.

His need grew more urgent. Reason fled as he unzipped his pants. He wanted her now. This was meant to be. No more waiting. He'd consider the consequences later.

The scratch of a key turning in the lock flashed him back to his senses. Springing away, he pulled up his zipper and tucked in his shirt. Cathy's face flushed scarlet, as she yanked her robe back on and tied the sash.

What rotten timing. He stifled a groan as the McGuire clan filed in, glancing curiously at him and Cathy. He couldn't say nothing had happened. One look at Cathy's swollen lips and tangled hair told the story.

With his lips tightly sealed, he glanced at Cathy and awaited a cue.

She competently filled the gap. "My, that was a short movie. It seems like you just left."

"We didn't see it. The seats were sold out, though it was showing on half the screens. We went there for nothing."

Dora's voice was unnaturally high, almost hysterical, more than warranted for missing a movie. The tone was strange, since Cathy's sister seemed so levelheaded.

Always the sympathetic, unselfish one, Cathy said, "Oh, that's a shame. Maybe in a few weeks it'll be less popular."

"Sure." Dora's voice came out flat as she hurried out of the room.

Now only Cathy's parents remained. They stood before Danny in quiet condemnation. Ted McGuire frowned, making Danny feel unwarranted guilt. It didn't help to know he'd feel the same if it were his daughter who looked like she'd just been had in the front hall.

Asking the favor felt awkward, but maybe the distraction would ease the situation. "Mr. McGuire, uh, I was wondering...I just got drafted by the Cyclones. They'll be sending me a contract. Would you mind looking it over?"

Ted's frown changed to a speculative smile. The offer apparently put everything in a new light. "Well, young man, congratulations! I'll be glad to offer my advice. Hey, this calls for a celebration. Nancy, where's the good bottle of champagne?"

As Cathy threw Danny a rueful look, he could almost read her mind. They'd carried on quite well with their own festivities until the rest of the family had arrived. Obviously the remainder of the evening would be lost in basketball discussions. With a sigh, Cathy excused herself. Relief stole through him as he watched her leave. Now that he'd come to his senses, he was glad of the interruption. He'd gone further than he'd intended. It wasn't right to get Cathy's hopes up and disappoint her.

As Danny sipped the champagne, Ted lectured about contract pitfalls. He insisted on examining the document word for word before Danny signed it.

Danny nodded absently. A creak from the direction of the stairs signaled Cathy's reappearance, this time clad in a form fitting tee shirt and molded jeans. He tried to focus on Ted's words, but out of the corner of his eye he followed Cathy's every move.

She sank down beside him. Her fresh scent permeated his senses, reminding him of what he'd seen beneath her robe. He wanted desperately to throw his arms around her and continue where they'd left off. Instead, he made himself listen to her father's legal advice.

It didn't take long before Cathy's eyes glazed over. His own had probably done the same. Legal mumbo-jumbo was too much to take at a time like this.

Danny rose. “Well, thank you, Mr. McGuire. You’ve been a great help.”

“Let’s not stand on formalities. Call me Ted.”

“Thanks, Ted. I’ll be in touch with you when the contract comes.”

Cathy followed him to the door. With an audience of two watching, he placed a chaste kiss on her waiting lips, then reluctantly stepped out into the warm summer evening.

A light breeze blew across his face. It was a night meant for loving and being loved. He longed to succumb to the gentle persuasion, but must remain firm. He’d had a narrow escape. He may not be as lucky in the future. He had to break up with Cathy. It was the right thing to do.

THE PHONE WAS ringing as Danny stepped into the apartment. He let his answering machine pick it up.

“You motherfuckin’ prick. You think you’re hot, but you’re nothing but pond scum.”

The unexpectedly angry words startled him. The voice sounded familiar, but the connection was scratchy. Frowning, he shook his head. There were all kinds of nuts out there.

Now that he was in the big time, he’d apply for an unlisted number.

A WEEK LATER RITCHIE invited Danny to his new apartment in the Logan Square district of Chicago. As Danny stepped inside, a loud chorus of, “Surprise,” rang out.

He’d been tricked, but of course he didn’t mind. Everyone important in his life was gathered to celebrate his success: all the McGuires, Tony and Tracy, along with his past teammates and buddies from school. The sight warmed him.

They all talked at once, speculating on what Danny should expect as a pro.

“Can I get your autograph before there’s a line?” Cathy asked with an impish smile.

At the sound of her voice, the familiar stirring rose deep within him. Her sparkling hair, infectious smile, her very presence, lit the room.

Standing next to her was Dora, looking mysterious and sexy in black jeans and an indigo sweater.

Ritchie eyed Dora speculatively. Danny frowned, then told

himself he shouldn't be jealous. He had no claim on Dora. Cathy was the sister he loved.

To reaffirm his feelings, he turned his attention to Cathy. Talk gravitated to Tony and Tracy's upcoming wedding. Cathy threw envious looks in Tracy's direction.

Fortunately, before any hints could be thrown, Ritchie stepped out of the kitchen and into the living room carrying a huge cake decorated with frosting in the shape of an orange basketball.

His "Good luck, old buddy," was echoed by the others, bringing a lump to Danny's throat. The people here were his family. He felt a special closeness to them all.

Tuning into his thoughts, Cathy squeezed his hand. Beside her, Dora smiled hauntingly.

IT WAS HIS first day as a Cyclone. Danny's fingers trembled as he unbuttoned his oxford shirt and slipped into the famous crimson uniform. The jersey material felt cool and soft against his fevered skin. Catching his reflection in the locker room mirror, he stopped and succumbed to a wave of sentimentality. He wished his family could see him.

On the night before Mary Alice's death, his sister had teased him about his basketball obsession. She'd ended up encouraging him, saying he could have anything he wanted if he tried hard enough.

"What do you want, Mary Alice?" he'd asked.

A wistful look stole across her face. "Oh, the usual fairytale stuff, you know, the virgin bride marrying the handsome prince. Then, a little later, a darling girl and boy, maybe a suburban home."

He couldn't resist asking, "Is Larry the one?"

Her forehead had puckered as she gave him a slight push. "That's my business."

The sound of the referee's whistle shifted his thoughts back to the present. The past was gone. Life went on and he was a part of it.

He stepped from the locker room and bounded onto the court. It was time to prove himself.

Living in the present was not a picnic. He no longer played for his alma mater. He had a job to do. If he failed, he'd be fired.

Such responsibility made him nervous, especially since he was the new guy on the block. Was he good enough?

Out of sync, he made mental errors in practice, letting his teammates get away with stuff he'd never have allowed at college. Coach Dexter frowned and corrected him.

Friday, after a week of Danny's non-stellar performances, veteran player, Ronnie White, took him aside in the locker room.

"Dan, I know you're good. You make three-pointers look like lay-ups. What you need to do is focus. Get in there and follow the action. Forget what people think, and just do your thing."

Danny stopped tying his shoes and flashed a grateful smile at the black man whose temples were tinged with gray. Ronnie had been around a while and didn't need to consort with a novice.

"Thanks, Ron. I'll do my best," he said, standing up.

Ronnie patted him on the back. "That's all you can do. You're not alone. We're all human. I've made my share of mistakes. You'll catch on."

The veteran was right. Danny had been psyching himself out. Instead of playing, he'd spent too much time worrying about what everyone thought. It was time to buckle down.

After the pep talk, Danny adopted an assertive attitude. It paid off immediately. He loosened up. He grabbed for rebounds and aimed at the basket. Thanks to Ronnie's encouragement, he made it back on track. Like a candle in the darkness, one person's kindness had been what it took.

Coach Dexter looked at Danny thoughtfully, then switched him to different positions to gauge the results. Finally he nodded. "Dan, I'm placing you at point guard. You've got the speed. You're making the long shots."

Danny didn't argue. He'd be happy anywhere.

Practices went fine after that. Exhibition season began. Danny discovered he enjoyed taking chances, connecting at outside baskets, pretending he was street playing. The crowd's cheers gave him a heady feeling.

ON A COOL, CRISP day in early October, Tony and Tracy stood at the altar of Our Lady of Lourdes Church with Danny, as best man, watching from the side.

A glance at Tracy's tiny form enveloped in the long white gown, along with the rapturous look on her face, told Danny she was totally right for Tony. Tracy had waited a long time for this to happen. She'd cherish Tony and treat him like a king.

What more could a man want? That is, a normal man who didn't have a fixation clouding his life.

The couple couldn't afford much, so after the ceremony, a small reception was held in the church's basement.

With Cathy seated beside him, Danny felt the familiar stirring of guilt. She was waiting for him. Watching another couple's happiness had to be hard on her. Because of that, Danny avoided her eyes.

TOMORROW EVENING WAS the season's opener—the game when Danny would prove himself to the world. To relieve the tension, he took Cathy to a Mexican restaurant. Unfortunately, his stomach was so knotted he barely picked at his taco. Over the rim of a margarita, Cathy smiled back at him, pain lurking in her clear blue eyes.

Her wounded look drove a nail through his heart. His temple ached. The upcoming game was forgotten.

He wasn't happy about what he'd have to do, but it was the right thing. Without Cathy, he'd be a lonely, empty man. Soon she'd be gone from his life. Cathy was not his for the taking. He had a mission to perform.

Staring across at her perfect face, he tried to imprint its features in his memory. He'd been a selfish cad and still was. The longer he waited, the harder it would be. Still, he couldn't do it.

He settled the bill, held out Cathy's chair and hardened at the whiff of her floral perfume. It was torture to be near her, yet it was worth it.

On the way home, he switched on the radio. Soft music wafted through the still night air. With Cathy beside him, he was transported to a place of innocence and beauty where he'd lived before Mary Alice's rape and murder. He wanted badly to stay in that happy place and ignore what lurked outside.

The lulling music was interrupted by a news bulletin. Another girl had been raped and murdered in the Lincoln Park area. A chill raced up and down his spine and his resolve tightened. He had to get rid of Kevin or he'd strike again when he was free.

To fill the gap, he talked about the upcoming game. Though he knew Cathy wasn't a sport's fan, she did her best to respond. She was his fan and that's all that mattered.

IT WAS ALMOST game time. The people who meant the most to Danny were seated in the arena waiting: Cathy and the rest of the McGuires, Tony, Tracy and Ritchie, along with thousands of cheering, frenzied fans. If he failed today, they'd all witness it.

The stadium darkened. The spotlight zoomed in on the Cavaliers' starters, then the Cyclones. Danny was not among them. Instead, he sat on the bench, poised for action, hoping to get his break. The first, then the second quarter began and ended. With each waiting moment, the padded seat became more uncomfortable. He wanted in the worst way to go out and do his thing.

With the third quarter almost over, Coach Dexter finally laid a hand on Danny's shoulder. "Get in there. We need some baskets."

Danny ripped off his warm-up suit. When he loped out onto the court, the lights blinded him. The din hurt his ears, flashing him back to the courtroom years ago. The grim reminder made it hard to think, yet he had to concentrate.

The orange blob sped his way. He grabbed for it, but it flew past. Stifling a groan, he saw the Cavalier player, Ralph Raven, retrieve the ball and dribble across the court.

That was not an auspicious start. Would Coach Dexter yank him out? Danny expected it, but the whistle didn't blow.

Before he knew it, he got another chance. His buddy, Ronnie White, passed him the ball. Danny grabbed it, broke away and headed for the basket. One of the Cavalier players, Big Ben Carter, appeared out of nowhere. The giant planted his mammoth body in front of Danny and knocked him in the arm.

He'd been robbed. That should have been his basket. Danny forced back his anger. He was in the big time and would get no breaks.

Well, he'd show everyone. He had to. Again Big Ben aimed. The ball flew off the basket. Danny jumped and caught the rebound. He passed it to Ronnie, who slammed in the tying basket. The crowd cheered. Danny smiled. At least he'd done something right.

Seconds later the whistle blew and he was pulled back onto the bench. The starter, Louie Larson, had gotten enough rest. A tied game was no place for a novice.

Danny chafed on the sidelines. Now he'd had a piece of the action, it was even harder to sit and watch. The score switched back and forth, with the players fighting like the fate of the universe was at stake. The result was a Cavalier victory by four points.

Outside the locker room, Cathy waited with a sympathetic smile and a box of candy. Danny shot her a rueful grin. "I'm sorry I didn't burn up the court for you."

Her eyes held confidence. "You did fine."

"Thanks, Cathy. I can always count on you for moral support."

But could she count on him? She had to be wondering.

His heart quickened at the sight of Dora standing in back of her. "Hi, Dora, did you have a good time?"

She nodded, golden eyes glowing. "Danny, you were wonderful, especially when you caught that pass from Ronnie. Too bad Ben elbowed you."

"You must be the only one who noticed," he said, feeling an instant bond.

"Of course I did," she said, smiling back at him.

Ted and Nancy offered congratulations, distracting his attention. Ritchie reached over to shake Danny's hand. "Hey, fellow, way to go. That was a great rebound. You're going places."

"Yeah, Danny, you did great," Tony piped up from behind. Tracy cheered, making Danny blush.

The praise was embarrassing. "I'm hungry. Let's get over to Tobasco's," he said.

They headed out the door. He could have picked anywhere to go, but had deliberately chosen Tobasco's as a way of memorializing the day his parents had died. They deserved a place in his memory today.

As he sat at the head of the long table and gazed across at everyone, a sense of loss crept in. He hoped his parents and Mary Alice would have been proud of him.

The pizzas arrived. Everyone joked and laughed, snapping Danny out of his somber mood. Being alive was wonderful. This was what life was all about, celebrating great moments with friends and loved ones. He reached for Cathy's hand.

Tracy smiled mysteriously. Tony cleared his throat. "Listen up, folks. We've got an announcement. Tonight's actually a double celebration. Tracy and I are having a baby."

Danny knew he should be happy for his friend, but all he could think of was what the news would do to Cathy.

Her eyes reddened as she offered congratulations.

The noose was closing in on him. What should he do?

Chapter Nine
Kevin

KEVIN COULDN'T SLEEP. It didn't help that Nerd Needham snored like a walrus and the others down the row joined in. The racket echoed off the concrete walls.

He was thinking again. It was the wrong time to do that. In the darkness, his brain wouldn't shut down. His fists clenched as he remembered what he'd seen that day.

Knowing Callaway had made the Cyclones, Kevin had sauntered to the rec room to check the prick's progress in the season's opener. He'd plunked onto the Formica chair and stared grimly at the screen.

Not far into the game, the announcer screamed, "What a rebound! Young Callaway's going places."

Not only that. The dude was by no means ugly. Kevin furiously stared at the deep blue eyes set in the movie-star like face, topped by dark, wavy hair.

Pedro blew a kiss at the screen and smacked his lips. "I want you, baby. You're sweet enough to eat."

The other inmates hooted.

That was it. With an angry scrape, Kevin pulled out his chair and headed for the door. He fumed the rest of the day and spun revenge plans.

If Callaway hadn't snitched on him in the first place, there wouldn't have been a trial or the need for a false alibi.

Somehow he'd find the perfect payback. In the meantime, like so many other nights, this one would be long.

By morning's light, he hadn't come up with a plan. In desperation, he turned to the *Chicago Sun-Times*. The subscription was a Christmas gift from the old man, a link to the past, his touch with the outside world.

Sitting on the edge of the bed, he opened the paper to the sports section, scanning it for mention of a certain basketball player. Nothing this time, but he'd keep looking. The more he learned of Callaway's habits, the better.

What used to be fun turned to torture as he forced himself to watch every Cyclone game. As the season progressed, so did Callaway.

Like gossiping biddies, the reporters harped on each bit and piece of Callaway's life. That's how a few months later Kevin learned of Cathy McGuire, a broad who hung around with Callaway.

Sprawled across his bunk, Kevin turned the pages of the sports section. He stopped when he caught sight of Callaway alongside a red-haired looker. His hands gripped the paper as he yanked himself up for a better view. What stared back set his heart thumping. She was a real princess, the sweet, wholesome type you wanted to fuck nonstop. The sight gave him a huge boner. He wanted her bad.

He couldn't have her. He was locked up in a cage.

Frustrated, Kevin tore the page, smashing it into tiny pieces beneath his heel. Hot, helpless rage engulfed him as he stared at the scattered papers, then at his filthy cell. He shouldn't be here. None of this was his fault. If it weren't for Callaway, he'd be free.

The prick had it all. Now, to top it off, he was poking a red-hot babe, while poor schmuck Kevin rotted in an infested box, wondering if he should bother to jerk himself off again.

Glaring, he glanced upward at his cell mate, Jonathon Needham, bookkeeper embezzler extraordinaire. Needham, as usual, silently stared into space. The nerd couldn't say two sentences in a row and wouldn't know a tit if it were stuck in his mouth. A solitary photo of his horse-faced ma was taped beside his bunk.

Not for the first time, Kevin wished Brad were back. At least he'd made the place bearable. They'd confided in each other and sympathized over the unfairness of their fates. Having a listening ear hadn't set Kevin free, but had helped him endure.

He wondered how his old buddy was doing. The last thing Kevin had heard, Brad and a few of the other "alums" had set in motion the plans Kevin had devised in electronics class. So far, they appeared to be succeeding.

Through a network of fake IDs, they'd obtained human resources positions at leading security firms and hired employees in the normal fashion, except for the chosen ones, whose purpose it was to scope out valuables in fancy homes. The scopers and managers stayed clean so no one could guess what valuable information they passed along.

Page two of yesterday's paper held two paragraphs about an art heist in Winnetka. Kevin wondered if his friends had pulled it off, but could only sit tight and wait for word. The grapevine was slow, but effective.

It hurt that he couldn't be out in the thick of it, instead of stuck in this tiny cell with the nerd of all nerds. Kevin sighed as self-pity set in.

He hated when he felt this way. Weakness was a curse.

Like a treadmill going nowhere, his mind spun back to the past, to what he'd almost had. He missed Mary Alice. He'd been so close to having her. After seven years, you'd think he could have gotten over it. He had to let go and be realistic. No amount of wishing could bring Mary Alice back. Forcing back angry tears, he kicked the papers beneath his foot.

One page stood out in the mess. Almost like a sign, a vision of long, red ringlets framing innocent blue eyes stared back at him. Cathy McGuire was one hot broad. Callaway didn't deserve her.

THE NEXT DAY the guard announced, "Green, you've got a visitor."

There was only one person who'd entered the prison gates to visit Kevin and that was his old man. Though Derek was a loser, he was family. The old man had lied for him and that meant something. Too bad he hadn't pulled it off.

This time Derek was all hyped up, rattling on about a broad named Sharon and bragging that her nipples were the size of quarters.

"She likes it on top. I don't even have to work," Derek confessed with a huge grin.

Before Kevin's imprisonment, Derek and Kevin had exchanged many such confidences and had outdone each other with exaggerations. That was then. Kevin didn't want to hear about it now. He'd warned Derek.

"What the hell're you doing? You know that stuff gets me hornier than hell and I can't get a woman. There's only self-service here, unless you're a dick smoker, which I'm not."

Derek looked sheepish. "Sorry, kid, I forgot."

"Well, try to remember next time before you open your trap, okay?"

His old man nodded. "Yeah, I see your point. If I were in your shoes, I'm not sure what I'd do." A mirthless laugh escaped him. "Maybe shoot myself, I guess. I can't go two days without a woman."

"Well, I don't have that option. Prisoners aren't allowed guns, for obvious reasons. Anyway, the way you're talking, if I had one, I'd go after you first."

Derek looked surprised at his son's bitterness. "I didn't mean no harm. Just making conversation."

They fished around for more topics to talk about. Fortunately, time ran out.

Derek rose. "I'll see you around, kid."

"Sure, Dad."

Kevin wretchedly watched the retreating figure. His only family member had walked out the door, possibly never to return.

As the guard led Kevin back to his cell, he felt like a lost and abandoned child. Hell, even children weren't left to rot in cages. If Derek were a decent father, he'd forgive his son and understand. A mother would.

That set him to wondering again about Ma. He didn't remember her and that made him feel gypped. He'd once heard from an uncle who'd passed on that when Kevin had been three, Ma had caught a thoroughly soused Derek balling a scroungy chick on the living room couch.

That's when the old lady had hightailed it out, abandoning Kevin to the old man's attentions. It could have been worse. Dad probably hadn't been thrilled about being stuck with a brat, but in his haphazard fashion, he'd done his best. Unfortunately, booze was the old man's curse and also Kevin's. If Derek hadn't been at the pub when Mary Alice was murdered, the alibi would have held.

Kevin sighed. There was no use dwelling on the impossible.

An hour later, Nerd Needham's horse-faced mother was announced as a visitor. The nerd smiled in anticipation and almost bounced off the bars.

Resentment flared in Kevin. Why couldn't his mother visit him? Where the hell was she anyway?

Mothers were respected. The inmates considered them the ultimate visitors. Steven Summers, in particular, spoke of his Mom as if she were a saint.

He'd once said, "Hell, that woman has no cause to love me, yet she cries each time she sees me. When I think of what I done by murdering her own mother, and yet Mama still loves me...well, it chokes me up inside."

Kevin wondered what unconditional love felt like, the kind that didn't choose between good and evil. If anyone loved him that much he'd feel all-powerful. It would be better than fucking a woman and hearing her beg for more.

Damn, he'd missed out on that whole mother-kid thing. There was only one person who could give it to him and he had no idea if she was alive or dead.

As he glanced around his cell, a hard knot formed in his stomach. He was on his own. No one cared about him but himself. He had to remember that.

That same night he had a dream, one he'd had before. He was a baby. His old lady was screaming at him.

"You're worthless. This is what you deserve," she said, thrusting him head first into the toilet bowl.

He sputtered as he hit the icy water. Just then, the old man rushed in, stuck his hands straight into the bowl and pulled Kevin out.

He awoke shivering. The prison heat was on the bum again. There was always trouble with the furnace, or so they claimed. Maybe they kept it cold to save money and make the prisoners suffer.

This place was hell. He wanted out, but had thirteen years left. Nothing would help, even being visited by his long-lost mother. If she did show up, she couldn't perform the miracle of getting him released.

A LONG TWO MONTHS passed before Derek's next appearance. Kevin pretended nothing had happened. He'd learned his lesson. From now on, he'd keep on Dad's good side.

To start with, he asked Dad for news of the old neighborhood. It had to have changed in the past seven years, yet for some reason, Kevin still felt part of it.

Unfortunately, Derek didn't know much of what was going on, except that the city was replacing some curbs. He was still fired up about the babe he'd babbled about on the last visit.

Kevin looked at his father incredulously. Derek never stuck with a broad this long. Could he be serious? Was he falling for Sharon? It was hard to believe, but maybe after all these years, the old man was settling down.

The idea was disturbing. If Derek did get remarried, Kevin wouldn't be his only family. Someone else would matter more. Derek wouldn't bother coming to visit. Fear and jealousy shot through Kevin, but he tried to appear nonchalant as Derek described the saint. Too bad she wasn't Kevin's real mother.

His mother had to be out there somewhere. He'd like to see her at least once. Where was she?

Kevin cleared his throat. With heart hammering, he broached the subject. "Dad, uh, I've been meaning to ask...have you heard from Ma recently?"

Silence stretched. Blinking rapidly, Derek looked across at Kevin, then said, "Shit, son, I must've forgotten to tell you...I probably got drunk that day... Hell, Gloria died about six years ago. She had pneumonia."

Kevin's heart plummeted. An immeasurable feeling of loss

gripped him. Until this moment, he hadn't realized the importance of seeing his mother at least once. Now it would never happen. Fate had robbed him of the opportunity.

He swallowed hard and smiled wanly, trying to hide the hurt. "Hey, don't worry about it. I was just wondering, that's all. Besides, the old lady was never around anyway. She never meant anything to me."

Derek looked relieved, then said, "You know, son, this time I'm doing things right. Sharon's a great gal and I'm being real good to her."

When the old man had left, the fear returned. What if Sharon decided to keep Derek from visiting him? If so, there would be no one left. Part of him said it wouldn't happen, yet the part that hadn't known a mother insisted it could. He had to be prepared.

That confirmed it. He better get used to loning it.

It wouldn't happen overnight. The next day, as was his custom, he comforted himself by pulling out his newspaper, the one evidence that Dad cared. He'd check on Callaway again. That would keep him busy. Before he could turn to the sports section, a headline caught his eye.

Copycat Killer Strikes Again, it read.

His hands trembled as he focused on the article. Another sweet-looking blonde had been raped and killed in the Lincoln Park area. Well, it served them right. When would the cops wise up?

A wild idea hit him. Would it work? Dare he give it a try? He hated to get his hopes up, but what was the alternative?

From the corner of his eye, he spied a fast movement. With fascinated loathing, he watched a cockroach dart across the floor. No chickening out this time. He had to do it.

Chapter Ten
Danny

THE PHOTOGRAPHERS AT the stadium weren't fast enough to catch Danny sprint from afternoon practice into a waiting taxi. As the cab wound its way through downtown Chicago onto Madison Street, heavy black clouds gathered, blocking the August sunlight.

Ten blocks further, the driver pulled up in front of Ted McGuire's Monroe Street office. Danny opened the door to translucent torrents of rain. They pelted the sidewalk, creating steaming eddies.

If the storm broke the heat spell, it would be a blessing.

Danny clutched his contract against his chest and darted inside. The air conditioning hit him, making his skin go clammy; in contrast, the air in the elevator was stifling.

On the tenth floor, the receptionist flashed a dazzling smile before leading Danny along a maze of pepper colored carpeting to the inner sanctum.

Ted McGuire rose from his desk. "Before you get comfortable, let me take a look at that," he said.

Danny passed him the semi-wet paper then lowered himself gingerly onto the edge of the tweed chair.

Cathy's father read it through, busily made notations in the margins, then looked up and smiled. "We'll see if this version gets past their attorneys."

Ted's eyes turned serious. *Here it comes*, Danny thought. He'd been afraid of this and had been tempted to go elsewhere, but that would have insulted Cathy's dad. He could almost read the man's mind. Ted's pride and joy was Danny's for the taking, yet he hadn't laid claim to her.

Ted leaned forward. "Well, young man, you've been with the Cyclones for a year and your career's steady on track. Maybe it's time to settle down."

"I'm thinking about that, sir." Danny said, rising quickly before Ted could pursue the subject.

He hated being impolite, but wouldn't be pressured into doing something he'd regret.

"Well, I better get going. I've got a cab waiting," he said, fleeing.

Miraculously he found his way through the desk maze to the elevator. As he descended, a sinking feeling not originating from the drop of the elevator gripped him. Cathy also knew about the contract.

With temples throbbing, he stepped outside.

The tension between him and Cathy had become as unbearable as the oppressive heat and humidity which the storm had not dispelled. Cathy wanted something he couldn't give her.

The time had come. He had to decide. The delay had already hurt Cathy. If he let her go, would it be right? If he didn't, what would happen later?

As he again settled into the cab, he remembered where they'd be headed in a few days, on Sunday. It wouldn't help matters. That's for sure.

THE CHURCH BELLS rang in the distance as Danny stepped out of the Magnolia Street apartment he'd called home since childhood. His shirt plastered itself to his back. Though it had been eight years since his sister had been murdered, August days like this reminded him of the trial. If none of it had happened, life would be simple.

It didn't help that his car felt like the inside of a hot cardboard box. With slippery fingers, he flicked on the air conditioning. As he gripped the steering wheel and pulled into the street, his neck knotted up. That was not good. He had to relax. He had to think of something else.

He took a deep breath and concentrated on the car's appointments, taking in the BMW's tan leather upholstery, the satellite radio, the other toys at his disposal. Since becoming a Cyclone, his automobile had been his one major indulgence. Other than that, he lived simply.

By the time he'd opened the door for Cathy, the car's interior had long since cooled off. Despite that, he felt the heat of her thoughts. Neither one of them said much as he drove past the tree-lined streets alongside Northwest Highway to the Vanettis' home in neighboring Jefferson Park. It hurt to realize that everything he'd had with Cathy would be over soon.

Unaware of the tension, Tony happily greeted them at the door of his bungalow and led them into a cozy looking living room.

"Tracy will be out in a sec, along with our new addition. How about iced tea or a beer?"

"Iced tea," they said in unison.

Tony darted away to fill their order, leaving Danny and Cathy alone. The silence lengthened. He filled it by glancing around. The furnishings were inexpensive, yet homey touches were evident everywhere, from the cross-stitched wall hangings to the lace doilies on the end tables.

As Tony reappeared with the cold tea, he caught the last of Danny's inspection. "It's not the Taj Mahal, but it's home," he said with a modest smile.

"It's very lovely," Cathy said graciously.

Though she came from a wealthy family, there was nothing pretentious about Cathy. Her unassuming attitude was one of the things Danny loved about her. It wasn't too late to change his mind.

"Hey, you two, have a seat," Tony said. "I was elected chef today. I've got things to do in the kitchen, but I'll be right back."

They settled silently onto the plump sofa. It was his first visit here, yet Danny couldn't help but feel at ease, despite the tension between him and Cathy. The place emitted warmth and comfort, as if it had taken on the characters of its occupants.

With Tony's fledgling ad agency up and running and Tracy minding the child, the Vanettis could barely afford their digs. Still, they appeared happy. His own family had been like that. Everyone had pitched in and they'd gotten by. The fact Danny was now wealthy meant little to him. There were more important things in life.

Tracy took that moment to waltz in carrying little Angela. "Here's our precious darling," she said.

The wanting look in Cathy's eyes tugged at Danny's heartstrings.

"Would you like to hold her?" Tracy offered Cathy.

Cathy nodded and the women gently made the exchange. Crooning softly, Danny's angel rocked baby Angela.

As he watched, his eyes smarted and he swallowed. God help him, Cathy deserved to be holding her own baby.

Angela's mouth puckered and aimed at Cathy's breast.

"Poor darling, you're hungry," Cathy said.

She turned to Tracy. "How often do you feed your little princess?"

Gazing proudly at her daughter, Tracy laughed. "Almost every minute. Sometimes I can't get anything else done."

She didn't seem too upset about it.

Cathy held onto Angela as if she'd never let her go. Danny's eyes were glued to them. They looked so beautiful together. How could he give this up? Instead of righting an old wrong, should he forget the past and lead a normal life?

He pictured a snowy evening of lying in front of a fireplace with

Cathy beside him, then afterwards a night of slow lovemaking. They wouldn't bother to be careful. If it were meant to be, they'd conceive a miniature Cathy or Danny.

How would Cathy look with her perfect breasts filled with milk? The thought made him want her even more.

His eyes strayed again to the Madonna-like scene. He yearned to keep Cathy, yet if he took her, he'd have to relinquish the mission he'd held onto for eight years.

Trying to force his runaway emotions into line, he gulped down the iced tea. He'd warned himself before. He had to be careful or his fantasies would get the better of him. He mustn't allow himself to weaken. Kevin must pay for what he'd done. His sister had been an innocent, yet she'd suffered and died a brutal death. Through no fault of her own, Mary Alice's dreams would never come true. She'd never marry her handsome prince and have children. Cathy could still do that, but not necessarily with him.

What was more important—Cathy or revenge?

Before Danny could answer the question, Tony stepped into the room. With raised eyebrows, he looked from Cathy to the baby.

"Danny boy, when are you going to break down and make an honest woman of Cathy? She'd make a great mother."

Cathy's face flushed a bright crimson. Ignoring Tony, she bent her head and smiled at Angela. Danny was not deceived. It wouldn't take long before the showdown.

It was obvious Cathy had pinned her hopes on him, expecting more than he'd offered so far. She had to be frustrated. With her intelligence and good looks, everything she'd wanted had come easily. She could get any guy she wanted, yet she'd chosen him. He had to be the biggest challenge of her entire life.

Selfishly, he wanted to hold onto her a bit longer. Life would be lonely without Cathy.

She looked at him strangely, awaiting his reply to Tony's question. Laughing self-consciously, Danny clutched at the nearest excuse. "Being a Cyclone has kept me so busy, I haven't had time to commit to anything else."

It wasn't a valid reason and he knew it. He daren't tell the truth. Tony sensed his reticence and filled the gap with basketball talk.

"Oh, Tony, I almost forgot," Danny said, pulling out a pair of season's tickets. "Maybe you could use these."

Tony's eyes lit up. "Thanks, man."

Knowing Tony's tight budget, Danny felt good about doing his friend a favor. Still, it didn't ease the sour feeling lodged in his gut as Cathy looked back at him in silent reproach. Although she'd taken the initiative suggesting their first date, throughout their relationship she'd never pushed him.

On the way home, Cathy didn't even mention the baby. His inner antenna told him she was hurt. He was afraid to say anything. Tears formed in the corners of his eyes. He blinked them away as the headlights of a station wagon packed with kids passed the BMW. What would he do without Cathy?

ON THE FOLLOWING evening, Danny took Cathy to a show rather than risk bringing her somewhere where they could talk. It was sad how their relationship had diminished. How long could the torture last? He had to put a stop to it.

The movie was supposed to have been a comedy, yet neither of them laughed. Later, when he pulled up to her parent's Georgian house, Cathy placed her hand on his arm. "Danny, we have to talk. I can't go on like this."

He sat silently, not making it easy for her, hoping she wouldn't press him.

This time she didn't give up.

"I thought you loved me and wanted to get married, Danny," she said in a trembling, determined voice. "Was I wrong all along?"

In pain he watched the street lamp cast a halo around Cathy's strawberry hair, making her look like a sad, lost angel. He'd known this moment would happen. He should never have accepted Cathy's love.

He looked deep into the innocent blue eyes, probably for the last time. He didn't want it to end this way. Her lips quivered. Any moment she'd cry. He didn't want to hurt her. Hell, he loved her. What should he say?

"Cathy, I wish I could offer you more. You deserve someone who'll marry you and give you children, but I can't."

Her eyes filled and a silvery tear dribbled down her cheek. He felt like a cad.

"But Danny, I don't understand. Why not?"

She was almost begging him, making him feel worse. This beautiful woman could have anyone in the world. What crazy quirk of fate had made her fall for him? The time had come for an accounting, yet he couldn't tell her. He had to protect her. In the long run, his cruelty would be a kindness.

Knowing what he had to do, he cringed inside. Why must he hurt the person he loved? "Cathy, I do love you. That's why I can't marry you. I've been selfish in holding onto you for so long. What I've done isn't right. I should've made the break a long time ago. You deserve more than I can offer."

"I don't understand," she barely choked out.

He was tempted to tell her. They'd been inseparable for two years. She knew almost everything about him: his obsession with basketball, his loneliness without his parents. She deserved an answer, especially after waiting so patiently. He hesitated.

Could he entrust her with his secret? He looked searchingly into the red-rimmed, innocent eyes, knowing what they were seeing wasn't him. She thought he was pure and good like her, yet inside he harbored evil vengeful thoughts.

He hedged. "A while ago, before we met, something rotten happened. It changed my life. I've never been the same."

"But, Danny, I love you just the way you are."

Her faith in him broke his heart. She was such a good person. She deserved better. He couldn't tell her. The corrosive hatred eating at him was not the sort of thing Cathy should have to deal with.

"I can't explain any more."

She tried to appear cold, but only succeeded in looking wounded. "All right, Danny. If that's the way you want it, I guess it's goodbye."

Blindly she fumbled with the door handle, then ran from the BMW and up the sidewalk, stumbling in her haste. He almost dashed out to help her, but stopped. It was better this way—a clean cut, with no repercussions.

Danny watched as she fumbled for the house key, then disappeared inside. The thud of the door reverberated through the night air, closing out an unforgettable chapter in his life.

It was done. He was free, but instead of feeling better, emptiness engulfed him. He'd thrown away something precious. Had he done the right thing?

WEEKS OF SLOW torture followed. Cathy didn't call. On game days, after Danny had suited up and stepped onto the court, he automatically glanced toward Cathy's empty seat. None of the other McGuires were present, either, not even Dora, who enjoyed going over the games with him afterwards. Apparently they'd heard the news and were not pleased. He'd lost another family and it hurt.

He'd relied on basketball as a refuge before, so he fell on it again, concentrating on his job. Despite his preoccupation, or maybe because of it, he managed to do well. Unfortunately, the person with whom he most wanted to share his accomplishments was not around to notice.

On a Washington road trip, he fought an overwhelming urge to call Cathy. Before, when he'd been away, he'd always felt better at hearing her voice. This time was different. He had only the remote control and Bruce Willis. His interest lagged. He fell asleep accompanied by the roar of a motorcycle on TV.

After the next game, he couldn't bear spending another solitary evening, so he joined the guys at Loco Louie's hamburger joint. Ronnie White told his usual jokes, making everyone crack up. Danny tried to join in, but his laughter sounded hollow to his own ears. The guys kept mentioning their wives and girlfriends, making Danny feel worse.

The end of the four-day road trip was almost a relief. When he stepped off the 747 into the airport, it really hit him. He had nothing to look forward to at home. The usual mob of reporters greeted him, but no one special. After throwing out a few random answers, he grabbed a cab.

Wearily he climbed the stairs to his apartment. When he opened the door, loneliness socked him. He was home, but it didn't matter. He was alone. The same gray couch where he and Cathy had sat laughing and munching popcorn stood in empty reproach, as did the rest of the apartment.

His thoughts drifted to the ones who'd dwelled here before, those who still held a claim to his heart. Was that Dad on the easy chair, shifting awkwardly trying to find a comfortable position for his back? Were Mom and Mary Alice laughing in the kitchen?

All this time had passed, yet it was still hard to believe he'd lost them. His eyes filled. This apartment held too many memories. He'd never wanted to before, but maybe it was time to move.

In defeat, he dropped his duffel bag on the floor and heaved a sigh. Out of the corner of his eye, he glanced at the answering machine on the coffee table. Its tiny red light blinked invitingly. His heart jumped. Cathy. It had to be her. If she'd made a move, could he ignore it?

If he could only hear her voice again, at least once. He pressed the button.

"Hi, pal..."

Damn, it wasn't her, but Tony inviting him for spaghetti the next day. Should he accept? Despite their longstanding friendship, he felt bad about going over there alone.

"Tony, uh, I don't think I can make it."

"What's up buddy? Ya got something planned? We're flexible. Let's make it Wednesday instead."

"I'm sorry. I'm just not up to it. I broke up with Cathy."

"Aw, Danny, you guys had something good going. What happened?"

Hearing the concern in his friend's voice made Danny almost blubber. He fought for control, though his insides crumbled. He was tired of it all. Everything was hopeless. He couldn't carry the burden alone. Perhaps if he explained, it would help. Maybe Tony, being so close to him, would understand.

"It has something to do with Mary Alice," he said almost too quietly.

Danny heard only the hum of the phone line, then Tony's cautious words. "Danny, that was a long time ago. I thought you'd gotten on with your life."

"I have, Tony, but there's more to it than that."

Something about Danny's tone alerted Tony. "Wait a minute, Danny, don't move. I'll be right over. We've got to talk."

Danny absently listened to the phone slam. His mind had already drifted away as, with great deliberation, he replaced the receiver in its cradle. Now it would come out. His friend would think twice about hanging around with a loon like him. That was understandable. He couldn't stand himself, either.

He didn't know how long he stood there in quiet desperation before the jolt of the doorbell startled him from his reverie. Without asking who it was, he dragged himself to the console and pushed the buzzer.

Tony's short frame whirled into the living room.

"Thank God, you're all right. Man, you had me worried. The way you were talking, it sounded like you'd freaked out."

Danny gave a small smile. "No, I haven't freaked out. At least, I'm not any different than I've been for years."

"Danny, why don't we sit down and talk this over, okay, buddy?"

Danny nodded, then sank onto the couch. Tony pulled up a chair across from him. He faced Danny, staring him straight in the eyes.

"All right, I'm with you. What are you talking about? How does what happened to Mary Alice affect Cathy?"

"Well, ever since then, I've had one thing on my mind and I can't get rid of it."

"You're not thinking..."

"Yeah, I decided long ago I'd make that scumbag pay for what he did. I'll never feel right until I do."

"Hey, Danny, I know how you feel, but you can't. The judge made the decision. Kevin got his sentence. You need to accept that. There's nothing you can do about it."

Danny banged his fist on the coffee table. "Damn right there is. I can erase that bastard from the face of the earth. He doesn't deserve to live. He should be dead like my sister."

"And then what? Have you thought of the consequences? Don't forget, man, you're in the big time. You've got it all and you can lose it all, just like that. What you're implying is premeditated murder."

"I know, but I've got to do something. It's not right what he did." Tears sprang to Danny's eyes. He hated the helpless feeling engulfing him.

"Danny, Danny, look at me. I'm your friend. I've always been proud of you, but this obsession of yours is dangerous. You've got to give it up before it steals your life.

"Just think of everything you have—there's Cathy, your friends, there's your career, so many good things. You can't throw it all away. Tell me you won't."

Danny stared into Tony's soulful brown eyes, knowing even if he ignored his friend's advice, Tony would still love him. He felt grateful for a friendship he didn't deserve.

Tony gazed at him steadily. Did he know something that Danny didn't? Confused, Danny searched his soul, this time not fighting the glimmer of hope sparking inside of him. Maybe he was a better person than he thought he was. Maybe he could forget the past. Maybe he was capable of living a normal life. All along, had he been using his hatred as a crutch against taking a chance at love?

One thing he knew. He disliked what he'd become. Hatred was a powerful habit and it soured everything. The moment Kevin had been convicted, Danny had also gotten a sentence, one inflicted by himself. His desire for revenge had wreaked irreparable damage on his life.

Tony and Tracy were so happy together. He wanted that with Cathy. Was it too late to abandon the goal he'd harbored for so long? His soul already felt corrupted. Could it be saved?

"What do ya say, Danny? How about giving yourself a break?" Tony asked in a confident voice.

The idea sounded appealing, but how could he give up what he'd held onto for so long? Yet if he didn't, in the long run, who would be the bigger loser, himself or Kevin?

Cathy loved him. Tony, Tracy and Ritchie did also. They saw

something of value in him. Why couldn't he acknowledge that his own life was worth saving? Why should he throw it away for the sake of revenge?

In his mind's eye, Mary Alice smiled back at him. She reminded him he could have anything he wanted if he tried hard enough. He wanted to love and be loved. That was more important than revenge. Why hadn't he realized it sooner?

As he slowly nodded, a giant burden lifted from his shoulders. Yes, he could do it. He had to. The alternative was hell. From now on, he'd ignore Kevin. When Kevin was released, let him live the rest of his life with a guilty conscience. That would be punishment enough. It was time to resume his own life.

The thought of how he'd treated Cathy left a bad taste in his mouth. He had to make it up to her. It was the right thing to do and he'd do it. As the enormity of his decision sank in, his heart beat fast. He'd make it work and it would be wonderful.

He stood up and crossed over to his friend. "Thanks, Tony. You've opened my eyes. I see what I should've seen long ago. You're a real buddy."

They shook hands. The handshake was a confirmation of his new life, almost a pact. He'd never renege on his word. From now on he'd channel his energy into positive directions.

"Hey, what are friends for, right?" Tony said, patting him on the back, sounding embarrassed. "Well, now that's settled, I'll just mosey on home to my wife and kid."

"Thanks again, man, I mean it. I won't forget."

After Tony had left, a sense of euphoria grew inside of Danny. He didn't have to wreak revenge. He could be happy and forget the past. Excitedly he planned what he'd say to Cathy. He'd beg her to forgive him, tell her he should never have allowed what had happened long ago to interfere with their future. He was tempted to pick up the phone right away, but restrained himself.

Everything must be perfect. Cathy deserved that. She'd put up with a lot. He had a lot to make up for. From now on, he'd give her the world. Through her joy, he'd find his. He just hoped it wasn't too late.

IT TOOK AN entire day for Danny to summon up enough courage to make his move. First, he called Cathy's home. Unfortunately, Dora's solid voice answered, instead of Cathy's ethereal tones. You'd swear Dora was the older of the two.

An unbidden thought flashed through his mind. If he'd met Dora first, would he have loved her instead? Physically he was attracted to both of them. Each represented a separate part of himself: one the dreamer; the other the realist. Right now, he was intent on embracing what was pure and good and forgetting the negative. Cathy's sister was too intense. He didn't need reminders of hardship and reality.

"Dora, is Cathy there?"

Dora hesitated, then launched into her piece. "Yes, she's upstairs. She's not happy with you, and I don't blame her. She's wasted too much time putting up with your games. I'm not telling her you're on the phone."

"Dora, slow down. I don't blame you for what you think, but there's more to it than you know."

"What possible reason could you have for leading her on and then dumping her?"

"Well, a valid one, but that's neither here nor there. I've decided to take the plunge anyway. Cathy's more important to me than anything else."

Dora's flat voice came back. "That's not good enough. I want a reason. You know, Danny, I'm really disappointed. I thought you were the best thing that ever happened to my sister, but I was wrong. I can't let her talk to you. I won't let you hurt her again."

"But, Dora—"

"No, and don't think of coming over here, either. I'll be guarding the door."

Things were getting complicated. Now he had to convince Dora before he could state his case to her sister. He thought for a moment. There had to be a way. He had to get Cathy back. He'd confided his story to Tony. Should he reveal it to Dora, including his past vow and his new resolution? His mind cringed at the thought of confessing again, yet it seemed the only solution. Since he'd already poured it out once, maybe it wouldn't be as difficult the second time. The main thing was that Cathy not find out.

Danny sighed. "Dora, could you meet me after the game tomorrow? Let's talk this over in a neutral setting, say, maybe Francine's in Mount Prospect."

The answering voice sounded a little excited, a bit unsure. Was there a chink in her armor? "Okay, Danny, but don't expect much. I love my sister."

"Believe it or not, I do, too. I'll meet you in front of the locker room, okay?"

"Sure, Danny."

On Saturday before the game, Danny glanced toward his reserved seats. He made out Dora, Tony and Ritchie. It felt good seeing some of his cheering section present, but its core was still missing.

When the starting point guard, Louie Larson, twisted his ankle, Coach Dexter called in Danny and allowed him to finish the game. Danny outscored and out-rebounded the other players.

"Callaway, keep up the good work," Coach Dexter said afterwards, patting him on the back as they entered the locker room.

Danny nodded, his mind already focused on the upcoming encounter. There was a lot at stake, probably his entire life. He had to talk sense into Dora.

A gorgeous woman stood by the door in the spot where he usually saw Cathy.

"Hi, Dora, I hope you didn't wait too long. Say, you're looking really nice today."

Danny strove to keep up the small talk as he fought back a growing attraction. Dora had come into her own. Her ebony hair shone brilliantly. Her hunter green pantsuit heightened the peach glow of her spectacular cheekbones. If he didn't want Cathy so badly, he'd be tempted to make a play for her sister instead.

"Thanks, Danny."

Her words came out breathlessly. The peach hue of her cheeks deepened. Cathy's younger sister wasn't as self-assured as she let on.

They drove in separate cars to the restaurant. It turned out to be a quiet, intimately dark place with small glass candleholders on red linen tablecloths. Danny felt a stab of sadness. Cathy should be here with him, not her sister.

Dora slid into the booth first, then Danny. As his elbow grazed hers, her eyes flickered momentarily. Danny put it down to a trick of the lighting.

Their talk skirted around the subject. They spoke of Dora's impending entrance to Loyola Law School. Undaunted by the prospect of long hours of studying, she was eager to meet the challenge. He had a feeling she could surmount any obstacle she wished.

As he listened, he grew mesmerized by her hypnotically glowing eyes. Before he could stop it, a startling image flashed through his mind: a nude Dora lying beneath him with shining amber eyes gazing upwards. He shook his head to clear it. He had to get a grip on himself. He'd almost forgotten his mission. Cathy was the one he wanted.

Sensing his withdrawal, her eyes clouded. Was she disappointed? Nonsense. She couldn't read his mind.

"Well, I guess, the legal profession isn't exactly of interest to you, Danny. There aren't many people who get as excited about it as I do. I know, let's switch to basketball. What about referee Burnham's call in the third quarter? Wasn't Andy Ransome over-guarding?"

They argued good-naturedly about the game's happenings. Dora, always the avid fan, showed remarkable insight. Her opinions about who was left in the game too long, who wasn't in the right spot to execute a play, who should be traded, made a lot of sense as usual.

Danny couldn't remember ever enjoying basketball talk as much. Sweet Cathy always tried to look excited when he rambled on about the game, but that was because she wanted to share the experience with him. Her actual interests lay elsewhere. Still, her unquestioning support warmed his heart and made him feel special. That reminded him. It was time to get Cathy back.

"Dora, maybe we better talk about why we're here."

Her glowing eyes dimmed. The restaurant's dark shadows settled on her lovely cheekbones. Her soft lips firmed. "That's right Danny. I know you're thinking you don't owe me a thing, that it's Cathy you should be explaining this to. Well, you've got to realize Cathy's a very dear, sweet sister and I just can't bear to see her suffer.

"I need to make sure you mean what you say and you're not going to hurt her again. It would be cruel if you came back and then decided to leave. She's not as strong as she lets on. Danny, she's let her whole life revolve around you, and you've ripped it apart.

"Sure, she's got her floral shop, but to a homebody like Cathy, that'll always be second. She needs you, but only if you'll stay. Otherwise, she'd be better off forgetting you and getting on with her life."

Her face reddened with emotion. Her trembling hands gripped the wine glass. "There, I know I've said a lot, but they were things that had to be said, things I've thought about for a long time."

Danny didn't know how to start. Before, he'd thought he'd been right to give up Cathy. Now he realized he wanted her more than he'd ever wanted to destroy Kevin. What he said now was important. He had to state his case emphatically enough to convince Dora. He was the lawyer and she the judge.

His throat went dry. He almost reached for his water glass, but resisted. "Dora, I mentioned to you about something that happened before."

She nodded.

"To understand my reasons, I've got to tell you about my older sister, Mary Alice. She was a beautiful person inside and out, the best sister anyone could have. As in every family, we had our differences, but bottom line is, we loved each other. She encouraged me. She told me I could have anything I wanted if I set my mind to it. If it weren't for Mary Alice, I wouldn't be a basketball player."

"Danny, I didn't know you had a sister."

"I did, but she's gone. She was raped and killed when I was sixteen."

Dora gasped, then placed her hand over his. "Oh, Danny, I'm so sorry."

He swallowed again, blinking back the tears which always sprang up at mention of his sister. "Well, anyway, when the cops came, I told them about an argument between Mary Alice and her classmate, Kevin Green. He'd been furious she wouldn't go to the prom with him.

"The police arrested Kevin. I testified at the trial. I'd like to think my testimony clinched his conviction. Anyway, instead of the death penalty, he got forty years. With good behavior, that turns into twenty in Illinois."

Danny grimaced. "The judge's excuse was Kevin's actions were the result of passion and not premeditated. All I know is he's still alive and will be released some day, but Mary Alice will never come back."

Dora sat silently, apparently marshaling her thoughts, still pressing his hand.

It felt comforting. Already he felt a bond developing between himself and Cathy's sister. He'd confided something important to her, yet it seemed right. Somehow he knew he could trust her with his life.

She loosened her grip and unconsciously traced her finger across the top of his hand, as if reluctant to relinquish contact. "Danny, something like that had to have left you with a horrible scar. Is that why you didn't want to get married?"

"There's more to it than that, Dora."

He snatched his hand away.

"Ever since the judge decided Kevin should live, I decided to go after him and give him what he deserved. I vowed to get even and put him in the grave where he belongs."

He watched Dora's drawn face for a reaction. She gazed back steadily.

"Are you shocked?"

"Not as much as you'd think. If anything happened to Cathy or Mom or Dad, I'd feel the same way. Yet, I'd hope to be strong enough to overcome that urge. There's a thin line separating a normal person from a criminal. Not crossing that line is the real test. If you're planning to step over it, you were right in the first place. It's best you don't see Cathy again."

"Before, all I could think of was getting even. I had to get back at Kevin as soon as he was released. Then my love for Cathy hit me out of the blue. Selfishly I didn't want to give her up, though I knew I'd eventually have to. I finally decided to make the break. I'd convinced myself it was for Cathy's good.

"It was too late. I'd waited too long. I love her too much. It hurt like hell without her. Still, I was sure I'd done the right thing. It didn't matter that both of us were miserable. It was the price I had to pay. No matter what it did to me or Cathy, I had to get even. I hurt deeply, but I wouldn't give up my goal."

"I can understand that, Danny."

"Thank God, I have a wonderful friend in Tony Vanetti. You've met him. He sits behind you at the games with his wife, Tracy."

She nodded.

"Anyway, Tony and I grew up together. We're tight. He accepts anything I do. Still, when he discovered how I'd been destroying my life by obsessing over revenge, he sat me down and we had a long talk. He convinced me to look deep inside my soul. He reminded me of what I'd be losing. He asked me why I was punishing myself for what Kevin did. He made me see that I'm important in my own right. I don't have to sacrifice my happiness because of what happened to Mary Alice."

Did Dora believe he'd changed? If not, all would be lost. Danny clenched his hands beneath the tablecloth. He must convince her.

"I'd always known revenge wasn't the answer, but hatred is a tough habit to break. In those few minutes with Tony, I examined myself thoroughly and didn't like what I saw. That's when I decided to put aside revenge and get on with my life. Cathy's love is more important than anything. I want to marry her and start a family. I'd give anything to make her happy. For too many years I've been caught up with my obsession, but now I'm free. I need Cathy to complete my happiness. What do you say, Dora? Will you help me get her back?"

Dora's eyelids sparkled with unshed tears in the candlelight. She sighed. "Yes, Danny, I'll help."

DORA WAS TRUE to her word. She phoned Danny the next afternoon and said she'd spoken to Cathy. She'd offered her sister a modification of what had happened, saying he'd lost his sister through death and then his parents. He'd been afraid of losing anyone else.

"Thanks, Dora. You're wonderful. I appreciate what you've done."

Her acknowledgment held a hint of sadness.

A few hours later, he was back at Cathy's door, shifting his feet, brushing lint off the lapel of his suit, trying not to be distracted by the odd thumping of his heart. He banged the knocker.

It seemed an eternity before the door opened. When it did, his eyes took in the most beautiful sight in the world, hopefully his future bride. The setting sun highlighted her strawberry curls. Her compact breasts tugged against a soft pink T-shirt.

Now that the time had come, he didn't know what to say. He felt as if they'd just met. Her eyes skittishly followed him into the house. It had only been a month, yet already they couldn't communicate. This was ridiculous. They belonged together.

"Cathy..."

"Danny..."

They both started to talk, then stopped and laughed.

He put his arms around her, pulling her close, feeling her breasts brush against his chest.

"Ah, Cathy, honey, I'm sorry. I know I hurt you. Can you forgive me?"

He felt rather than saw her nod, as she pressed closer to him. Could she love him despite the hell he'd put her through? All he could do was hope.

She felt so good next to him. His body hardened. He ached to prove his love. They were so close she had to know what was going on. He didn't care. His lips claimed hers. A gentle kiss turned into something frighteningly intense as their pent-up emotions were released. Her lips were soft, the nectar sweet.

His mind swirled. He stepped back. His tail bone jammed into the doorknob, reminding him of where he was. Now was not the time to behave like a caveman. He wanted Cathy to remember tonight for the rest of her life.

"Cathy, why don't we go somewhere nice? There's something I have to ask you."

Hope surfaced in her eyes. "Sure Danny. Let me change and comb my hair. I won't be long."

Before rushing up the stairs, she threw him a parting look, as if she was afraid he'd disappear. He didn't blame her. The old Danny would have left. The new, improved Danny had decided to start a new life and Cathy would be its fulcrum. If she rejected him now, his world would crumble.

"For you I'd wait forever," he whispered toward her vanishing figure.

After about ten minutes she reappeared, wearing a sunny, scoop-necked dress and looking glorious. He wanted her badly. God help him if she changed her mind. She seemed interested enough, but he couldn't blame her if she refused him. At the thought, cold sweat broke out on his forehead.

He'd made reservations at Regina's, an intimate Italian restaurant in Arlington Heights, where they'd eaten once before. They stepped inside the quiet darkness. Regina's was more upscale than Francine's, where he'd taken Dora to dinner. For a moment, a picture framed in his mind of Dora's lambent eyes shining back at him in the candle glow.

He shifted his focus. Tonight was Cathy's. He mustn't blow it. Barely glancing at the menu, he ordered the first thing he saw, which was an antipasto plate. He didn't feel like eating. He had to know where he stood. How should he begin? Calling the waitress back, he asked for a bottle of Dom Perignon.

"I've never had this before," Cathy said, fingering the wineglass.

Before she could raise it, he gently disentangled her fingers and slid the glass away. He placed his palm on top of hers. "Cathy, there's something I have to say. I know it's taken me way too long to get around to this, but I hope you'll forgive me anyway." Swallowing hard, he looked into her innocent blue eyes. "I love you, sweetheart. I've always loved you, from the first moment I saw your strawberry curls in front of me in class."

She smiled shyly. Her hand trembled and he gripped it tighter.

"This is where I get down on my knees. I'm going to look like a fool, but to prove I mean what I'm saying, I'll do it in front of the whole restaurant."

She watched mutely, as he climbed down before her. Desperately he went on, "Cathy, darling, I love you. Would you do me the great honor of becoming my wife?"

There, he'd said it. He'd gotten the words out. It had taken a lot of guts, but he'd done it. Now it was her turn. What would she say? She could make him the happiest man in the world or the sorriest man alive.

Her eyes filled as she stared down at him. She was taking way too long to answer. If she didn't want him, couldn't she say it and get it over with?

The silence lengthened. *Cathy, what are you doing to me?* he asked himself. Well, she had a right to torture him, though it wasn't usually her style.

"Yes, Danny, I'd be glad to marry you. I love you, too." Her voice broke.

"Thank God. Cathy, those were the longest few minutes of my life."

As he got up, he pointed to the window. "If you'd have said no, I'd have jumped right out there." He laughed to relieve the tension.

She joined him, then added, "Danny, don't worry. I'd have never said no. I've always loved you."

He turned serious. "Cathy, I'm sorry for hurting you. There were things in my past I should've buried long ago. They had nothing to do with you. I should never have let them stand in the way. You're the most important person in my life."

"Don't be sorry. You have a right to your feelings. You've worked everything out and that's what's important. We can go into our marriage without any surprises lurking in the background. It's better that way."

His future wife was more understanding than was good for her.

At that, the waitress arrived with the salads.

"Well, now maybe I can eat. I don't know about you, but suddenly my appetite's enormous," he said, flashing a suggestive leer.

She blushed charmingly at the double entendre. With a flustered expression, she reached for her fork. He did the same. They lingered over the meal, enjoying its significance.

In the candle glow, Cathy's eyes took on an azure hue, sparkling with excitement. He felt good inside, knowing he was making Cathy happy. He brushed aside any lingering doubts about Kevin. That episode was over. From now on, Cathy was his life.

Chapter Eleven
Kevin

A FEW WEEKS AFTER Kevin's desperate letter had gone its way, his former lawyer, Dominski, deigned to make an appearance. "Mr. Green, I've got good news."

Kevin's heart thumped. "What do you mean?"

"One of the officers redid the evidence room and found the missing Callaway DNA samples lodged between two of the cabinets. I might be able to help you."

This couldn't be happening. He hated to get his hopes up. It would be doubly hard if he were disappointed. "Just get me out of here."

"I'll do my best."

Dominski snapped open his briefcase and extracted a long yellow pad with green lines. "Tell me exactly what happened."

This time, Kevin told him the real truth. When he was through, the public defender said, "If you'd told me that sooner, you might've saved yourself some grief. Anyway, there's still hope. I'll send an evidence technician around for DNA samples." Dominski stood up. "Hang in there, good buddy."

Kevin smiled wryly. They hadn't seen each other in eight years and Dominski called him buddy. Hell, if the public defender pulled off what he'd hinted at, they'd be friends for life.

After Dominski left, Kevin's thoughts alternated between excitement and fear. He'd been let down before. What if the appeal didn't work?

He dreamed Technicolor visions of the outside world where he sauntered around the block, smiling and whistling, a free man.

He had no peace after that. While he carried out the daily grind, he clung to the thin thread of hope dangling in front of him.

A month after the meeting, he stood in the kitchen, grasping a slippery pot, trying to concentrate on scrubbing. His mind resisted, flying off on tangents. What would freedom mean?

He had to get out. So much was waiting for him. According to Brad, the security scam ran high. If Kevin joined him, he'd be sitting pretty. Freedom had to happen. But what if it didn't?

At the thought, the pot slipped through his fingers and clanged onto the cement floor.

Steve Summers drew his head out of the oven he'd been cleaning and gave Kevin a searching look. "You're acting strange, boy."

Kevin glanced carefully around, then dropped his voice. "I might get out," he said, letting the forbidden hope creep into his voice. "They found the missing DNA. It might spring me."

A flicker of regret flashed in Steve's eyes, but he was kind enough to say, "Man, you don't know how lucky you are."

"Don't I know it. That is, if all goes well."

Kevin tackled the pot again, but the grease remained embedded. He ignored the buildup, rinsed the pot and placed it on the steel counter.

"I'd like to take you along, good friend," he said, patting Steve on the back.

"Get those slimy hands off me," Steve said, laughing good-naturedly.

Kevin felt a rush of pity. It was a damn shame the poor fucker couldn't get out. One lousy mistake and the guy's life was ruined.

He'd made a mistake, too. The consequences had been costly. Through a bizarre chain of events, he'd lost a good portion of his youth. He bit his lip. Sure, he'd told Mary Alice he'd see her dead before she went out with anyone else. People said things like that when they were mad. It had been his rotten luck Callaway had picked up on the exchange and broadcast it to the court room.

Bearing down on another scummy pot, Kevin reveled in the familiar rage. He'd been victimized because everyone believed he wasn't good enough for Mary Alice. Only he knew what she'd actually thought. That got his thoughts going on another tangent. He hadn't had a piece of ass in years. He couldn't exactly remember how it felt, but couldn't wait to find out.

What if, heaven forbid, he couldn't perform? Would his dick hang there as limp as the wet towel he was gripping? Sweat broke on his forehead. He angrily swiped at it with the back of his hand.

When he got back to the rec room, he sat by the TV and devoured the sight of Mighty Woman. Those breasts were enormous. As he watched, he grew hard as cement. He needed a fuck bad. He hadn't been this horny since he'd been put in the slammer.

The jeering of the other inmates distracted him. They'd switched the channel and were hamming it up over a corny movie. A smarmy woman was reeling in a dopey man who didn't have a clue as to what she was up to. He watched curiously as the couple professed their undying love for each other. It was bull, yet he couldn't tear his eyes away. They looked so happy.

Then the wife got knocked up and the sappy husband couldn't think straight. Kevin snorted. What puke. Such a pain to drag around a screaming monster.

Something slipped into his mind, bringing him up short. His old lady had copped out, leaving behind her a screaming brat named Kevin. How had his old man coped?

A rush of gratitude spilled out before he could stop it. His eyelids grew wet. Derek had to love him.

Chapter Twelve
Danny

INDIAN SUMMER IN Chicago was bright and beautiful, with a hint of coolness. Danny shielded his eyes from the sun's glare as he dashed into St. Vincent DePaul, the campus church of DePaul University. By dropping a false lead, he'd evaded the reporters, sending them scurrying to St. Raymond's in northwest suburban Mount Prospect.

Danny almost tiptoed up the side aisle to the sacristy. Nervously, he awaited a glimpse of his bride. Much had taken place since he'd proposed to Cathy two months ago, throwing them both into a whirlwind of activity. They'd decided to get married right away, before the fast approaching basketball season. By some miracle they'd thrown everything together, including the many things women found so important: the wedding gown, bridesmaids, the works.

Such touches added to the solemnity of the occasion. Vows before a justice of the peace would not do for his Cathy. He wanted this to be a special day to remember. That meant an official ceremony in a church, conducted by a priest and witnessed by close friends and relatives.

Through it all, he'd been so busy he hadn't had time to think, much less be scared. Now, as he stood waiting, he couldn't help but wonder if he was doing the right thing. Maybe he should have given her up, but it was too late for regrets and doubts.

He shook off a feeling of uneasiness as, on cue, the music began. Petite Marianne, Cathy's college friend, led the parade in an ankle-length gown, tightly clutching a bouquet of daisies and chrysanthemums. Next came Dora, head held high, advancing regally up the aisle. Her long, black locks offered a startling contrast to her lemon hued gown. It clung like a designer's creation, emphasizing her perfect proportions.

Even from a distance she looked way too tempting for his peace of mind, especially since Dora was not the woman he was marrying. As she drew near, he could make out wet eyelashes and shiny cheeks. Biting her lip, she stared ahead, apparently not seeing him. Obviously she was moved by the sentimentality of the occasion. It wasn't every day her sister got married.

He'd avoided her lately. Dora was dangerous. She radiated sexual attraction and she knew too much.

The familiar chords of the wedding march marshaled Danny's thoughts into line, reminding him there was but one woman in his life. His eyes scanned the back of the church, searching for a glimpse of his bride.

At the sight of her, all sparkly and bright, his heart leapt. Ted McGuire gently held Cathy's arm, as if she were a figurine. She approached Danny, looking so lovely she seemed otherworldly, too perfect for this earth.

As Cathy stood beside him, the enormity of the step he was taking hit home.

God, please let this be the right thing, he prayed as he gazed into the childlike eyes of his bride. He loved this woman. He wanted only the best for her.

The service began. He tried to pay attention, but his mind drifted back to a few days earlier. In a final attempt to relinquish his past life, he'd visited St. Peter's Church in downtown Chicago. Through the anonymity of the confessional, he'd admitted to sins of hatred and intentions of murder. Father Francisco hadn't pressed him for his identity or the intended victim's, but had given Danny this advice: "Son, remember the Bible: '...do not avenge yourselves; leave that to God's wrath, for it is written: Vengeance is mine; I will repay, says the Lord... Do not be conquered by evil but conquer evil with good.'"

He'd gone on to say, "By wishing harm on others, you harm yourself. On the other hand, if you make others happy, you'll by rewarded by happiness."

The words made sense. After absolution, Danny emerged, feeling cleansed and whole, determined to follow the good priest's advice.

He was now at the crossroads. Today he was altering his life. A different priest stood before him, asking him to exchange vows. As he repeated the words, "I, Danny, take you, Cathy, to be my wedded wife," he was pledging more to her than she'd ever know. By consecrating himself, he was embracing peace and joy and thrusting aside hatred and bitterness.

Through a wet blur, he slipped the gold ring onto Cathy's finger. The sun shone brightly through the stained glass windows, illuminating his angel's face, a sign of the sacredness of their pact. Almost afraid to sully her perfection, he bent to kiss his bride.

The reporters had caught up with them by the time the wedding party reached the Savoy, where the small reception would take place. As he helped Cathy out of the limousine, myriad light bulbs flashed. He shielded her as best he could from the onslaught of pressing bodies. It was difficult not to be annoyed, especially when he saw the disappointed look on his bride's face. This was a private occasion, not meant to be shared with everyone.

Where were the security guards he'd ordered from Alert Advantage? Lots of the other players used them. This was the first, maybe the last time he'd hire them.

"I'm sorry, Cathy," he apologized.

A bright mask slipped over her face. "That's okay, Danny. It's not your fault."

Of course it was. If he had a regular job, this wouldn't happen. Damn it, he couldn't do that. Basketball was his lifeline. It had seen him through too many tough times.

They got to the door. The reporters pressed, trying to follow the couple inside.

"Hey, give us a break," Danny said, firmly shutting the door in their faces. Inside, he found the guards racing down the hall.

"I'm sorry, sir. Someone told us you'd be using the other entrance," one of them said.

That's right. The original plans had been to enter by the front entrance. He and Cathy had changed their minds and decided to go around the back, forgetting to relay the change in plans. Well, what was done was done. Breathing a sigh of relief, he left the guards stationed at the doors.

He and his bride walked arm-in-arm into the hall. Now they could relax and enjoy themselves.

As the rest of the world retreated, Cathy's face glowed. The guests enthusiastically tapped their wine glasses. Her lips grew red from his kisses.

He managed to eat a few bites, then was treated to a performance by the O'Malley step-dancers, a surprise arranged by Nancy McGuire. As the Irish jigs played, an earnest, dark-haired boy caught Danny's attention. With startlingly white shirt and vibrant vest, he couldn't have been more than six, yet he kicked up his heels with the best of them.

Danny whispered to his wife, "Maybe we'll have our own little dancer soon."

With a wide smile, Cathy nodded.

Then the lights dimmed and the band played. The evening passed in a happy blur. All too soon he was holding Cathy tight, moving in time with the familiar chords of "Let Me Call You Sweetheart," followed by the last dance. Pressing his bride close, he realized how fortunate he was.

One day maybe he'd have enough courage to ask Cathy what she saw in him. For now, all he could do was marvel at the vibration of her heart beating in unison with his while they whirled around the dance floor.

Then it was over. Exiting through the back door, they slipped into a waiting limousine. They sped down the Kennedy Expressway to O'Hare International Airport. Under assumed names, they boarded a plane.

Nine hours later they arrived in Maui. With leis dangling around his and Cathy's necks, Danny sat contentedly in a cab winding its way up the verdant hillside to the Christina Hotel. When they reached the penthouse honeymoon suite, in keeping with the time-old custom, he carried his bride over the threshold. Gently he set her down on the plush lavender carpet.

They silently faced each other. His heart pounded fiercely.

The lovely Cathy smiled back at him with trembling lips. Beneath the gauzy, cream colored dress, her breasts rose and fell rapidly.

"Cathy, darling."

He bent to kiss her open lips, then reached to gently knead her shoulder blades.

At that, a sigh escaped her and her body swayed toward him. Reaching out, he luxuriated in the texture of his bride's sparkling curls. With a slight touch, he turned her face to his and gazed into the lovely, passion-filled eyes.

Still watching, he inched his fingers slowly downward, unfastening her zipper. At that point, she closed her eyes, too embarrassed to reveal her innermost thoughts.

He laid feather light kisses across his darling's smooth skin. Soon the dress shimmered to the floor, yet there were other encumbrances to remove. Cathy's pert, confined breasts swelled above her lacy bra. Nervously Danny reached for the clasp, fumbling with clumsy fingers until it gave.

As his hands caressed the freed creamy mounds, a moan escaped her. His tongue traced a downward path within the freckled valley. More obstructions awaited him, which he removed with moist hands matching his body's temperature. Soon she stood, face flushed, in all her radiance.

"Don't be embarrassed. You're beautiful," he whispered as he hurriedly divested himself of his clothes.

Reverently he touched her. She sighed and reached out for him with shy fingers turning ever bolder. He whisked her up and carried her into the bedroom.

There he lowered his new wife onto the velvet comforter of the four-poster bed.

"Now, Danny, please," she begged.

He plunged in, feeling the wet smoothness close in around him like a moist glove. She gasped, whether from pain or pleasure he had no idea. He began slowly, savoring the precious moments.

Doing his best to please Cathy, he held out as long as he could. Soon her breath shot out in loud spurts, matching his. Outside, the waves ebbed and surged in time with the rhythm of the earth.

He couldn't wait any longer. In a dizzying paroxysm, he released himself inside of her. Cathy surrounded him with answering quivers.

When it was over, they clung to each other. She kissed and tasted him, her lips moving slowly downward.

He tentatively asked, "Cathy?"

She fulfilled his half-spoken wish.

Cathy was such a giving person. There was nothing she wouldn't do for him. He was hers for the taking as her lips claimed every inch of him. He didn't know if he deserved such happiness, but he dared not question it.

A riotous explosion shook him and he cried out with pleasure.

That was not enough. Soon he was plunging back inside her, as close as he could get. This was heaven on earth. Perhaps if they were lucky, a reward would be theirs in nine months. If so, he'd welcome the extension of their love.

Locked in her arms, he fell asleep to awake to a perfect morning. When room service rang, they hastily threw on their robes. The bell hop wheeled in huge plates of scrambled eggs, melons, sausages, bacon and crescents.

Danny instructed him to leave breakfast on the balcony table. He and Cathy nibbled as they sat overlooking the ocean. Soon the food was abandoned as they hurriedly disappeared inside.

Time sped forward until only two days remained. They'd spent most of their honeymoon indoors.

"Honey, why don't we go down to the beach?"

She smiled and nodded.

Like the newlyweds they were, they held hands in the elevator going down. After they'd spread their towels on the sand, she lay face down. He protectively applied lotion on her back.

With his fingers skimming across the soft flesh barely covered by the turquoise bikini, he felt the tension mount. She shivered beneath his touch. He gently turned her over and saw her eyes darken with passion.

Furtively he glanced around. "How about it?" he whispered.

She bit her lip, but didn't protest when he draped the towel over them. He divested himself of his trunks, pulled off the bottom of her suit and entered her, with the sand beneath them, surrounded by the glories of nature. As the waves pounded and their bodies merged, the once demure Cathy responded with abandon.

Afterwards she replaced her suit with shaky fingers, then looked up at him with her heart in her eyes. That was too much.

"I better cool off," he said, throwing on his trunks.

She laughed knowingly. Cathy was no longer an innocent, but a full-fledged woman. On her, it looked terrific.

They ran into the waves, splashed and taunted each other under the sun, then strolled along the water's edge, laughing as their feet sank into the sand.

With such fair skin, it wasn't long before Cathy's shoulders turned pink.

"We better get you indoors," he said.

Danny prided himself on being her protector, though, at the moment, he had more than protection in mind. He proved that time and again during the remainder of their honeymoon.

All too soon, they were forced to abandon their make-believe world and pack for the flight home. One consolation was that on their return, they had something to look forward to. Between exhibition games and Cathy's work at her new floral shop, they'd squeezed in enough time to discover a dream home in the quaint, tree-lined Sauganash section of Chicago.

The brick country-style house rested on three acres of land, affording ample space for any new additions to the family, plus the garden of Cathy's dreams.

When they arrived at the front door, he again carried her over the threshold. They happily settled in, he tackling the wallpapering, she planting bulbs in anticipation of spring.

Minding the flowers, Cathy was in her element. When she wasn't at home, she lost herself amidst the nosegays and greenery of her florist shop. Conscientiously she tended her domain, not only puttering with arrangements, but also performing the tiresome minutiae of utility bill payments, bookkeeping and cleanup. It wasn't Cathy's style to sit at home and let Danny provide for her.

She was perfect. He didn't have to remind himself how lucky he was. Whenever he ventured out with his wife, men stared at her in admiration. Her beauty drew guys like a magnet, yet she seemed unaware of her power. Her eyes were only for him. The knowledge of her love made him humble yet proud. And to think, he'd almost given her up. Thank God he'd come to his senses.

Danny's good fortune extended everywhere. He was now dubbed the team's sixth man, the next best thing to being a first stringer. Life was wonderful.

At Christmas, the family congregated for dinner at Cathy's parents' home. His wife sparkled in a tartan silk vest over green toreador pants. He caught short glimpses of Dora in a cranberry sweater as she sped back and forth from the kitchen to the dining room.

After a delicious roast lamb and accompaniments, they all retired to the family room and sat contentedly. Dora volunteered to clean up, refusing Cathy and Danny's offers of help. As soon as she'd rejoined them, Ted, removing his arm from Nancy's shoulders, asked, "What about those presents?"

"Sit back...I'll hand them out," Dora said in a cheerful voice, though her eyes glinted brightly.

Why was she keeping so busy? Did she feel out of place in her own family?

Danny eyed Dora as she reached for the presents beneath the tree. Her earrings sparkled in the semi-darkness. The Christmas tree lights cast a twinkling glow, illuminating her face, making her look sexy and mysterious.

"Here, Danny."

He let go of his wife's hand. Dora's fingers brushed his as she handed over Cathy's present. Ignoring the unexpected tingle, he turned and extended the gift-wrapped package to his wife.

At home later that evening he and Cathy exchanged their own private gifts beneath the seven-foot tree they'd picked out themselves at the forest preserve. Among its ornaments was one labeled Our First Christmas, which Cathy had discovered at a craft fair. They glanced at it and exchanged smiles.

Pushing aside disturbing thoughts of the lonely figure beneath that other Christmas tree, Danny gathered his wife into his arms. He made love to her amidst the twinkling lights of their own tree, while the aroma of pine needles tickled his nose. Life was good.

BY THE START of February, basketball season was in high gear. Now that Danny had become a valued member of the team, he was awarded more playing time. Things were going along great, but there was a down side. With success came recognition. He was often besieged and interrupted at inopportune times. It wasn't easy to play the gracious star, but he did his best. He remembered what it felt like to be an underdog.

After a particularly horrendous trip to the grocery store where they were mobbed and jostled, Cathy asked, "Danny, can't you find another job?"

"You don't mean that," he countered. "Isn't it fun being famous?"

In his heart he knew Cathy didn't want the spotlight, just him. Well, compromises had to be made. Stuff had to be put up with. Nothing was perfect.

A WEEK LATER, HE sat on the bench, eagerly awaiting his playing time. It was an uninspiring game, five minutes into the first quarter, when Coach Dexter pointed to him. "Danny, get us some points."

He sprinted out. Ronnie White stood surrounded by Blazers, so he passed to Danny in the back court.

Danny pivoted away from the Blazers' center for a reverse dribble. As he spun back, the Blazers' point guard blocked him. Cornered between the opposing center and guard, Danny had no room to maneuver. His right foot landed hard on the other guard's. A shooting pain flashed through his ankle. His right foot crumbled beneath him. In a cold sweat, he sank to the floor.

Dr. Jack Halman, the team physician, rushed onto the court. After a cursory exam, he said, "We better get you to the hospital."

Danny felt like bawling, but not from pain. In the bounce of a basketball, his career may have ended, his dreams dieing. He bit his bottom lip as he was carried off in a stretcher.

Cathy appeared beside him, frowning with concern. "Danny, are you all right?"

A fresh wave of pain hit him, making him grit his teeth. "My foot hurts like hell. I have to go to the hospital."

"I'll go with you."

They quietly rode in the ambulance, amidst the wail of the siren.

When Danny arrived at Northwestern Hospital, he got the VIP treatment. A technician whisked him into a cubicle, took x-rays, did an ultrasound, and sped off. Danny awaited the results, nerves wreaking havoc on his stomach. Had his career ended before it had begun? What would he do without basketball?

It seemed forever before Dr. Halman approached. "Mr. Callaway, you've got a badly torn tendon. Healing such an injury can be more difficult than a broken bone. You're going to need surgery."

Fighting waves of disappointment and pain, Danny swallowed hard. "When can you operate?"

"I'm flattered by your confidence, but you need a specialist. He'll be along soon."

Maybe Dr. Halman had painted a worst-case scenario. Maybe the foot doctor would have better news. Half an hour passed before a middle-aged man in jeans and a polo shirt strode in and shook Dr. Halman's hand. "How's it going, Jack? I came over as soon as I heard."

He turned to Danny and shook his hand. "It's an honor to meet you, Mr. Callaway. I'm Dr. Warren Mason. Okay, let's have a look at that foot."

Unfortunately Dr. Mason's diagnosis concurred with Dr. Halman's. Danny need surgery, but it would have to wait until the swelling had subsided. In the meantime, Dr. Mason applied a temporary splint.

An hour later, armed with anti-inflammatories and pain pills, Danny exited the hospital in a wheelchair.

As he waited for a taxi with Cathy, the enormity of his situation hit him. This might be it. His career could be over. What would he do? Basketball meant almost as much to him as his wife. His life had been just right the way it was. Damn it, he better not lose basketball. The disturbing prospect haunted him, keeping him awake well into the night.

He wanted the surgery over, yet cringed at what could be the final result. The two weeks inched by. Finally, he again lay in a hospital room, this time getting prepped. Soon his fate would be decided.

He prayed, but wondered if God would listen to him. He wasn't blameless. After all, he'd plotted to kill a man. How much weight did repentance carry? As the Demerol in the IV entered his bloodstream, he resigned himself to fate. He had no choice. What would be would be.

PAINKILLERS FOGGED DANNY'S brain. A wavy figure approached. It had to be Dr. Mason, which meant the surgery was over. There was something Danny had to ask, but he couldn't remember what it was. Suddenly it came to him, along with a stabbing fear. How was his foot? Was it whole or had it suffered irreparable damage?

The doctor said something, but Danny couldn't make it out above the pounding of his heart. "What did you say?"

"Mr. Callaway, I did the best I could, but it was tricky. I can't guarantee a complete recovery. We'll have to wait and see."

That didn't sound good. Danny looked around wildly, his gaze settling on Cathy to his right. Her eyes held pity and something else that looked like relief. He knew she disliked his road trips, also his popularity.

Her reaction seemed like a betrayal. Maybe if he were a better man, it wouldn't bother him. What had happened wasn't her fault. It was only an accident. Only his life.

He'd never liked whiners, yet this time, he couldn't help resorting to self-pity. His injury couldn't have come at a worse time. He'd just begun to make a name for himself. If he didn't recover, he'd never know how far he could have gone. He pursed his lips to keep from crying from frustration.

Dr. Mason patted his arm. "Don't give up. You've still got a chance. In a few weeks, we'll see about therapy."

The man knew what Danny was going through. Maybe he was a sports fan. Danny flashed him a grateful look. He'd cling to the slim hope and run with it. Okay, maybe in his present condition that wasn't the right terminology. He smiled wryly.

As he was wheeled out of the hospital and helped into Cathy's Infiniti by the nurse's aid, his foot throbbed mercilessly, almost mocking his determination to get better.

On the way home, he broached the subject with his wife. Without taking her eyes from the road, she said, "Danny, remember there are other things besides basketball. You're healthy. You've still got your foot, though it may not be as strong as before. It might be something you'll just have to accept. Everything happens for a reason."

In a way she was right, yet her attitude seemed overly simplistic. The familiar irritation rose inside him. She'd be happy if he never stepped foot on a basketball court again.

She pulled into the driveway and opened the passenger door for him. Frowning, he balanced himself on the new crutches and hobbled into the house. The damn things were a nuisance. He hoped they wouldn't be permanent.

The peal of the telephone jangled his spastic nerves. Cathy rushed to grab it. "Oh, hi, Dora, we just got back. Everything's going fine."

She didn't seem too upset about his injury itself, only the fact he'd made it through surgery okay. Her attitude was getting to him. Did she have any idea how devastated he was?

Cathy handed him the cordless phone. "Honey, why don't you tell Dora you're okay? She sounds worried."

He felt lightheaded and his foot killed him. Still he had enough strength left to yank the phone from Cathy's hand. "Hello, Dora," he said.

In the background, Cathy cheerfully said, "I'll get some soup going."

Fighting a feeling of desertion, he concentrated on the caller.

"Danny, are you all right?"

Dora's concern was palpable. She really cared.

He couldn't control the quaver in his voice. "Well, not really. I'm worried." He told her about the doctor's prognosis, then said, "I don't know what I'll do if I can't play basketball."

"That's terrible. I know what playing means to you. I'd give anything to help. The best thing to remember, Danny, is: don't give up. If you try hard enough, you can make it back."

After the sting of Cathy's traitorous words, her sister's advice was like a soothing balm. She really understood. He wasn't alone. Having Dora's support meant more to him than she'd ever imagine. He swallowed a lump in his throat.

"Thanks, Dora. I needed to hear that. You're right. I've got to try."

Despite that, after he hung up, his spirits plummeted. It was hard to be optimistic when deep inside he had a horrible feeling.

Tony and Ritchie dropped by the following afternoon, momentarily succeeding in distracting him with jokes and antics. As soon as they'd left, depression set in. The familiar questions sped through his mind. What if he couldn't play? What if basketball were taken away from him? What would he do?

The phone rang all weekend, driving him crazy. Reporters, friends, ex-schoolmates, everyone wanted to know what he didn't know. He wished to God he could enlighten them.

Sunday night, the phone again interrupted their dinner. Cathy moved to answer it. She returned with a pleased expression on her face. "Danny, I'm having Dora drop by tomorrow to keep an eye on you."

His heart banged as swift fear vied with riotous elation. "But Cathy, I don't..."

"I know you don't think it's necessary, but I'd feel better if she were here. Dear, it's important I get to the shop. An audit plus lots of other things are waiting there for me. I don't want you alone."

He opened his mouth to protest, but she placed her finger over his lips.

"Honey, it's too soon for you to get around. We can't take a chance on your getting worse."

He relented, but felt uneasy. Cathy thought she was doing him a favor, but she might be causing more harm than good. If she could read his mind, its contents would not be pretty. He still felt unhappy about Cathy's unspoken relief over the possibility of his leaving basketball. He didn't want to resent her, yet he couldn't help it.

He loved his wife, yet at this point he felt extremely vulnerable. It was not a good time for Dora to be around. The seeds of doubt had been sown and he was powerless to ignore them. Cathy's sister understood him. Right now he needed to be with someone like that, someone who'd encourage him and tell him he still had a chance.

He glanced at Cathy, but her innocent face revealed no idea of his torment. He'd keep it that way. She must never guess. There had to be a way out of this. "Doesn't Dora have law school?"

"Yes, but remember, she's through early on Mondays, so she can get over here by three-thirty. I told her the key will be under the flowerpot, so you won't have to get up. You'll see. It'll all work out fine. She'll fix dinner and that'll give me a break, too. I may have to stay late at the shop."

He almost choked on his food. Feeling like a craven coward, he badly wanted Cathy here to protect him. Appetite gone, he pushed aside his plate.

That evening he couldn't sleep. No matter which position he tried, he was uncomfortable. His foot hurt despite the medication. On top of that, anticipation welled inside of him at the thought of seeing Dora. He hadn't seen her since Christmas and next week was already Valentine's Day.

A picture stole into his mind of Dora wearing the cranberry sweater, sitting alone under the McGuires' Christmas tree. The ornament-shaped earrings glinted in her ears, catching the reflection of the flashing tree lights. Her eyes flashed with unshed tears. Her full breasts strained as she passed over the brightly wrapped presents.

He'd told himself then, as he did now, it's wrong to lust after your wife's sister.

He and Cathy had made love that very night under their own Christmas tree. The urge had been strong, but had he given into it to block out the image of Dora? How would it have felt to have Dora beneath him instead?

As soon as the traitorous thoughts slipped into his mind, he wished he could take them back. It wasn't right to think of Dora as he lay beside his wife.

His ears caught the sound of Cathy's soft breaths. She was his angel. She'd put up with a lot. To be honest, he had to admit his road trips were rough on her. After a long day at the shop, she had to feel lonesome stepping into an empty house. He shouldn't blame her if she wished he had another job. Yet he did. And he knew Dora didn't share Cathy's feelings. Resentment flared. Why couldn't Cathy be more like her sister? Swearing inside, he punched the pillow.

The next morning, after his wife had left, he sat upright with anticipation in the wing chair, his bad foot braced on the ottoman. A thin afghan placed by Cathy lay across his lap to ward off possible chill.

By two o'clock, though it was too early, he was already listening for the sound of a car engine. The television was on, but he couldn't concentrate on it. He was bored with sitting around. Dora would be a welcome distraction.

The sleep he'd lost the night before finally caught up with him. He didn't hear the key turning in the lock.

Suddenly she was beside him, her hand reaching to lift the fallen afghan. When he moved, she jerked her fingers back. Her full breasts hung almost even with his mouth and jiggled inside the gold turtleneck sweater.

She caught the direction of his gaze and blushed. Her flickering eyes turned the same burnished gold as her sweater. It was no use pretending everything was fine. He was deathly afraid of this woman.

"I'm sorry I woke you up. Does your foot hurt a lot?"

God, she was magnificent. He could only stare at her. The silence stretched. He had to say something. This was embarrassing. "I've got drugs. I'm managing," he finally answered.

She nodded, assuming a cloak of professionalism. "Well, I better get started with dinner. Cathy told me she's got a pot roast around here somewhere." She almost ran from the room.

The vibrations remained. He sat in his chair, bewildered and upset, wishing for, yet not wanting, Dora to come back into the room. After all, there was only so much a man could take.

With the familiar sound of pots clanging, reason returned. The kitchen was Cathy's domain. Dora was an interloper and didn't belong there. His face hardened. He loved his wife. He would not let anyone destroy their relationship.

Fortunately, Dora didn't test him. Only once did she assist him into the bathroom, then wait discreetly outside. Other than that, she kept her distance, preparing their meal, occasionally sticking her head into the family room to check up on him.

By five-thirty, she announced dinner was ready. Fear shot through him. He wasn't prepared to sit across the table from her. What truths would he be tempted to blurt out?

Just then the front door opened.

"That smells wonderful. Did everyone eat already?"

Danny saw Dora frown, then compose her face. "Hi, Cath. We're just getting ready to sit down."

"How's my patient?" Cathy asked, bending over to brush Danny's cheek.

He kissed her with surprising intensity, breathing in her fresh floral scent. "I missed you," he said, relief flooding through him. Thank God his sweet angel had rescued him.

"Well, now I'm back. I finished earlier than I thought. Why don't we all sit down and eat? It's not every day we have Dora here to prepare a nice meal for us. We can't let it go to waste."

He hobbled to the table and concentrated on doing justice to Dora's cooking. As he did so, he focused on his wife. Cathy was his all. He loved her. He mustn't forget that.

After apple pie á la mode, they all retired to the family room. Not long afterwards, Dora rose to leave. "Well, I've got another three chapters to read for a test tomorrow."

Amidst high praise for her culinary skills, she took off. As soon as the door closed, Danny felt himself relax. He'd had a close call. He'd never put himself in that position again.

"Cathy, can you help me?" he asked his wife, who was seated next to him at the table.

She frowned in concern. "What is it honey? Does your ankle hurt?"

"No, something else needs attending to." He shot her a leering grin.

"What about your foot?"

"We'll work around it," he said, reaching for Cathy, his only salvation in a crazy, mixed-up world.

THE FOLLOWING WEEK he saw Dr. Mason. "Danny, let's start with that therapy and see how it goes."

Danny uncomplainingly practiced all the foot exercises and fitness routines. If he didn't succeed, it wouldn't be for want of trying.

That still left the remaining hours of the day to fill. He found himself thinking too much. It didn't help to read the blurb in the

Chicago Tribune about Kevin filing an appeal and demanding a DNA test. Mary Alice's rape and murder, as well as Danny's own role in Kevin's conviction, were outlined in detail in the article as well.

Apparently, after all this time, the missing DNA samples had been relocated in the evidence room.

Danny snorted. Kevin was definitely guilty. Why did he even bother with an appeal? Didn't he know how sophisticated the tests were?

He hobbled up and tossed the paper into the recycle bin. Thank goodness Cathy hadn't seen it. He still hadn't told her what had happened and didn't want her to learn this way. She had no idea of the suppressed hatred and bitterness that lingered inside him, threatening to burst out at the slightest provocation. She thought he was different.

The back door swung open. Guilt flashed through him.

"Should you be on your feet?" Cathy asked.

He sat down awkwardly. "You're right, but it's already Monday. All that Sunday paper stuff was getting in the way."

"Darn, I never have time to read that," she said, reaching into the fridge to prepare dinner. He could make it himself, even with a bad foot, but she enjoyed playing homemaker.

"The therapist said my foot's getting better. There's still hope I might play."

A frown crossed her face as she pulled out two Cornish hens. "Danny, like I've said before, it's not the end of the world if you don't go back. There're plenty of other things you can do."

He watched her rinse the poultry. Basketball meant a lot to him. She just didn't get it. Maybe he shouldn't have married her. Lately they didn't seem as compatible as he'd thought.

Dora understood. In fact, she'd encouraged him to get back to basketball. Why couldn't Cathy? Had he married the wrong sister?

"What did you do today?" Cathy asked, straightening up after placing the birds in the oven.

"Not much, as always." Maybe that was it. He needed something to occupy himself with. Then he wouldn't get these crazy ideas about ditching his wife.

The next morning, he grabbed the phone and dialed Dean's Computers. A temporary job as a software technician was available. With his solid computer skills, the company was only too happy to take him on.

After a two-week brush-up, he hit the trenches. When distraught callers presented their problems, they had no idea they were speaking to Danny, the basketball player. To them, he was a savior rescuing their computers. Their undying gratitude gave him satisfaction, but it was a poor substitute for his fans' approbation.

He still watched the games, even though it hurt to see his teammates play without him. He ached to rush out and help, but could only sit impatiently with his foot propped.

For the first time he understood what it meant to be disabled. It was depressing to think some people had no hope of recovery. The thought made him doubly appreciate what he'd taken for granted. If his condition did improve, he'd be forever grateful to God. Father Francisco had said something to him in confession about making others happy. When his condition stabilized, he'd definitely do some charity work.

In the meantime, he continued with therapy. The cast was cut off.

Who knew it would be so hard to do such simple things as wiggling his toes or bending his foot? It was amazing how the nerves and bones were connected together in such a fashion that, if one part hurt, the pain traveled to another.

AN ARDUOUS SIX months of alternating depression and hope passed. The swelling began to subside, as did the pain. The crutches were abandoned. Tentative steps became confident ones.

Then one day with a smile, his therapist, Marie, said, "Mr. Callaway, you're amazing. Your ankle's almost back to one hundred percent."

Dr. Mason was so pleased he released Danny without restrictions. Barring unforeseen circumstances, he could continue on where he'd left off.

He could play again. It was like a miracle. Danny's heart pounded with joy. He couldn't wait to get back into the game.

He had to. The season was over. Practice wouldn't begin for two long months. Three-fourths of a year had passed since he'd set foot on a basketball court. Would his game suffer? Would his ankle hold up?

Chapter Thirteen
Danny

DANNY HAD JUST walked a novice through partitioning a hard drive when the doorbell rang. He wasn't expecting anyone, but welcomed the intrusion. Marking time until the start of basketball season was chafing.

The peephole revealed a face he hadn't seen in years. His stomach churned as he opened the door.

"I hate to bother you like this," Bill Rosenberg said, "but I've got news that's best said in person."

Now what? Did Kevin win his appeal?

Rosenberg assessed the custom-made furniture and matching drapes before sitting on the wing chair where Danny indicated.

"Mr. Callaway, something unexpected has come up. It appears we've been dead wrong about your sister's case."

"How's that?"

"You remember the boyfriend, Larry Murphy? Well, he's just been arrested for the rape and battery of a young woman named Nancy Woods. DNA tests also link him to the Lincoln Park copycat killings. It appears Murphy also may have killed your sister and pinned it on Green. The test results will be back any day now and we'll know for sure."

Danny sat speechless. Larry couldn't be the killer. It had to be Kevin. Kevin had seemed guilty. Also, Kevin had threatened Mary Alice. Larry was her boyfriend and had no reason to harm her.

"I don't believe it. Kevin had the greatest motive. Maybe Larry copied him."

"That's unlikely, but we're checking all aspects," Rosenberg said, rising. "Well, I've got to go. I'll keep in touch."

After the man had left, anger and nausea warred inside Danny. Kevin had to have killed Mary Alice. Would the bastard get off without completing his sentence? That meant justice would not be served, unless Danny took the law into his own hands. He'd sworn not to get involved, yet he couldn't let Kevin get away with this.

He dared not dwell on the alternative, yet the thought slipped past anyway and refused to go away. What if Kevin were innocent? If so, Danny was the one mainly responsible for convicting an innocent man.

How could he live with himself? How could Kevin forgive him?

Chapter Fourteen
Kevin

THE APPEAL PROCESS went grindingly slow. Kevin's case sat at the tail end of a long line of inmates demanding DNA tests. Months dragged on as he waited in frustration. Didn't Dominski have any clout? Couldn't he push things along? It was nine months since he'd offered that string of hope to Kevin, enough time for a woman to have a kid.

Discouraged, he trudged into the rec room where he found Pedro surfing the remote. For a second, a familiar face flashed on the screen before a cartoon figure replaced it.

"Hey, flick that back," Kevin yelled.

"All right man. Don't have a Chihuahua."

Kevin ignored him and listened to the newscaster.

"Officer Nolan Woods discovered his sister in the process of being raped and beaten. He chased the alleged perpetrator, Larry Murphy, and caught up with him a few blocks from the scene. Mr. Murphy is now being held at Cook County Jail, pending criminal sexual assault charges. The victim lies in critical condition at Weiss Memorial Hospital. If Nancy Woods dies, Larry Murphy will face charges of first degree murder. Stay tuned for further developments."

Kevin sat stunned. It all clicked into place. Hell, he'd been a dunce. Larry had raped and killed Mary Alice, not some perverted stranger who'd happened along. Why hadn't he realized that before? It made sense. Mary Alice must have told Murphy she'd changed her mind about going to the prom with him and he'd been majorly pissed off.

He had to hand it to Murphy for the brilliant cover-up job on the witness stand. The sob story about having sex on the day of the murder after discussing their wedding plans had choked up everyone and deflected suspicion. Murphy had colossal nerve. And he would have pulled it off if he hadn't been so greedy. Wasn't Mary Alice enough?

That didn't get Callaway off the hook. The jerk should have realized Kevin loved Mary Alice and hadn't meant what he'd said that day.

None of that mattered at the moment. The big question was, what about the appeal? How long before he could get out of this joint?

The sperm samples had to prove his innocence. Now he could reveal what had really happened and not be afraid. The truth was he'd cut through the alley to meet Mary Alice, after she'd suggested they meet in front of her apartment. She'd said she had news for him. He'd never know what that news was.

At sight of her still form lying on the ground, he'd stared in disbelief. The sound of approaching footsteps had scared him. What if the person who'd killed Mary Alice came after him?

He slunk further back into the alley and then fled when Otto Meyer turned on his porch lights.

Trembling and soaked with perspiration, he'd stepped into the apartment he shared with Derek. It was empty. The old man was on a binge again.

When Derek did make his appearance a few hours later, Kevin had already showered and plunked himself down on the couch in front of the TV.

Sure, he'd been a coward for not sticking around when he'd discovered the body. He should have known better than to make up a phony alibi about his old man being home with him, but who could blame him? Why would anyone believe such a farfetched truth?

Now he realized he should have tried anyway. He should have spoken up at the trial, even though Callaway had sounded sincere, and even Dominski had been convinced of Kevin's guilt.

The only way out of the mess had been to pretend remorse for a crime he hadn't committed, so he could get himself a better sentence. Even that hadn't worked. He'd not gotten off lightly. He'd bungled everything big time. He should have had more confidence and told the truth. If he'd played his cards right, Murphy would have been rotting here instead.

That was all in the past. This was now. He had to get in touch with Dominski.

Chapter Fifteen
Danny & Kevin

CATHY WAS AT the shop again when District Attorney Bill Rosenberg made his second appearance. The look on the man's face confirmed Danny's worst fears. DNA didn't lie. Larry Murphy was the guilty party. With a sick feeling, Danny realized he'd been responsible for sending an innocent man to prison.

"It's my fault. Kevin and my sister had an argument, and I blew it all up out of proportion. I'll never forgive myself," he admitted.

"Mr. Callaway, don't take it to heart. The evidence pointed at Green. If it makes you feel any better, I'm as much to blame. I should've dug deeper and gotten to the truth."

No, Rosenberg had done a good job. He wasn't the person who'd held a vendetta against Kevin.

After the man had left, guilt swirled inside of Danny like a dust storm. He'd have no peace unless he made amends. Maybe facing Kevin would help. Kevin would be released soon. Danny was almost tempted to wait until then, but forced himself not to. He deserved the punishment of witnessing firsthand what his vindictiveness had caused.

The next morning, while Cathy was working, he drove the thirty miles to the prison. In a sick fog, he underwent an embarrassing body search. He listened to the guard call Kevin on the phone.

The dreaded moment arrived. As Danny gazed through the glass partition, he almost didn't recognize the person on the other side. He should have realized Kevin would have changed, but his imagination had not supplied the details. An unblinking, stone-like visage stared back at him.

Nine prison years had lent a pasty sheen to Kevin's complexion and added extra lines around his eyes and mouth. The once-sandy, straight hair was tinged with gray and shortened to a crew cut. Kevin was no longer an angry teenager, but a hard, embittered man.

One thing had not changed. Those cold, sea green eyes bore without forgiveness into Danny's own, refusing to grant what he needed most: absolution. He didn't blame Kevin. If the situation were reversed, he'd react the same.

"I'm sorry for not trusting you. I'm sorry I put you in here. I'd do anything to take it back," he said to the unblinking statue.

Kevin was quiet. When he did speak, the response was jarring. Danny had no defense against Kevin's accusations. Every word was true. Shame and remorse rose inside of him. There was nothing he could do to give Kevin back his lost years.

"Would money help? I've got plenty. Name your price," Danny finally said in desperation.

"You won't get off that easy."

A chill raced up and down Danny's spine. For a moment it seemed Kevin was actually guilty.

After that, Kevin clammed up. Danny sat and waited until visiting time was over. Then, head bent, he stumbled out of the room.

Chapter Sixteen
Kevin

KEVIN COULDN'T SLEEP. Since last month, when the DNA tests had been run and Larry Murphy had confessed, everything had moved with rapid speed. Kevin's appeal was heard and granted. The result was that tomorrow he'd be a free man. His mind couldn't catch up with the idea.

How should he act? This cell had been his only home for the past nine years. He hated to admit it, but he was petrified to step out into the real world. He almost wanted to commit a real crime so he could stay here.

What the hell was he thinking? Shit, he'd been waiting for freedom forever. He'd been man enough to handle a prison hell hole. The real world had to be a cinch.

At daybreak, the morning whistle shrilled, rousing the prisoners. Kevin did not awaken because he'd never fallen asleep. Now, when he needed his faculties, he felt confused and exhausted.

He groggily followed the guard into the mess hall. Dumping some mushy oatmeal into his mouth, he reminded himself that soon he'd sink his teeth into a lumberjack breakfast of pancakes, sausage, and eggs. He'd cram it all down until he was stuffed, then gorge himself even more. Man, how he craved decent food.

The commissary issued Kevin a regulation suit. It itched like hell. He'd never liked suits anyway.

The fat-assed warden called him into his office. "Mr. Green, soon you'll be a free man. Unfortunately, it appears you shouldn't have been imprisoned here in the first place. You're not the first person to endure such a calamity, so let me give you a little advice. Don't be bitter. Go out and make good the rest of your life."

Easy for you to say, Kevin thought, nodding blandly. He'd agree to anything at this point, though he knew the pompous jerk in front of him couldn't care less about what had happened. Why should he? It wasn't him.

Fighting a simmering rage, Kevin followed the guard back to his cell. There he gathered his meager belongings. They consisted of a small pile of *Playboys* and auto mechanic magazines, an ancient radio, and a nine-inch black-and-white TV—not much to show for being holed up for so long.

"Okay, let's go," the guard said.

This was it. Trembling seized Kevin. He couldn't move. Then, as if in a dream, he stepped out of his cell and floated past an endless line of bars. A bombardment of cheers and obscenities greeted him.

Midway down the line, Steve Summers reached out. "Kevin, my man, let me know how it is out there."

Kevin swallowed a huge lump in his throat. Without Steve, he'd never have survived. This part was rough. He'd die before setting foot back in this hell hole, but that meant never seeing Steve again. "Don't worry. I will," he said, gripping his friend's hand tightly, trying not to look surprised as he felt the exchange of a small piece of paper. What was that all about? Maybe a goodbye message. Nonchalantly he transferred it to his jeans pocket.

MAKING HIS WAY down the lengthy corridor, he listened to the echoing sound of his footsteps, a reminder of the hollow existence he'd led for the past nine years.

He and the guard reached the last gate. Kevin shifted his feet, so nervous he wanted to piss. The ring in the guard's hand jangled as he tried out different keys.

"Come on, come on," Kevin muttered beneath his breath.

The guard stood still, then turned to Kevin. "What'd you say?"

Panic made Kevin's heart race. Could he be thrown back in for bad behavior? "Nothing," he answered in a subdued tone.

Satisfied, the man tried another key. It finally turned the lock. With a creak, the gate swung open. Kevin's heart galloped. He felt so lightheaded he almost passed out. He couldn't believe it. He was free!

The gate clanged behind him. He was outside—alone and disoriented. Panicking, he searched for a familiar face, but no one was in sight. All he could see were endless miles of open fields and a vanishing highway. Where was Dad? Derek had promised to be here at eleven. It was already eleven-thirty. Had Derek gotten drunk? How could he reach him? There was no phone around to make a call.

Anxiously he scanned the horizon. Derek had to come. He wouldn't let his son down, would he? Sure, Sharon was first in Derek's life since their marriage several years ago, but Derek's only son had to mean something. This was important. Dad had promised to pick him up. Also, he'd offered to pay Kevin's first month's rent in a new apartment. Kevin bit his lip. He longed to be stretched out in his own pad, enjoying his first taste of freedom. He didn't want to be standing here on tired legs waiting.

Trying to still his jitters, he forced in a deep breath. The refreshing September air felt good as it settled in his lungs. Not to panic. The old man had never been punctual. He'd show up sooner or later.

Kevin was so lost in thought he didn't notice the weathered Ford pickup approach.

"Get in, son," Derek called out.

With relief, Kevin climbed onto the tattered seat. As the cab rolled, he bounced. The jolt of the broken springs didn't bother him. They were familiar. Derek had never owned anything decent. Knowing next to nothing about auto mechanics, he'd run every vehicle he'd ever owned into the ground. Besides new springs, this particular truck cried out for a tune-up. That was one department where Kevin could pay back the old man.

Derek's threadbare jeans and tattered T-shirt testified that paying an extra month's rent for his son would put a big dent in his wallet. A rush of gratitude filled Kevin, making him smile. He wasn't the only one in the old man's life, but he still counted. It felt good to be wanted. The world wasn't so bad after all.

After a few hours, they reached the north side of Chicago. Derek pulled up in front of an aged wooden building. They climbed a rickety staircase to the fourth floor. At the third door to the right, he handed Kevin a key. "This is it, son. All yours."

Kevin's hands trembled as he turned the key, a symbol of his freedom. For too long, others had controlled his comings and goings. His stomach knotted at the remembrance. He wouldn't think of that now. He only wanted to enjoy the moment. He pushed open the door, stepped inside and glanced around. The apartment was small, but clean, and furnished with second-hand discards. The worn, gold-colored sofa looked like the same one he and his old man had shared ages ago.

The tired fixings didn't matter. This place was infinitely larger than a jail cell, and all his. At last he could do what he wanted whenever he wanted. He was struck dumb at the enormity of the thought.

Mistaking Kevin's silence, his father said, "I know it's not much, but when you get a job, I'm sure you can do better."

Kevin already felt possessive about the place. "Thanks, Dad. I really like it. You're great."

He hadn't planned it, but suddenly he reached out to hug Derek.

Neither of them had ever been openly affectionate, but today was special. Right now he wanted to throw his arms around the world.

Derek broke away quickly. “Well, I better get going. Sharon’s waiting.”

Kevin nodded absently, already basking in his newfound freedom.

It didn’t take long to unpack. Afterwards he wandered into the kitchenette. Surprisingly, the cabinets and refrigerator were already stocked with groceries and utensils. Such details were the mark of a woman. He’d never met her, but maybe Sharon wasn’t so bad after all. She was his stepmother and they were family. Maybe she could be like a substitute mother.

He shook off the sick feeling which invaded him at the thought of never seeing his own Mom. Today wasn’t a day for morbid thoughts.

First, he may as well set things up. He threw his meager store of underwear and socks into the scarred dresser. With that done, he placed his tiny television onto the battered stand. The picture flickered, then stilled. He scrounged for the bag of Fritos he’d seen in the cabinet, then plunked himself down.

A favorite episode of *The Three Stooges* was on, the one where the bee got stuck in the fancy lady’s dress and she danced all over the place. He laughed loud and long, as if he’d never seen the program in his life. It felt good to let go. It seemed strange not to have a guard yell at him to pipe down. Here he had no curfew. He watched TV late into the night, until his eyes grew heavy and he nodded off.

When he awakened, out of habit he listened for the morning whistle, but only heard static. Could it be broken? As his memory returned, relief flowed through him. He was a free man. What an awesome thought. Prying open his eyes, he watched in fascination as the rays from the sun streamed from the window onto the television screen. Man alive, what a marvelous sight.

He still couldn’t comprehend that he was free and the nightmare was over. His head spun and he felt high on hope.

The state of euphoria lasted a few short weeks until reality set in. He had to find a job, but who would hire him? He’d been innocent, but was still labeled a jailbird. Who would believe him?

He had to locate Brad somehow, so he could hook up with him on the security scheme. In the meantime, he’d settle for something less lucrative to keep from mooching off the old man. A few blocks away at the drug store, he uncovered a crumbling phone book, where he looked up the State of Illinois employment office. After taking a five-block hike, he climbed onto the bus.

When he got to the office a few miles away, the place was jammed. A glance at his competition revealed an ugly, motley crew. Kevin's complexion was prison-pale, but his ill-fitting suit couldn't disguise his broad shoulders and trim waist. Exercise and weightlifting had relieved his boredom. Now he was reaping the benefits. He decided he looked a hundred percent better than any of the creeps here, that's for sure.

Eventually he got to the front of the line, where an old hag presided behind a grated window. She looked like she'd never felt a dick inside her in her life.

Time to turn on the old charm. He flashed a seductive smile. Though it was rusty from lack of practice, apparently he had enough left in reserve to dazzle the old biddy. She fluttered her eyelashes and forked over a long list of available jobs.

"Take your pick," she said.

She'd probably offer her body if he asked.

The room smelled surprisingly like prison B.O. Stifling an urge to hold his nose, he slid behind a classroom-like desk. Hadn't these losers heard of soap and water? He knew he smelled good. Every day he took extra time in the shower to wash away the prison smells. He'd never reek again.

Time to find that job. He glanced at the first sheet, applying what he'd learned about controlling dyslexia, forcing his mind to recognize the written words. There were scads of white collar jobs, but he despised reading. Deciphering this tedious list was bad enough. He needed a job where he could use his hands. There were a few maintenance positions, but they required experience, as did those of electricians. Would jail time count? That would be too embarrassing to list.

Wait a minute—Wally's Repair Shop needed a mechanic. He could do that. He was a whiz at assembling and disassembling motor parts. Also, he was a genius at diagnosing car problems. This job looked right up his alley. Hopefully Wally wouldn't be too particular about background.

He got his interview. Wally quizzed him on alternators, speedometers and brake lines. Satisfied, the man took him on. The pay was low, but it was a foot in the door.

It didn't take long for Kevin to settle in at Wally's. He liked testing the BMWs and Jaguars and pretending they were his. He enjoyed the twenty-minute breaks in the morning and afternoon and the hour off for lunch.

A few weeks later, he was lounging in the break room and reading the oil-stained *Tribune*, which made its rounds to all the mechanics, when he happened to glance at the sports page. Pro basketball season would start on Friday. Word was out Callaway had gotten the thumbs-up to play. Would his ankle last? Columnist Wilbert Woods, ever the optimist, predicted Callaway would make it through sheer determination. Others were cautionary, saying the injury was tricky.

Kevin gripped the paper tightly, crunching its corners. Why must he get reminders of something he wanted to forget? God, he hated Callaway. If it weren't for him, Heartland would not have happened. And the jerk had had the audacity to come and visit. If it weren't for curiosity, Kevin would have refused to see him. Danny Callaway had looked sick to his stomach as he gazed at Kevin through the glass.

"I'm sorry as hell," he'd said. "Can I make it up to you?"

The great Danny Callaway had begged for forgiveness. At first, Kevin hadn't replied. He'd watched as the prick sweated. He'd refused to make it easy on him.

"Please, I'll do anything," Callaway had pleaded.

Kevin had smiled with disdain. "You should've thought of that a long time ago, you prick." He'd gestured around the dismal looking room with its once-white, now-gray walls. "This is your fault. You're the one who got me in here."

"How was I to know it was Larry?" Callaway had asked, in a rising voice.

"You shouldn't have jumped to conclusions. As far as I'm concerned, you're guiltier than Murphy," Kevin had said flatly.

He'd looked straight into the star's groveling eyes and said, "You could've saved me. Now live with what you did."

Callaway had next offered money. No way would Kevin let him get off that easy and had told him so. Then he'd clamped his mouth shut, a signal for Callaway to leave. If he'd had less pride, he would have taken that dough.

Kevin's ruminations were cut short by a stern voice.

"Break's over, Green. Constance Jennings needs the Chrysler."

Swearing to himself, Kevin rose. Assistant Manager Brian Barnes, the owner of the grating voice, was the one horsefly in the ointment here. Barnes always rode Kevin's ass, never giving him a break. If only he could smack the jerk...but then he'd lose his job.

Kevin drove around the LeBaron to Mrs. Jennings, who didn't waste her sweet breath on even a thank you. As she slipped into the driver's seat, she purposely let her skirt ride up, revealing a flash of long legs. His cock rose to the occasion. He barely restrained himself from jumping in beside her.

A fellow mechanic, Mike Evans, caught Kevin's look, and whispered, "Forget that one. She's a prick teaser."

With a regretful shrug, Kevin set his sights on a dented station wagon. His practiced hands glided over the rocker panels, envisioning Constance's luscious body. It had been a long time since he'd had a woman, yet he still recognized the signs when one wanted him.

Why not? He was still a hunk.

Chapter Seventeen
Danny

IT WAS A MONTH since Kevin's release. Though Kevin was free, Danny suffered in his own prison of guilt, tortured by what he'd done. He tiptoed on the edge of a precipice, where one wrong move could fling him into a dark abyss.

As he sat across from Cathy in the kitchen's sunny alcove, he picked at his cold scrambled eggs. His thoughts roamed far from the brilliance of the bright fall day. Guilt plus a sleepless night equaled a bad combination.

When he'd injured his ankle, all he'd wanted was to play again. Since his return, he'd been so distracted his playing had suffered. This time the sin he'd committed was so serious even basketball couldn't save him. For some reason, his teammates didn't fare any better.

With red-rimmed eyes he looked across the table at his wife who was glancing idly at the front page of the *Sun Times*. A sliver of alarm ran through him. He usually scanned the paper before she got it. She flipped through the pages. He fought a rising concern. So far, he'd been lucky enough to keep information about the trial and its aftermath from her.

A broken water main on Delaney Street had flooded her store, Cathy's Creations, along with neighboring stores. She'd spent countless hours supervising the restoration and had had scant opportunity to pay attention to anything else. Her misfortune had been a blessing.

His buddies and Dora knew about Kevin, but they'd agreed to keep silent. Even Cathy's parents had acknowledged it was best to protect her.

He almost felt as if he was conspiring against his wife instead of shielding her, yet he knew it was for the best. The knowledge would rock her foundations. She'd never understand.

He tried not to stare as, with the coffee cup in one hand, Cathy turned from one page to the other. When she slammed down the mug, he almost jumped.

She was way too quiet. She focused far too long on one article.

Frowning, she glanced up. Their eyes met. His heart plummeted. She knew.

"Danny, why didn't you tell me about this?"

No use pretending. He wouldn't insult her by playing dumb. "I didn't want you to have to deal with it," he said, slowly putting down his fork, abandoning the pretense of eating.

He hadn't wanted this to happen. He'd always hoped to protect his wife from the consuming hatred that had haunted him before he was married. For too long he'd wished Kevin dead. The good priest had been right. God should be the one to exact revenge. Only the Almighty knew what was in each person's soul.

Cathy's eyes looked wounded. Her bottom lip trembled as she tried not to cry. "Danny, it seems I really don't know you. Seeing this makes me wonder what other things you've kept from me."

Her words punched his gut. He couldn't answer. He'd botched everything from the beginning. He should have come clean before the wedding, but had been afraid of seeming unworthy. Cathy had always existed on a higher plane than he did and seemed incapable of grasping the nature of evil. He hadn't thought she'd understand the real Danny, the dark-souled sufferer he'd kept hidden from the world.

Strangely enough, he'd been able to spill it all out to her sister. Dora seemed capable of handling anything he dished out. She'd been exposed to the black marks of his soul and hadn't been put off. Had he married the wrong sister? Danny had no opportunity to dwell on that. His wife was all wound up.

Now that she'd started, she pressed on. "I feel so sorry for that poor man being stuck in jail all those years. How could you do that to him?"

"Believe me, Cathy, I thought he was guilty."

"I understand you made a mistake, but what about now? Is there anything you can do to help him? With all your basketball money, there has to be some way to make good."

"He refuses to speak to me, much less take my money."

"Speaking of money, haven't you made enough? Why do you insist on playing? You know I hate you're on the road so much. After the injury, I'd hoped you'd respect my wishes, but you've been going to practice anyway. On Friday, the season will begin all over again. Then you'll be away most of the time. Can't you give up basketball? Won't you do that for us?"

The sweet angel he'd married had morphed into a witch before his eyes. Perhaps living with him had changed her, or maybe he hadn't known her after all. Of course, even before she'd married him, though she'd never thrown it up to him, she'd lived the life of a rich man's daughter. As a wedding gift, her dad had deposited a generous sum into their joint account, which Danny had refused to touch. He prided himself on making it on his own. Money was not the issue and never had been. It had nothing to do with basketball.

He had enough trouble dealing with Kevin, without throwing basketball into the mix. Did she have any idea what he was going through?

They hadn't seriously discussed his occupation before, but now it was out into the open. Resentment shot through him. He'd been wrong about Kevin, but on basketball he would not cave in. "I'll never give up the game, no matter what."

Her head snapped back as if hit. Sobbing, she pulled back her chair and rushed from the table. Damn, if she refused to accept something so important to him, their marriage was on shaky ground.

By Friday, a deep chill still permeated the air. After a silent breakfast during which they pretended to eat, Danny threw his wife's ticket on the table.

"That's in case you change your mind," he said before stomping out.

He knew she wouldn't be there, yet later, when he stepped onto the court, he glanced toward the stands. The other members of his cheering section were present and accounted for, but Cathy's empty seat stared back at him accusingly. Reminding himself he still had basketball, he squared his shoulders. He'd hold onto it as long as he could.

His timing was off. Nothing clicked. He played hard, but felt as if he were foundering on quicksand.

After a huge Cyclones loss, he pulled into the garage, entered the silent house and closed the door softly behind him. He missed his wife. He'd hurt Cathy and had to put things right. She wasn't in the kitchen or the family room. Had she left? His breath caught at the thought. He was afraid to look further. At the door to the living room, he paused, catching a whiff of her fresh floral scent. In the darkness, he almost didn't see the slight figure seated in the wing chair.

He dared not turn on the lights. He couldn't bear to see tears marring the beautiful face. He came up behind his wife and placed a tentative hand on her shoulder. "Cathy, honey, let's not fight. I know I was wrong to keep important things from you, but I was doing it for us. I'm not perfect. I can't even promise to give up basketball. All I can say is I love you."

She sobbed quietly, but didn't pull away.

Perhaps there was still hope. Gathering her tightly in his arms, he rocked her back and forth. “Cathy, I love you. Please give me another chance.”

She pulled away and gazed at him silently, with the look of a disappointed child.

Gently wiping the tears from her cheeks, he pressed his lips firmly on her trembling mouth. “Please, honey, don’t give up on us. I need you.”

With a soft sigh she wilted, sinking against his chest.

His hands fingered her tangled curls. “I know I can’t be here for you all the time, but, Cathy, honey, maybe we can do something about those lonely nights of yours. It’s time we got a little someone to keep you company.”

“I’ve always wanted that, Danny.”

“Maybe we haven’t tried hard enough.”

They spent the rest of the evening making slow, tender love.

IN THE ENSUING weeks, neither of them spoke of Kevin, or of Danny’s decision to keep playing basketball. At times he caught his wife glancing at him hesitantly, as if she couldn’t make up her mind. They spent more time than ever making love, but sometimes it seemed they were only going through the motions.

Were they trying to conceive a child out of love or to prove they still loved each other? There had to be something left to salvage. He needed Cathy as much as he needed basketball.

His preoccupation did not go unnoticed by Coach Dexter. “Callaway, snap out of it. You’re hurting the team. Leave your personal life behind when you step onto the court.”

Coach was right. It wasn’t fair to accept a huge sum of money and not do his best. It was time to buckle down.

Danny couldn’t pinpoint when the transition occurred. One day he foundered, the next day everything clicked. He caught fire, scored fantastic shots and burned up the court. The fans ate it up. When he heard their cheers, he felt warm inside. He could almost believe his life was perfect.

Under his leadership, the team made it to the playoffs, then fought their way up the ladder to the last game, which was scheduled for Chicago. The evening before, Danny felt his stomach contract.

Cathy noticed his pained expression. “Are you all right?”

“I think I’ve got the flu,” he said, dashing away. He barely made it to the bathroom in time.

He spent a good portion of the night there. By morning, he was exhausted and still cramping. With fumbling fingers he tried to fasten his shirt, but the buttons kept slipping out of the holes.

Cathy stepped up to him and placed a cool palm on his forehead. "You're crazy. You can't go in."

Ignoring her advice, he climbed unsteadily into his pants. People depended on him. He couldn't let his teammates down. Cathy didn't understand.

Red blotches sprang to her cheeks as her voice rose. "It's only a game, Danny. Stay home. They can do without you."

He gritted his teeth. "Cathy, show some respect. You've got your dreams. Let me have mine. I don't demean your flower shop, do I? I'm going now and don't try to stop me." His head pounded. He didn't want to battle his wife as well as his illness. Why couldn't she understand how important basketball was to him?

Cathy gave him a long, searching look. Shaking her head, she grabbed the key ring and marched to her car. Wobbling, he followed her.

"Get in," she ordered.

Neither of them spoke on the way to the stadium.

On leaden feet, he stumbled onto the court. Perspiration sprang to his forehead. Before long, his jersey grew clammy and clung to his skin. Continuing on was torture, yet he did it anyway.

In the first quarter, a Houston guard tripped him. Danny's head spun. The room blackened for a second, then cleared. No one noticed. He righted himself and went on.

The remainder of the game passed in a pain-filled blur. Each time he tried to score, the ball bounced off. His teammates gave it their all, but fell short, with three of them fouling out and being replaced by second stringers. He was far from par, but didn't dare leave.

At the final buzzer the Cyclones dejectedly made their way back to the locker room, lucky to have lost by twelve points. Danny felt miserable knowing if he'd played at his peak, the team might have stood a chance.

Cathy brought her Infiniti around to the player's exit, swung open the door and said in a quiet voice, "Danny, let's go home."

With teeth chattering, he climbed in, then huddled in the passenger seat. She sighed, but didn't preach. He couldn't have handled that. He was miserable enough.

The germ lingered for an entire week. When he'd finally shaken it, the scale showed he'd lost eight pounds.

The fact that the team had gone so far, only to lose anyway didn't make him feel better. It was difficult to set aside his disappointment, but he had to. He must go on, as he'd done in the past. The trick was to keep busy. As usual, Dean's needed help, so he signed on to work in the off season.

Even that made him feel guilty. He was working to maintain peace of mind, but in doing so was stealing a position from someone who could use the money.

The baby project went ahead full steam. Now, more than ever, Danny craved closeness with his wife, maybe because they no longer seemed on the same wave length. Perhaps they never had been. Despite that, for some reason, the physical attraction between them remained strong.

A LATE AFTERNOON IN mid-September found Danny at home, restless and lonesome. An idea formed in his mind. Why not surprise Cathy and take her somewhere romantic for dinner? He ached to be with her. If they pretended things were right between them, maybe they would be. He jumped into his BMW, his mind too preoccupied to enjoy the last vestiges of summer clinging to the oak and walnut trees lining his driveway.

After he'd pulled up to the shop, he hesitated. Who was this woman he thought he loved? The artful displays in the window had been arranged by the same loving fingers that had often stroked and enfolded him. At the thought, need burgeoned inside of him. Dinner was forgotten.

Glancing inside, he saw two elderly customers milling about, content to look. He glared, willing them to leave. Perhaps they caught a glimpse of his threatening face, for suddenly they fled.

The coast was clear. He stepped inside, locked the door and pulled down the blinds.

"What are you doing, Danny?" Cathy asked in a frantic voice.

"The store closes in half an hour, right?"

She nodded.

Though no one else was near, he bent down and whispered in her ear. She blushed to the roots of her fiery red hair, but didn't say no. Encouraged, he removed his shirt. When she saw he meant business, she let out a half-hearted protest. He continued undressing. Her eyes grew round when he stood before her with his arousal in plain view.

She swallowed and unconsciously licked her lips. It was all the signal he needed. He reached to unfasten the top button of her dress, then placed his hand beneath its cloth and onto her soft skin. He did the same with each of her buttons, moving slowly downward.

Her eyes filmed with passion. She seemed almost in a trance as she followed him to the center of the tile floor, where he lifted the dress over her head. With practiced hands, he removed her bra and cupped her upturned breasts.

She moaned in pleasure as his teasing fingers caressed, then withdrew, slipping off her nylons, then her panties. Gently grasping her wrists, he lowered her down onto the cool tile, then positioned her on top of him.

As their skin touched, fire bolted through him. Cathy was his. They were meant to be together. To reaffirm their closeness, he pushed himself into her as deep as he could. She gasped.

"Are you all right?" he asked.

Before she could answer, the door knob rattled.

"You locked it, didn't you?" she whispered.

"You saw me."

Tensely they waited for the intruder to leave. After what seemed like forever, the footsteps receded.

"Now where were we?" he asked.

The added element of danger spiked his senses, making him more aroused. His ears were attuned to each sound, picking up Cathy's small, panting breaths, the ticking of the wall clock, the trickle of water dripping from the faucet.

Very close to him, his wife's fragrant womanly scent blended with that of the roses and orchids. Her breasts brushed against the hairs on his chest, as he slipped between her damp, yielding thighs.

She arched and quivered. He answered with an acute explosion. That wasn't enough. He pushed in deeper and deeper, murmuring "Cathy, Cathy."

She lay over him, hugging him close. They moved in unison with each other. He couldn't get enough of her. At this point, he didn't care who broke the door down. Fireworks ricocheted through him.

He reached up and brushed a strawberry curl from his wife's glistening forehead. "Cathy, my love, you really are something."

She smiled down at him tenderly. "Danny, I have a suggestion."

"Anything, my sweet," he said from his vulnerable position beneath her.

"If we're going to do this for a while, could we go somewhere more comfortable?"

Thank goodness she hadn't said stop. Apparently, she also felt this amazing closeness and didn't want to lose it.

Rising, she led him into her cozy, plant strewn office to a couch beneath the chintz curtains.

He needed no further encouragement. Gathering his wife into his arms, he laid her gently on the couch, where they continued on in comfort, exploring each other thoroughly, almost as if the experience were brand new. They didn't stop until well past midnight, when she pled exhaustion and they agreed it was best to round up their clothes.

He abandoned his BMW and brought up Cathy's Infiniti. They said little on the ride home, yet it was a peaceful silence. She rested her head on his shoulder, reminding him of the old days. Was it too late to go back?

SINCE THEY'D BEEN married, Danny knew that Cathy had always been disappointed at the arrival of her "monthly visitor." It was doubly hard when they visited friends with children. She deserved a baby. Why couldn't she conceive? The pressure built inside him to give Cathy this one thing she wanted. If they had a baby, the child would be something they could share.

Six weeks after what his wife had labeled their "floral madness," he found a flush-faced Cathy unwrapping a test kit in the bathroom.

The sight tugged at his heartstrings. Would this be another disappointment? He had to prepare her for failure. She looked way too excited.

"Cathy, calm down. It could be another false alarm."

She ignored his advice. After she'd performed the procedure, she sat on the bed with legs shaking and lips moving in silent prayer.

Bracing her for another letdown, he sat beside Cathy and took her elegant fingers into his large palm.

When the timer rang, she let go and almost tiptoed into the adjoining bathroom. He followed, holding his breath. Would this be like all the other times?

Cathy picked up the stick.

"Oh, my God," she cried, dropping it, before he could see what it read.

She spun towards him. He didn't have to ask the result. He'd never seen his wife look more beautiful. Her entire being glowed, from the top of her sparkling strawberry hair to the tips of her dainty toes. He stared back wonderingly.

"Danny, Danny, you're going to be a Daddy," she squealed, throwing her arms around him.

His eyes filmed over as he said a silent prayer of thanks. He didn't deserve this wonderful reprieve, yet God had been gracious enough to give it to him.

Cathy sobbed. He pulled out his handkerchief and gently wiped her eyes.

"Sweetheart, don't cry."

"I can't help it. I'm just so happy. I've hoped so long for this to happen, but never thought it would."

"This calls for a celebration," he said, lifting her up and carrying her back into the bedroom. He lit a scented candle, turned the volume low on the CD player and gently made love to her.

Afterwards, he rubbed her stomach and said crazy things like, "How was that, Bernie? Did we wake you up?"

Her laugh tinkled, reminding him of the day they'd met in class. "You can't be serious, Danny. I will not allow you to name our child such a corny name."

"Don't worry. We've got time to come up with something better."

"Thank goodness." She reached out and ruffled his hair.

After that, he and Cathy existed in their own private world, marveling at the miracle growing inside of her, savoring their concealed knowledge, forgetting their differences. They were on the threshold of something new, exciting and scary called parenthood.

The world was ripe with a summer that stretched into October. As he watched Cathy wend her way through her magnificent gardens, she reminded him of a fertility goddess. Her flowery children blossomed and thrived under her touch. She cared for them all, down to the tiniest alyssum.

After another month, her breasts filled and her waistline thickened. By mutual agreement, they decided to break the silence.

They invited the McGuire family for dinner on Veterans Day to share the news. He wished his own family could be present, but what might have been could never be. Life was good. The growing seed inside of Cathy overwhelmed everything else.

He'd just finished dusting the bottom of the family room coffee table when the doorbell rang. He rose to answer it. Ted and Nancy were first to arrive, followed by Dora, who, as usual, looking disturbingly attractive. Her cream colored mini-skirt displayed her never-ending golden legs. Her matching cashmere sweater set his heart pounding. Her perfect, upturned breasts couldn't be disguised. They swelled out, as if begging to be touched. Her amber eyes glowed. She was amazing.

"Do you have any iced tea?" Nancy McGuire asked, jarring

Danny from his spell.

Eager to escape, he turned toward the kitchen.

"Let me get it, Danny," Cathy offered, stepping out of the dining room where she'd been arranging a centerpiece.

"That's okay, honey. Sit down and relax. I'll start the steaks."

He was already babying her and Cathy was eating it up, enjoying the attention. After all, her pregnancy had been a long time coming.

Dora intervened. "You do the steaks. I'll get the tea."

Before he could protest, Dora had followed him into the kitchen. He didn't need her around, but it would be impolite to refuse. Before he knew it, she'd closed the door and cornered him. Though it was a large kitchen, he felt as if its dimensions had shrunk. She stood next to him, so close he breathed in her spicy cologne. Its scent hinted at danger and wild rhapsody.

As if unaware of her power, she gazed earnestly at him. "How are you dealing with Kevin's release?"

The familiar guilt stabbed him. With a start, he realized his mind had strayed from Kevin since Cathy had become pregnant. He didn't need this reminder.

"He shouldn't have been put there in the first place, but it's too late to change that. I try not to think about it," he said tersely.

Dora nodded. "That's the only way to look at it."

His forehead pounded. He'd never get over what he'd done. Why had she brought it up today of all days? Of course, she couldn't know of today's significance, since he and Cathy hadn't broken the news. It was silly to think Dora was punishing him.

Irritated, he reached into the cold refrigerator to pull out the steaks, then thrust them onto the preheated stove top grill.

Dora inched over, stationing herself directly across from him. When he glanced up, he was so close he could make out the throbbing blue veins on her slender neck. His mind shut down, as his temperature rose to match the grill's. The steaks sizzled. Something had to give.

"What about that iced tea?" he asked pointedly

"That's right," she said, grabbing the pitcher and vanishing.

That had been close.

His surcease was short-lived. She returned, asking if she could be of more help.

"I can handle it, Dora."

"Well, Cathy's busy talking to Mom and Dad. She looked so excited I didn't want to interrupt her. I know with the shop and all she doesn't get a chance to visit them often." Clearheaded Dora kept babbling on, as if nervous. “Why don’t I get everything out in the meantime?” she said almost to herself.

He ignored her as she pulled out the potato salad, relishes and other side dishes, then carted them from the kitchen to dining room. Why didn’t Cathy come in and rescue him? Her pregnancy didn’t make her helpless.

Of course, the answer was she didn’t know anything was going on. Her blissful ignorance kept her in the other room chirping away.

He tested the center of a steak. Pink was turning to brown. He better get them out.

Dora stood next to him, eager to help, as he deposited the sputtering meat onto the platter. He balanced the growing load as he reached for the last steak on the grill. Before he could object, she grabbed the platter. He stubbornly clung to it.

“It won’t hurt for me to help,” she insisted.

The husky timbre of her voice sent goose bumps up and down his arms. She could easily get a phone sex job, not that she needed one.

Averting his eyes, he relinquished the platter into her capable hands. He stabbed at the remaining steak, tossing it onto the dish. Grease popped and splattered on her hand. She flinched and the plate wobbled. He reached for the platter, just as her hand tightened over it. Their fingers connected. A searing jolt flashed up his arm. The plate almost fell, but he managed to straighten it out.

They stood frozen. Then, with concern, he looked into the eyes he’d avoided. A thin sheen of tears laced them. Her lips trembled.

“Dora, are you okay?”

She cradled her hand, which already bore a red welt. An urge came over him to bend down and kiss the pain away. He was ashamed of himself for considering it. With a stricken look, Dora nodded at him, though he could see she was hurt. Were her tears from the burn or something else? He dare not ask.

“Are you sure you’re all right?”

She nodded.

“You better put something on that. I’ll bring out the steaks.”

“Sure, Danny.”

After she’d left, his heart continued its wild hammering. His fingers trembled. He couldn’t believe this. His wife was in the next room with their baby growing inside of her, yet here he was fighting an urge to jump her sister. He hadn’t wanted this to happen. He wouldn’t let Dora come between them, not after he and Cathy had made everything right. He shook his head, trying to clear it of the image of the flinching Dora.

The door swung open again. He groaned inside. How much more could he take?

Thankfully this time it was Cathy. "Danny, I'm sorry for not helping. What can I do? Are the steaks about ready?"

He glanced at his wife, as if seeing her for the first time. The sun poured down from the kitchen skylight and radiated over her glorious strawberry curls. He stood transfixed, soaking in her ethereal beauty. His fairy tale princess rivaled nature, like a gift from above. His heart ached, thinking of how he'd betrayed her in his mind. It wouldn't happen again. Especially now, when she had that special someone growing inside of her. His heart swelled at the thought.

"Danny, what about the steaks?" she repeated.

"They're ready now. We got a little delayed. Dora had an accident."

Cathy's forehead puckered. As if on cue, her sister reappeared with her hand wrapped in gauze. Guilt hit him at the sight.

"Don't look so upset. I'll survive," she said.

"Glad to hear that, Dora," he said before turning to his wife. He'd known all along that Cathy's sister was dangerous. This proved it.

When everyone was seated, he and Cathy exchanged a special look. It was time.

Danny began grace. "Bless us, Oh Lord, and these thy gifts, especially for the new gift of life you've so generously bestowed on our family."

Nancy McGuire's head shot up. Her hand flew to her chest. "Young man, you almost gave me a heart attack, but I'd gladly die from such a nice surprise."

Ted reached out and pumped Danny's hand. "It's about time."

Danny laughed in embarrassment. "Well, it's not as if we weren't trying."

Dora sat still, tears streaming down her face. Finally she rose and embraced her sister. "I'm so happy for you."

Cathy beamed and said, "Dora, I want you to be the godmother."

Dora nodded. A sad, happy smile flitted across her face.

After that, they all talked at once. The sound of their excited voices drowned out Danny's disturbing doubts. He'd have to act as if nothing had happened. He couldn't let on he felt more for Dora than he wanted to.

Chapter Eighteen
Kevin

KEVIN FROWNED. HE'D wasted enough time. He had to get ready. Where was that address he'd gotten from Steve? The night he'd been released, he'd dug the paper from his jeans and put it in a safe place. Oh, yeah, it was under the coffee can.

Sticking the scrap of paper into his back pocket, he yanked at the door of his rusty clunker. It stuck. One of these days he'd work on it.

He turned the key. The engine, the loving object of his attentions, roared with eagerness to transport its master to whatever destination he desired.

With little effort he found the rundown warehouse. It was exactly where he'd heard it would be, in the Uptown District. Its ground floor housed a sporting goods store. He'd heard rumors of what the entire subterranean length of the building contained.

An African American Mexican pushed open a curtain and stepped out, holding an oil rag and a rifle.

"Are you Max Gonzalez?" Kevin asked.

"Yeah, that be me."

"My buddy, Steve, said you could help me find something."

"I been waiting for you. What'll you be needing?"

"Something powerful and efficient."

"No problem. Follow me."

Still holding the rifle, Gonzalez locked the door, then led Kevin through a long corridor and down a dark flight of stairs to a room which seemed to be all counter. Only after Gonzalez stepped behind it, did the man lower his rifle and lean it to the side.

At sight of what the man was guarding, Kevin understood his paranoia. This was a dangerous business. His heart pumped double time as Gonzalez pulled open a felt-lined drawer and withdraw a gleaming .357 Magnum.

He aimed it at Kevin.

It had to be a test. Kevin stood there unblinking, then said, "I hear you also give shooting lessons. How much?"

The man chuckled and lowered the gun. "Since you know Steve, you get a special deal."

Kevin agreed to donate a substantial portion of each of his paychecks for Max's instructions. That meant subsisting on hot dogs or peanut butter and jelly sandwiches for a while, but it would be worth it.

With the business end settled, he was granted a grand tour of the adjoining soundproofed rooms. He took pleasure in picturing Callaway's face on each target.

HE CARRIED OUT his lessons faithfully. The rooms where he learned and refined the art of shooting became almost as familiar as his tiny cell at Heartland Penitentiary.

"Stop canting," Max screamed, straightening the gun when Kevin tilted his wrist.

"Stop flinching," was another favorite gripe.

Often Kevin got so pissed he felt like turning around and plugging his instructor. That wouldn't work. The gun was loaded with blanks.

Perhaps it was his determination. At any rate, it didn't take long before Kevin's instructor said, "Hey man, you're a natural. It's like you were born to shoot."

That was true. Kevin enjoyed the feel of the rubber grip as well as the recoil sensation speeding up his arm. Both spelled power.

Bang, bang, take that, Callaway.

KEVIN RUBBED HIS eyes. He'd worked eight hours, then had gone for practice at the shooting range. It had been a month since he'd sent out his feelers. He better check the mail just in case. Maybe this time it would be there.

As he riffled though the junk mail, a plain white envelope fell to the floor. What was that? With heart skidding, he swooped it up and tore it open. The single index card inside read, *T. Walker, 7.*

His hands trembled. He'd expected it, but couldn't believe it was happening. Finally he'd be able to bust out of the repair shop. It couldn't have come at a better time. Barnes was driving him crazy. Also, there was that matter of Constance Jennings. His face grew warm at the thought.

He wished he'd never dug up the bitch's phone number from the invoice. When he'd made his proposition to her, he should have had a clue.

The cool voice had said, "My man's out of town. You'll do."

Well, a fuck's a fuck, he'd thought. Beggars can't be choosers. She'd be the first in forever. She came on cool, but underneath she had to be hotter than hell. The possibilities stiffened him

Afraid to jinx anything, he'd kept word of the rendezvous from Mike Evans, intending to fill him in on it later.

From the start, she was different from the others. In the old days, the babes he'd had were shy, young and willing. This number was composed and well-preserved at around forty.

When she'd slipped off her slinky dress, he'd gaped. He wasn't prepared for the sight of huge breasts jutting out over tiny abs.

His eyes darted to the blonde thatch peaking between her legs. He swallowed hard.

"Do you like what you see?" she asked, raising her eyebrows.

He nodded quickly. Not taking his eyes off her, he hurriedly discarded his clothes. Were those boobs real? He reached out to check.

"Don't waste your time on the incidentals. I want it now," she ordered.

"All right. Let's do it," he said, flicking off the switch to darken the room.

"No, leave it on. It's my turn. I want a good look at you."

Whatever. He turned the light back on. He hadn't counted on Constance's eyes fastening on his dick like a pigeon eyeing a morsel. Did he meet her expectations?

She shrugged. "I've seen larger, but yours will do."

He felt himself shrinking. That had never happened before. His face burned.

Frowning, the bitch put her hands on her hips. "I'm not wasting my time."

Before he knew it, she'd pulled her dress back on and vanished out the door, leaving him alone and mortified, thanking heaven he hadn't bragged to Mike.

That embarrassing crap was behind him. He was back in the big time.

KEVIN STEPPED UP to the garish billboard at Walker Cinema. Hmm, the action flick looked good. Too bad he didn't have time to catch it. When the cashier asked for seven-fifty, he blinked hard. Shit, how long had movies cost that much?

At seven sharp he stepped from the lighted lobby into the darkened theater. After his eyes adjusted, he made out two couples in the last row groping each other. Remembering the debacle with Constance, he frowned.

The place was huge. Would he have to check each row for Brad?

Someone poked him in the ribs and whispered, "John."

Kevin slipped into a nearby seat, waited a few minutes, then sauntered into the lobby, then the bathroom. At the sink, he easily spotted his buddy. Though Brad had put on a few more pounds, he still wore the same crew cut as in prison.

Guys were getting last-minute leaks in before the show got started, so Kevin washed his hands to kill time. His fingernails were always greasy anyway. Finally the coast was clear. Brad made the first move.

"It's been a long time, my friend," he said, patting Kevin on the back.

Kevin nodded. "Yeah, man, and it could've been longer if they hadn't found that DNA stuff."

"I wasn't sure you wanted to get in on the action...you know, now your slate's officially clean."

"Hey, I've got eyes. I read the newspaper each day. I deserve a piece of the action. It's not like I'll get myself caught or anything."

Brad smiled. "You're damn right. There's always room for the genius who cooked up the action. You'll be a freelance electrician, right?"

Kevin nodded.

"Anyway, as we'd planned, we now have personnel managers occupying key positions at major security firms. Along with hiring civilians who are not in the know, they dip into our special list of freelancers. Of course, you'll be at the top of the list and can pick and choose your targets." Brad reached into his wallet. "You'll be needing this, Ed Anderson."

The license's fuzzy picture showed a blue eyed man with carrot colored, shoulder-length hair.

Kevin squinted, then grinned. "Okay, I can do it."

A wig and contacts were easy. It'd be a hoot posing as this guy Anderson, scouting out mansions and rummaging through the jewelry boxes of unsuspecting owners. Along with drawing up blueprints which led to the goodies, he'd perform some legitimate chores as installing security systems.

Also, there was that other matter, the one he wouldn't mention to Brad. At thought of it, his lips pursed. The word forgiveness was not in his vocabulary. He had a score to settle.

Chapter Nineteen
Danny

DANNY FELT THE heat as the Cyclones caught fire. The fans flagged the flames, swamping the players and begging for autographs wherever they went.

A boisterous vanload followed Danny home one night, pounding on the front door, refusing to leave, forcing him to call 911. His profession was catching up with his private life. Now that his wife was pregnant, he couldn't take any chances. As they waited in the family room for the police to arrive, he held Cathy tight. Their home was supposed to be a haven, not a fortress under siege.

"I hate to do this, but we've got to install a security system. We could also use a guard or two."

As she opened her mouth to protest, he placed a finger over her lips.

"I know, Cathy. Things won't be as private, but we can't think of only ourselves."

She gave him a telling look that said it all. She hated sharing their lives with anyone. If he weren't a professional basketball player, security wouldn't be necessary.

He wouldn't give in.

She sighed. "Okay, you can put in the electronics, but I won't have any guards around the house. I wish you'd get a regular job. Then we wouldn't have to worry about all this."

Sirens and disappointed moans from the fans signaled the arrival of the police. He stepped outside to speak to them. When it was over and he came back in, Cathy had already gone upstairs to the bedroom. He sighed. By now, he'd hoped she'd have learned to accept his occupation. Anyway, right now the issue of what he did for a living was a moot point. The fans already knew him. If he quit, it wouldn't make a difference.

More attempts to invade their privacy occurred in the following weeks. He was a star. His picture was plastered in the papers, on TV, everywhere, yet he didn't feel any different than before. After each Sunday afternoon home game, he and Cathy opened their home to family and friends. Everyone had a good time devouring pizzas and rehashing what had happened at the game.

Ritchie had married Marilyn, whom he'd met in a night school accounting class, and they'd promptly produced twin boys.

Tony, Tracy and Angela were usually in attendance, as well as Ted and Nancy McGuire. Dora and her best friend, Margaret Lynley and her daughter, Tory, and sometimes Cathy's friend, Marianne Manning, and her husband, Charles, showed up.

After word got out about the prospective new addition to Cathy and Danny's family, the wives huddled together like field marshals making battle plans, while Cathy grilled them with countless questions. It was an exciting time.

Almost overshadowing the commotion on the home front was the team's success, which continued unabated through winter and into the spring. The Cyclones had come into their own. This year they possessed both the necessary talent and depth, with Dave Connors new at center and Andy Ransome back as guard.

With an easy defeat of the Sonics by eighteen points in the regular season's final, hopes for a Cyclone national trophy ran high. They were headed for the playoffs.

The team jumped past each hurdle and loped through the first and second rounds. In the third, they faced an at-home nail-biter.

With the home team behind by three points and four seconds to go, Danny threw out a three-pointer and was promptly elbowed by a Peregrine player. Fortunately, the referee noticed.

It was crunch time. Danny stood at the line, eyeing the basket, knowing he must get the ball through the hoop three times. Sweat dripped down his forehead. A hazy film blocked his eyes. He swiped with his wristband. He'd done this before. Why did it seem so hard this time?

He steadied himself and aimed. The first throw swished through, but there were two more to go. Behind the basket, Peregrine fans waved towels and banners, screamed and blew horns, doing their best to distract him. He had to block them out.

Taking a deep breath, he extended his arms. Obediently, the ball wound into the net.

Just one more. That's all it would take. His heart thumped as if it would burst from his jersey. Trying to calm himself, he took a deep breath and aimed.

In horror he watched the ball hop around the rim, slow itself, then spiral.

As if by some hidden force, it drew itself back into the hoop. At the beautiful sight, he let out a sigh of relief. That was close.

The crowd went insane. His ears hurt, but that didn't matter. He caught the fervor and jumped up and down, grinning and flashing a victory sign.

"Let's go," Coach yelled.

Amidst a rain of congratulations and flying objects, Danny sprinted into the locker room. One more game to win, five days from now, and the championship would be theirs. Could they do it?

As he drove home, the cell phone rang. He smiled. It had to be Cathy congratulating him. She was uncomfortable with the baby due in sixteen days and hadn't been able to make it to the game. He understood why she couldn't have been present, yet it was a shame she hadn't been there with the rest of his cheering section to watch the victory.

"Hi, Cath," he said, pressing the speaker button as he turned a corner.

"Danny, please hurry. I don't feel good."

His hands tightened on the wheel. His neck knotted. He was at least forty-five minutes away from Tahoma Street, where he wanted to be. "Did you call the doctor, Cath?"

"I did. He said to go in."

"I'll call an ambulance."

"No, I want you here with me. I'll wait."

"Honey, just go in, please. Anything could happen. Don't take chances."

A truck rounded the corner and almost sideswiped him. He swore and blasted the horn, then sped up. Damn, he was too far away.

He'd been on the road when the security system had been installed. Cathy had insisted it was enough. She'd been adamant about not allowing guards on the premises. He should have overridden her. Then she wouldn't be alone.

"Cathy, can you hear me?"

He heard a moan, then silence. "Cathy, Cathy?"

With trembling fingers, he punched 911, stated the situation, and asked for an ambulance.

The drive home was a nightmare.

"Please, God, let her be all right," he prayed.

If anything happened to Cathy, he'd never forgive himself.

He hit the speed dial for the McGuires, then remembered they'd left for vacation five days ago. Nancy had wanted to be well rested before the new arrival appeared.

Who else could help? He punched in Dora's cell phone number, but got voice mail. She was probably out celebrating with the rest of their friends, who knows where. Thank God, he'd decided to come home right away. He only hoped it wasn't too late.

Danny dashed from the BMW into the house. It was empty. Cathy had to be on her way or already at the hospital. He sped down Devon, then Harlem, to Resurrection Hospital on Talcott, where she would have headed. The two-mile trek seemed like a hundred. When he arrived, the emergency room was jammed. Lines stretched long before the admittance clerks' windows.

Where was Cathy? Was she all right?

"Please, please, could I ask something?" Danny said, shouldering his way past twelve people in front of him.

"Wait your turn," a beer-bellied man with a bandaged arm yelled.

"I need to find out about my wife. Can someone help me?" Danny insisted.

A gray-haired clerk took pity on him and beckoned him to the side. "What's her name, son?"

Fear made his throat go dry. "Cathy...uh Catherine Callaway."

A voice yelled, "That's Danny Callaway. I thought I recognized him."

He didn't want people prying. He only wanted his wife.

"She's in there," the clerk said, pointing at a closed door. He rushed toward it.

"You can't go in without an access card," the clerk yelled.

An orderly came up behind Danny and slipped his card through. Danny dashed in beside him, then stood, confused, in the middle of the brightly lit floor. Curtain-drawn cubicles lined its perimeters. Which one of them contained Cathy?

A round desk stood to the right behind which a young nurse wrote on a clipboard. He stepped over and cleared his throat. "Is Cathy Callaway here?"

"And you are?...Oh, you're that basketball player, Danny Callaway. Great game tonight."

He nodded impatiently.

"She's this way, sir," the nurse said, smiling and leading him across the room.

The antiseptic smell was strong, bringing back unpleasant reminders of when he'd had his ankle surgery at Northwestern Memorial Hospital. A baby cried. An old man groaned. While the rest of the world played, here people clutched themselves in pain and fought for their lives. Fear clawed at his stomach.

The nurse stopped abruptly in front of him, making him almost bump into her. She pushed aside the curtain to a cubicle.

Cathy lay still, her skin as pale as the sheet she lay upon. Her red hair and freckles stood out in contrast, reminding him of blood. An IV was stuck in her arm. A nurse and doctor conferred nearby.

Danny rushed to her side. "Cathy, honey, I got here as fast as I could. Are you all right?"

She didn't move or speak. He waited a fear-filled moment before he saw her force out a weak smile. Seeing her in pain wrenched his gut.

The doctor took him aside. "Mr. Callaway, everything went faster than we'd expected. She lost a lot of blood. The good news is you've got a fine, healthy eight-pound boy."

"What about Cathy?"

"We didn't have time for an incision, so your wife suffered an extensive rip to the peritoneum. She lost a great deal of blood, but has stopped hemorrhaging. We're carefully monitoring her blood count as a precaution. The best prescription is a few weeks of bed rest."

Danny blinked back sudden tears. If only he could have been here with Cathy instead of being stuck in traffic.

A nurse poked her head in. "The room's ready, doctor."

"All right, then. Let's get Mrs. Callaway to the maternity ward where she belongs. The baby's already up there."

Danny followed the gurney as Cathy, sleeping the sleep of the exhausted, was transferred to a private room in the maternity wing.

With Cathy situated, the nurse, carrying a small bundle, approached Danny. "Would you like to see your son, Mr. Callaway?"

He swallowed a sudden lump in his throat, then gingerly picked up his child.

Glancing down, he was surprised to find the same black hair as his. The sight tugged at his heartstrings. This child was a part of him. It even looked like him. Since the baby had been inside Cathy for so long, it had seemed only hers.

The following morning, Dora joined them. By then the baby had been named Sean and was contentedly nestled in his mother's arms. Cathy was already regaining color in her cheeks. The doctor was satisfied enough to promise her release from the hospital the following day...as long as she followed orders.

Danny's gift of pink tea roses and baby's breath sat on the window ledge, along with a baby shoe flower arrangement from Dora, plus various other flora from family and friends.

"This place looks like your shop," Danny teased, smiling at his wife.

A quick frown crossed her face, followed by a valiant smile. He knew she hated leaving her shop even for a day.

"That reminds me," Dora said. "I better get over there and open up."

Smiling through sentimental tears, Dora took one last look at the new addition, then hurried away. She'd be busy, working half-days at the shop and half-days at the law firm.

When Cathy's parents had heard the news, they'd wanted to rush straight home, but Cathy had insisted they finish their vacation.

"I'm not the only woman in the world who's had a baby. Don't miss out on your vacation," she'd told them.

Yes, Cathy was something. She handled everything perfectly. She'd even convinced her parents to stay put. He smiled at her tenderly. She'd waited for this chance a long time. Thank goodness it had happened.

That night he didn't sleep. The house seemed empty without Cathy. The next morning he was only too happy to drive her and Baby Sean home. Now there would be one more person to fill the rooms.

Cathy wanted to sleep with the baby right next to her, but Danny knew she couldn't get better that way.

"Remember, Cath, the doctor wants bed rest. You need to get strong again."

She bit her lip.

They hit on a compromise. When Cathy needed to sleep, Sean would be put into the cradle beside the master bed. With that settled, Danny concentrated on other matters. In all the excitement, he hadn't given much thought to the playoffs. The team was counting on him, baby or no baby. That meant, no matter how much he didn't like it, he'd have to leave Friday for practice in L. A. The championship game was on Saturday.

Cathy couldn't manage on her own. Something had to be done.

With some juggling of schedules, they managed to get Dora's friend, Margaret, to help at the shop. That left Dora available to stay with her sister.

The only hitch was Saturday, when they both would attend Margaret's daughter's graduation ceremony and party afterwards.

That made him uneasy.

"Cathy, people get crazy around playoffs. I know we went over this before and you didn't want guards, but I'd feel better if you humored me this once. I'll tell Alert Advantage to send over a guard. It'll only be for the final game."

"I don't like it. I want us to be a normal family."

Sean took that inopportune moment to let out a wail, punctuating her statement and diverting his mother's attention.

Danny sighed, wishing Cathy would be more accepting of his profession. He knew everything couldn't be perfect, yet whenever she slammed basketball, she hammered him.

FRIDAY AFTERNOON, DANNY stepped into the bedroom to say goodbye. Cathy was propped atop two huge pillows with Sean cuddled safely in her arms. In her pink cotton gown, with eyes puffy from sleep, she looked almost like a child herself.

He caught his breath at the tableau, then stood still taking in the sight. Smiling, he reached down and planted a kiss on Cathy's lips and another on Sean's forehead. He had to be the luckiest man alive. At the door, he turned for one final look. The drapes were open. Late June sunlight streamed onto their faces. They looked so vulnerable, almost lost on top of the giant bed. How could he leave them?

"Hell, this is rotten timing. I wish I didn't have to go."

Cathy nodded resignedly and turned to Sean. He shook off a creeping feeling of jealousy. He couldn't fault her. He'd been the one to suggest a baby as a substitute for him.

On the limousine ride to the airport, he had plenty of time to mull over his new status, wondering if he'd already been relegated to second best.

The air was humid as he boarded the plane. The sky darkened. Guilt and unease combined to form a niggling headache behind his temples.

He'd called this morning to hire an extra security guard, just in case. Cathy and Sean would be in good hands. Professionals would be present every minute to watch over his family. Also, Dora would stop by later in the afternoon. Why couldn't he relax?

To take his mind off a growing uneasiness, he opened a computer magazine he'd bought at the terminal. The problem was every ad seemed to reflect Cathy's pale accusing face, pleading with him to give up basketball.

Chapter Twenty
Kevin

KEVIN ACCEPTED ODD jobs at security firms, biding his time, knowing it wouldn't be long before Callaway came a-knocking.

When the call came, a man named Ed Anderson installed the alarm system, with the lovely Cathy looking on, babbling about how she really didn't want it, but had to have it because of her husband's road trips.

As he listened, he ducked his head to hide a grin. Also, to keep from reaching out to grab her.

Even in her intensely knocked-up condition, Mrs. Callaway was a looker. He felt like sticking his tongue into her talkative mouth, then jamming himself deep inside her. He knew he'd come real good, not like with Constance "Bitch" Jennings.

He barely restrained himself. While Cathy jabbered on about babies and basketball, he installed cameras and bugs in the smoke alarms, thermostats and other spots in the Callaways' joint.

From then on, he'd known all about the Callaways' comings and goings. What he'd especially enjoyed was watching the lovely wife remove her clothes. Until lately, the couple had done the deed almost every day. The bitch was a real turn-on, making sexy mewing sounds whenever she got hot. Just once, he'd like to stick himself inside her, but that wouldn't fit his plan.

He'd hardened his heart at the sight of mother and baby arriving home from the hospital. Had his Mom ever looked at him like Cathy Callaway looked at her brat?

It was almost time.

The day before the big game, from his vantage point parked down the block, Kevin watched Callaway leave for the airport. Smiling in anticipation, he gunned the motor and drove away.

Callaway had left, with no clue of the tragedy which awaited him. Soon the "Great One" would sink to his knees. Even sweeter was the fact it would happen at the happiest moment of his life. He'd never know what had hit him until it was too late. Then the score would be settled.

That night Kevin was so fired up he couldn't sleep. Everything had to go exactly right. He set two alarms extra early, just in case.

The next morning he stationed himself behind the Callaways' front bushes. A bug bit him. Stifling a curse, he shifted his weight. The leaves rustled. He held his breath, but no one came to investigate.

Everything was in place. Three weeks ago, he'd written to Anthony Edwards and asked for his wife Miranda's address, telling him he'd have a tiny delivery for her.

In prison, Anthony had been heartbroken at the loss of his son. He'd wanted another baby for his wife's sake, but under the circumstances, couldn't do that.

Kevin had never confessed to Anthony that he'd told Billy Holliday about Anthony's squealing to the guard about the hash. He still couldn't get over how Holliday had killed Anthony's kid. This would be a great way to make it up to him.

Kevin's legs cramped and grew numb. Wasn't it time for the blasted guard to take a break? Kevin had worked with Todd before. The sap couldn't last long without a nicotine fix. Some security.

The door slammed. Todd whizzed by, headed for the back.

Kevin stepped out. He wore the distinctive Alert Advantage green jacket, but in a larger size than usual. Underneath was a matching uniform.

Gingerly he reached for the package beside him. At the doorstep, he carefully set down the box, switched off the alarm, picked up the package and slipped into the house.

Knowing where he would find Cathy and the baby, he climbed confidently up the stairs. He shifted the package, then lightly knocked on the semi-open door. There was no answer, so he knocked harder.

"Who is it?" a soft voice asked.

"Mrs. Callaway, it's me, Ed Anderson—you know, the guy who installed the security system. I'm on duty. How are you doing?"

Her uncertain voice floated back. "Oh, I thought Todd was working today. I just saw him a few minutes ago."

"Not to worry. He'll be back later. He had some personal business to attend to. In the meantime, he wanted me to keep an eye on things. Can I come in for a minute? I've got something for you."

"Sure, Ed," she answered, though her voice still sounded uncertain.

He stepped into the bedroom. As he'd envisioned, Cathy Callaway was seated on the bed, with the baby's cradle to the left. The volume on the TV was set so low he could barely hear the announcer.

He cleared his throat. His voice came out louder than he'd

intended. "Mrs. Callaway..."

She raised a finger to her lips, smiled, and pointed to the cradle. "Please don't wake him. He's finally asleep."

Perfect.

He lowered his voice. "Mrs. Callaway, I've got a surprise for you. It's from your husband."

He stepped between the crib and the bed. As he handed her the package, her face lit up.

"Now, ma'am, you've got to promise not to open this until the end of the game. That's what your husband said."

Kevin had taken great pains to wrap fancy gold paper around the box and finish it off with a giant silver-and-gold bow on the top.

He could tell she was dying to rip it open. He didn't blame her.

"Thanks so much for bringing this up to me," she said, eyes shining.

Kevin gazed back, almost hypnotized. Her eyes were as blue as the summer sky. Her hair sparkled. Just looking at her took his breath away. Maybe he should take the package back. She'd done nothing to him.

Idly she fiddled with the fancy bow. His heart pounded. Just then the phone rang as he'd planned. She reached for the receiver on the other side of the bed.

He turned and slipped the sleeping child from the cradle into his coat. The boy didn't let out a whimper as Kevin rearranged the covers so it would look like he was still in the crib.

"Who's there? Danny is that you?" Cathy was saying.

With the boy tucked in his coat, Kevin said a quick goodbye and made his escape.

Hearing her voice still saying, "Hello, hello," he rushed through the hallway, then down the stairs.

KEVIN RACED TO his van down the block from the Callaway's mansion. The brat woke up and let out a tentative wail.

"Shut up or I'll bring you back," he muttered, pressing his hand over the small mouth.

He was tempted to do just that, but something inside him said no. God would never forgive him if he did. At the van, he reached into the glove compartment, grabbed the duct tape and fastened it over the brat's mouth.

"There, scream all you want. It won't do you any good," he said, depositing the kid on the back seat under a pile of newspapers. There, now no one could tell.

He switched on the radio and honed in on the see-saw battle. The Cyclones must win or his revenge would not be complete. When Ronnie White blew a shot, Kevin almost missed the expressway ramp leading to uptown Chicago.

"Shit, get with it, man," he yelled.

He wove through traffic, exited at Lawrence Avenue, and dropped the kid off at Anthony's wife's place.

On the way back, he almost rear-ended the slow, old fart in front of him. Finally, with five minutes left on the game clock, he made it back to the end of the Callaways' block. It was almost show time.

Chapter Twenty-One
Danny

THE SCORE REMAINED tied. With only a few minutes left in the fourth quarter, the din was deafening. Danny had to rely on instinct to perform his maneuvers. Like a wolf guarding his territory, he defended the basket.

So far, he'd contributed ten rebounds and forty points. They meant nothing if the team lost. The Crows refused to go down. With every Cyclone basket, a Crow racked up as many points. Both teams were ravenous for the meat of victory.

Though his head was sweat-soaked and his eyes stung, Danny focused on the ball. The clock ticked in his head, reminding him they had to pull ahead or all would be lost. At times like this, he wondered why he was a player.

With thirty seconds left, he wove back and forth, searching for a break. The Crows were wise to his tricks. They pushed and pressed, leaving no room to pass.

Miraculously, he found an outside chance, though he'd have to backdoor it. Ransome had the ball. No one looked clear, yet the Crows' guards veered to the left. Danny took two quick steps to the right toward Ransome, then stopped and broke for the basket.

Ransome caught on and threw the pass. The ball flew into the air, Danny grabbed it, jumped up and dunked, only to crash straight onto the Crow's guard, Paul Charles.

The referee called the foul against Danny, though it wasn't his fault. The basket didn't count. Biting back an obscenity, he lined up with the other players. Charles missed the first, but easily made the second, placing the Crows ahead by a single point.

With eight seconds left, Danny felt the game slipping away. He wouldn't let go. Winning was the most important thing in the world, almost an affirmation of his existence. He'd sacrificed a lot for basketball's sake. It must not be in vain.

Danny pictured Cathy in their bedroom watching TV as she held Sean. This win would be for them.

Everything led up to this moment. He wouldn't blow it.

Hoping a pass could get to him, Danny positioned himself a few steps past the free throw line. The Crow players swarmed around him like gnats. Trying to confuse them, he ducked back, then to the side.

Out of nowhere it came. The ball whizzed from the center line straight to the far end in a desperation pass. Danny jumped up and grabbed for it. Magically it landed in his fingers. He pivoted, then arced the ball as the whistle blew. The crowd grew silent, watching the descent.

It slid in. Pandemonium broke lose. They'd done it! The Cyclones had won the championship!

Voices chanted "Danny, Danny," as his teammates hoisted him on their backs and carried him around the court. Missiles glanced off him, but he didn't care. It was all part of a marvelous moment he'd never forget.

He was on top of the world. What more could he ask for? He had a beautiful wife, a newborn son, more money than he could dream of, and the championship to boot. He might look stupid with this wide grin on his face, but somehow he couldn't wipe it off. He had so much to be thankful for.

Yes, he'd had some rough times on and off the court, but they'd all been worth it. They made today's happiness that much sweeter. God forbid, but if anything happened right now and he couldn't play again, he'd always have this one shining moment to remember.

When they reached the locker room, his teammates finally set him down, only to turn champagne bottles onto him, squirting the icy liquid onto his sweaty head. He ducked, but not too hard. The cold felt good.

He finally was able to dart away and pat his buddy, Ransome, on the back.

"Hey, we did it," Ransome said, looking as stunned as Danny.

Ronnie White ran over to slap Danny's hand.

The place was a madhouse, with everyone screaming and yelling. Over the din, reporters jostled around the players with their microphones. Danny answered whoever caught up with him, but knew he wouldn't remember anything he said. How could he? He was in shock.

The fans cheered and chanted, demanding another glimpse of the players. It was only right to go out.

Danny yelled above the din, "One time around, okay?"

Against common sense, the team ran out and flashed "V" signs. The security guards frowned as they ran alongside trying to protect them.

On the sidelines, fans climbed on top of each other, attempting to swipe the hoops off the baskets. With all the pushing and shoving, the hoops got twisted and tangled. Danny saw one guy fall to the floor and stumble up just seconds before getting trampled. No one wanted to leave. The world had gone completely bonkers for one glorious reason—the Cyclones had won the championship!

Policemen preserved one section of the court inviolate. There Danny stepped out to accept his MVP award. His heart burst with happiness as he held the glinting trophy high. Cameras zoomed, lights flashed. His future was as shiny as the bright lights surrounding him.

Cathy had to be watching, along with what might be the family's future basketball player.

When Danny again stumbled through the crowd and into the locker room, the reporters stuck more mikes into his face. With his mind already flying ahead, he quickly answered their questions.

He wanted badly to break away and share the victory with Cathy. He hadn't seen Sean in over a day, but he could still picture his child's tiny, perfect face. It was amazing how he already missed the baby, not to mention his mother. Cathy had to be impressed. Now she'd understand why he'd sacrificed so much.

Dora might also be there. Maybe she'd seen the ending basket. Maybe she'd transferred some of her excitement to her sister.

Radio newscaster, Terry Torrence, stepped up to Danny with a mike.

"How does it feel to win the championship and the MVP award?" he asked.

"Better than you'll ever know."

Danny politely answered other questions, then looking straight into the lens, said, "Cathy, I love you. And tell Sean that Daddy loves him, too. I'll be home real soon."

It wasn't easy, but Danny finally managed to break free from the revelers, get to his locker and open it. He reached into his duffel bag for his cell phone and punched the quick dial, but only got a click. He wiped his hands on his wet, sweaty jersey, then dialed the long way, with the same results.

Strange. He'd never had trouble with his phone before. Well, tons of calls had to be going out. That must be the problem.

Sighing, he went in search of a land line. He vaguely remembered seeing a phone on the wall of the locker room.

The trouble was Ronnie White was already there with five other guys clustered around.

With each passing moment, he felt an increasing urgency to reach

Cathy. It was almost as if he didn't speak to her right now, he never would.

A fine time to get superstitious. Most people acted that way before a game. When he got home, he and Cathy would have a good laugh over that. Also Dora.

At the thought of her, his heart quickened. More than her sister, Dora would appreciate what the championship meant. Not only was she an avid sports fan, but she understood the sacrifices necessary to earn something important. She'd studied long and hard to ace her bar exams and was making great strides as a competent attorney.

Too bad the rest of the clan was still gone. Ted and Nancy were in Ireland. Tony, Ritchie and their broods were fishing in Canada. They'd made reservations months before anyone could guess the Cyclones would make it to the playoffs.

Tony, good buddy he was, had offered to stay home, but Danny had insisted he go. His friend worked hard and could use a vacation.

He broke off his thoughts to check the line by the telephone. Hell, it was getting longer. Instead of wasting time standing around and thinking, he should have gone up there. There had to be another phone around somewhere.

As he dodged through his partying teammates, a soggy towel stung his face. Fighting back an unreasonable irritation, Danny returned the volley. Everyone was having a great time. Why was he so uptight? By letting a minor inconvenience upset him, he was missing out on all the fun. He might never experience anything like this again.

The noise echoed down the hallway as he checked the small rooms bordering it to no avail. He was becoming obsessed. All he could think of was finding the precious phone. There had to be one.

A door to the right stood partially ajar. He flicked on the light and discovered a long vinyl table with Crows paraphernalia propped against the wall. Several folding chairs were stacked against it. His trained eyes spied the black phone at the end of the table.

Letting out a sigh of relief, he reached over and shut the door. His search had paid off. Now he could speak to Cathy without everyone listening. He punched in the numbers. The phone clicked.

He swallowed hard in disappointment. The worries he'd kept at bay leaked out. Was something wrong? Were Cathy and the baby all right? Where was Dora?

He had to get a grip on himself. Probably a squirrel had bitten the telephone wire. Damn, why had it happened today of all days?

Still you'd think Cathy or Dora could have called him on the cell phone to congratulate him and let him know everything was all right. They had to realize he'd want to reach them.

Maybe they couldn't get through, either. Cathy didn't believe in cell phones, but Dora had one. Maybe they'd used hers and he hadn't heard the ring over the racket. He punched the Caller ID button, but no numbers were listed. No new messages appeared.

Wait a minute. He'd programmed Dora's number onto his phone when Cathy got pregnant. He scrolled, then punched Dora's number. It rang, then switched to voice mail.

Where was everybody? And what about those guards? Weren't they supposed to report to him? Hell, he was paying them good money. Some security.

With growing uneasiness, he made his way back to the locker room and stepped into the shower. As the accumulated grime from the exhausting game fell off him, his skin tingled, reviving him.

When he emerged, he felt refreshed and optimistic. His team had won the championship. Nothing could go wrong. Instead of staying over tonight, he'd hop an early jet, get home and celebrate with his family.

He'd just managed to slip into his street clothes when two uniformed men appeared in the locker room doorway. The shorter one was yelling something, trying to communicate over the din.

Ronnie must have heard because he shouted, "Danny, he's asking for you."

Now what? Not another delay. At this point, all he wanted to do was get away. He had to loosen up. This stuff was all part of winning. These guys were probably here to escort him out. The fans had to be hysterical by now, ready to kiss or kill.

Plastering a smile on his face, he approached the policemen. "I'm Danny Callaway. I hear you've been looking for me. Are you my protection?"

The policemen exchanged a silent look. Neither one cracked a smile. Apparently they had a lousy sense of humor. It was just his luck to get two deadbeats. Maybe they were Crows fans. That would explain their grim expressions.

He wouldn't let them rain on his parade. "Hey, don't look so down. Next year the Crows'll get another chance. Of course, I can't guarantee we won't beat them again."

One of them blinked. Danny glimpsed a flicker of sympathy in his eyes. A quiver shot down his spine.

The taller one asked, "Mr. Callaway, is there somewhere we can speak in private?"

The other glanced around the crowded room, as if he'd rather stick around and celebrate.

Danny's mind blanked. His heart pounded madly. He couldn't think, much less remember the layout. He was afraid, deathly afraid. Any second the boom would fall. He didn't want it to happen.

Not today, please, not when everything was going right. Please don't let it be Cathy, Sean, Dora or anyone else he cared about.

The three of them strode out of the locker room, then down the hallway. Danny found the small room where he'd tried to reach Cathy. With shaky fingers, he reached for the switch. The fluorescent fixtures cast off a garish glow. His mind spun back to when the porch light had shone on his sister's prone body. Would this be as bad?

Danny glanced at the short policeman, who quickly looked away, then made a show of pulling out three folding chairs and opening them. That done, the officer said, "Well, why don't we sit down and talk."

With a smile that didn't reach his eyes, his partner said, "That's a good idea, Hank."

After they were seated, the short one cleared his throat. "Mr. Callaway, I'm Officer John Harding and this is my partner, Hank Donnelly."

It was taking too long. What did they want? Why didn't they get it over with? "Okay, what can I do for you, gentlemen? What's so important you had to drag me out of the locker room at the height of a championship celebration?"

He smiled uncertainly. Maybe if he pretended nothing was wrong, nothing would be. The other possibility was too frightening.

"Mr. Callaway," John Harding continued, as if Danny hadn't spoken. "Do you have friends or family in L.A.?"

"No," Danny answered. "My wife and sister-in-law are at home with my newborn son. The rest are on vacation."

What difference did it make? What was the man getting at?

Harding took a deep breath and sighed. "Well then, I'm afraid I've got some bad news. Apparently there was an explosion in your home."

The news hit him with a wallop, sucking his breath away. He'd been braced for the worse, but was still unprepared. A sick feeling spiraled through his throat and down into his gut. "Cathy?" he croaked through parched lips.

"I'm sorry, sir. Your wife perished."

No. That couldn't be. He'd talked to her right before the game.

She couldn't be gone.

Another thought hit him. "The baby?" he whispered.

"We don't know yet, sir. So far, we can't find any evidence of the child. Perhaps the boy was dropped off somewhere."

"Cathy wouldn't allow that. The baby's less than a week old. Sean had to be with her."

There must be a mistake. It was a different house, not his. He had a security system and guards. Cathy and Sean had to be safe.

And Dora? What about her? She was supposed to have gone over there after the graduation party. Not her, too, please, no. He had to ask. "Was anyone else found?"

"Yes, another adult."

His heart skipped a beat. He squeezed his lids shut. Oh, God, not Dora, too. Flowing dark hair and golden, knowing eyes flashed through his mind. He'd ignored Cathy's sister too often out of self-preservation, knowing in his heart that he felt more for her than he should. Now he could never make it up to her.

Gone was that magnificent, independent spirit. Dora had had so much to live for. She'd been going places in a man's world, but now would go nowhere. It was such a waste. She could have given so much.

A familiar roiling sensation hit him. He remembered this feeling—one he'd never wanted to feel again.

Trying to take his mind off the pain, he glanced around the small room. His eyes rested on the Crows' pennants and banners. They were a melancholy sight. All the lost hopes of so many people. For every winner, there was a loser.

In the background, the revelers carried on. His eyes filled with tears. Everyone was so happy. Everyone but him. Once again, he was alone. This was too much. He couldn't stand it.

He pushed back his chair and headed for the wall. He pounded his fist harder and harder into it, hitting the painted bricks, not feeling the pain, not hearing the officers ordering him to stop. He was in hell. The rest of the world didn't exist.

"No, no, it's not true," he repeated like a mantra.

Officer Donnelly ran out, then reappeared with the team physician.

"Can you give him something? He's injuring himself."

Dr. Halman nodded and reached into his bag. "All right, Danny, stop that."

Danny turned in the direction of the new voice.

"This should help."

He barely noticed the prick of the needle as it sank into his arm. Through a fog, he heard the doctor ask the officers what had happened.

Donnelly said, "His wife and baby were killed. Their house exploded."

Dr. Halman shook his head. "That's a terrible shame. And what a time for this to happen."

Doctors had to be accustomed to death, but Danny knew this one cared more than others for his patients.

Still, he didn't want anyone's sympathy. Right now, it didn't matter if he lived or died. All he wanted was to sink into the beckoning blackness and disappear.

As the drug flowed through his veins, a numb lassitude took over, carrying with it a strange calmness. That was good. He never wanted to feel again. Feeling only brought pain.

"Danny, where are you staying tonight?" Dr. Halman asked.

"I just want to go home."

"I'm sorry. That's not possible. You have no home to go to."

"I can't stay here. I'm going back to Illinois."

The officers exchanged a look. Donnelly addressed his partner, as if Danny weren't standing next to them. "Is that wise? Do you think he can manage?"

"Look at me. I'm right here," Danny said. "I'm a responsible adult. I can get by. Besides, I don't know anyone in this city."

Dr. Halman pursed his lips. "You've got a point. Give me the name of someone to call and I'll make sure you're picked up at the airport. The team will be leaving in the morning anyway."

Danny fumbled in his shirt pocket and pulled out his cell phone. Furrowing his brows, he tried to get his clumsy fingers to scroll through the list. Everything looked blurry. What did it matter? Wasn't everyone who was important to him either dead or on vacation? Who was left?

Out of frustration, he tried last number redial. The display showed Dora's number. Pain shot through him. Dora was gone. God, it hurt so badly. Now he could never tell her he loved her.

Dr. Halman looked across at the display. "Do you want to call, ah, Dora McGuire?"

"We can't," Danny said in a whisper. "She died, too. She was at the house." Lightheadedness hit him. Maybe he'd pass out and never wake up.

Officer Donnelly cut in. "No, Mr. Callaway. Your sister-in-law arrived at the house after the explosion."

Danny looked uncertainly at the officer. "But you said two adults died."

"From the garment scraps discovered next to the other body, we believe it could've been a security guard," Donnelly said.

He'd forgotten he'd hired another guard. Tears sprang to his eyes as relief washed through him. Dora had been spared. Thank you, God. If she were here right now, he'd wrap his arms around her and bury his face in her breasts. Dora was strong. He needed her.

The world spun on its axis. The officer steadied Danny as he swayed.

From what seemed like far away, he heard the doctor call someone. He knew they were talking, but his mind was elsewhere, coping with the realization of how much he cared for Dora. The thing about drugs was they made people accept the truth.

The doctor placed another call, then grabbed his business card and wrote on the back.

"All right, let's get you to the airport. I've got an early plane lined up. I'll call your sister-in-law with the details."

Danny stumbled to the door, the doctor's arm around him. They passed a cheering crowd, but he didn't have the heart to wave to his fans. A lifetime ago the Cyclones had won the championship. He'd been happy then, when he'd had a wife and baby to come home to. Now he didn't even have a roof over his head.

The one consolation was Dora. He thanked God again for sparing her.

DANNY STARED AT the blackened sky from the 747's window. Were Cathy and Sean out there somewhere? They had to be. They couldn't have been wiped away as if they'd never existed. There had to be something after death, some kind of place for souls to spend eternity. God had to be watching over them, along with the rest of his family. He wished he could join them. Earth was hell.

The ride passed in a dull haze. Before he knew it, he'd grabbed his duffel bag and stumbled across O'Hare's buzzing terminal, where a mob of reporters awaited him.

After several "No comments," he broke away, pretended to head for the luggage area, but instead zagged in the opposite direction. The ruse worked and he lost them.

Outside the terminal, not one familiar face was in sight. Maybe Dora was inside somewhere. Or maybe she hadn't come. His shoulders slumped. His fogged brain refused to formulate a plan. Where should he go? Should he stay at a hotel?

A cab pulled up. Luckily the driver didn't recognize him. Danny lowered himself inside and closed the door. Before he could give directions, he heard a banging on the window.

"Danny, wait. I'm here."

He glanced out. Dora's eyes were red. Her hair stuck out wildly. She looked out of control. He'd never seen her like this. He stared at her stupidly.

"Sir, where to?" the cabby asked.

Confused, Danny glanced again at Dora. Should he go with her? She looked even more dangerous than he'd remembered. He rolled down the window.

"Please, Danny, come back with me. You can't be alone right now."

He shook his head. "No, Dora, I better not."

"Danny, don't be stubborn. Get out of the cab. You can stay at my parents' house. Family should stick together at a time like this."

She was right. He shouldn't be so selfish. They were family and should be together. She had to hurt as much as he, probably more. After all, he'd only known Cathy a short time. Dora had been her sister for many years.

"I changed my mind," he told the driver, fishing into his pocket and handing over a twenty.

As his foot touched the sidewalk, he almost pitched over. He steadied himself by putting a hand on Dora's shoulder. "You're right, Dora. I'm sorry for being so selfish."

The amber eyes gazed back at him with a stricken, hungry look. Then she seemed to pull herself together. "Wait here," she said. "I'll bring the car around."

He had to lean on the post to keep from falling. This was too much. His wife and baby were dead. Besides that, he had this insanely hot feeling about his sister-in-law. It was wrong to think that way at a time like this. For God's sake, his wife and child had just died.

Damn! If he hadn't gone to the final, he could have been with them. Maybe if he'd been there, they'd have been saved. If not, he could have gone down with them and that would have been fine.

"Okay, Danny, I'm here." A gentle, firm voice spoke from far away.

Wearily he climbed into the forest green Acura.

With practiced ease, Dora pulled out. Since he'd avoided her as much as possible, she'd never driven him anywhere before.

As he would have guessed, she merged onto the Kennedy Expressway with controlled, deliberate movements. Though not overly aggressive, she didn't relinquish her rights.

She was probably just as precise when she practiced law. Her father must be proud of her.

That reminded him. "Have you heard from Ted and Nancy?" he asked.

Dora turned her head briefly, time enough to reveal the tears forming in her eyes. "They don't know yet. I haven't been able to reach them. They're still in Ireland. I'll try again at the house. I know they'll need us when they hear. That's why it's best if we stay there."

It didn't matter where he stayed. Still, if it helped them, he'd do it. "You're right. This will tear them apart."

Dora nodded, fingers tightly clutching the steering wheel. The car slowed. Impatient drivers honked behind them, but she seemed unaware of their existence.

"I don't know how I'm going to tell them. I still can't believe it myself. It's a nightmare."

"I know what you mean." He wished to hell he didn't. If only Dora didn't have to go through this as well. No one should have to bear such pain. If her parents were lucky, they wouldn't hear of it for a long time. Let them enjoy themselves while they could.

Horns honked. A Jeep loaded with teenagers sped past.

Dora bit her lip and focused on driving, marching the Acura toward its destination. While she drove, she related her side of the story. He didn't want to hear it, but he knew she had to get it out.

"I went to Chicago for Tory's middle school graduation. You've seen her. She's been at your open house before."

Danny nodded. She was a sweet kid.

"The auditorium was packed. I couldn't believe how huge the class was. When her name was called, Tory clutched that diploma like it was pure gold. She'd worked so hard to get it. Studying hasn't been easy for her after the car accident that injured her head.

"At the party, I got to see some of the game. When it was half-time, I called Cathy to tell her I'd be home before it ended. I hadn't counted on a jack-knifed truck on the expressway and an hour and a half backup." Dora grimaced. "I guess that saved my life. Otherwise I'd have been in the house, too." Her fingers trembled.

"Thank God, you weren't," Danny said softly.

For a moment Dora was silent. Then she continued. "When I'd last spoken to her, Cathy told me she had a package you'd left for her with one of the guards. She was going to open it at the end of the game. She sounded so excited and touched that you'd thought of her. She'd always been jealous of your basketball career."

Danny frowned. He hadn't left a gift for his wife, but he should have. It would have been a nice touch. Now it was too late.

"I didn't," he started to say, then stopped.

Maybe it had been delivered to the wrong house. Such trivialities didn't matter at a time like this.

Dora continued, "Anyway, I listened to the game in the car. When you won, I just knew Cathy had to be proud of you. I could hardly wait to get over there to celebrate. It was taking forever. Then, a few blocks away, the roads were closed. Police cars and fire engines were everywhere. As I approached, I saw shooting flames and smoke in the distance, yet it didn't sink in. The whole mess was just an inconvenience. I had to get by. I had to be there with Cathy. And I could hardly wait to see my godchild-to-be again."

She took a deep breath. "Then I got closer. I saw the top of your home was blown off, and the bottom had collapsed into itself. I just couldn't believe it. I dashed out of the car and tried to get into the building, but the firemen stopped me. I was hoping for a miracle, that somehow Cathy or Sean had survived, though deep inside, I knew that was impossible."

She shuddered. "Not the way that house looked. No one could have made it out alive. Anyway, I ran up to an officer and told him who I was. The man looked at me with such pity that right then, my heart broke. He told me they'd found Cathy's remains, along with her wedding ring."

"Oh, my poor Cathy," he whispered.

He hadn't thought he could feel worse, but he was wrong. Hearing the actual details drove a dagger through his heart. His body shook. "They said they can't find any evidence of Sean. He's nothing but ashes. It's as if he'd never existed," Danny said in a voice choked with tears.

"I'm so sorry, Danny. Sean never had a chance. It's not right."

"At first, they said two adults were found. For a moment, I thought one of them was you. It was bad enough hearing about Cathy and Sean, but when I thought you were gone, too..."

She looked across at him. A glimmer of something like hope shone in her golden eyes. Then they dimmed. "I was the lucky one. One of the guards died instead. Oh, and there was another guard out back. While he was being carried out on a stretcher, I heard him say something to a policeman about an Ed Anderson."

Through a fog of pain, something clicked in Danny's mind. "Oh, Ed Anderson. He's the man who set up the security system while I was on the road."

"Maybe he made a mistake with the wiring or something. Maybe that's why the house exploded."

Danny sighed tiredly. "I don't know and it doesn't matter. Whether it was a gas leak or electrical problem, or anything else, none of it makes a difference. Nothing can bring Cathy and Sean back. I just hope they didn't suffer."

He knew it was a vain hope. His shoulders shook and he shielded his eyes, trying to hide the tears.

Dora turned the corner and pulled up in front of the house. She flicked off the ignition, then also burst into tears. Somehow they were holding each other, sobbing out their hearts. An aching tenderness swept over Danny as he shared her misery. This was not the Dora he was accustomed to seeing. It had taken her sister's death to break down the thick wall of her self-control.

He wouldn't dwell on trivialities. He had to help Dora get through this. He'd dealt with tragedy before. She was new to the game and trying desperately to cope.

Her breath came out in shudders. Her golden eyes looked wounded. He drew out his handkerchief and gently wiped her wet cheeks.

"Let's go inside," he said.

Chapter Twenty-Two
Kevin

UNABLE TO KEEP still, Kevin paced his apartment, grabbed a whiskey bottle and grinned like a chimpanzee. He still couldn't believe he'd pulled it off.

After dumping the kid in the back seat, he'd gunned the motor and headed to Miranda Edwards' apartment in the uptown district of Chicago.

Not waiting for her to answer the doorbell, he slipped a credit card beside the door jam and gained entrance. He huffed up the stairs, then rapped on the door Anthony had said would be hers. It was answered by a dark-haired woman who looked like she hadn't missed many meals.

"Here, take this," he said handing over the kid.

She gazed longingly at the brat. "For me?" she said in a high, thin voice.

"Yeah, all yours. Anthony and I are buddies, you know. I owe him a favor. This kid needs a home and you qualify. It's that simple. And, remember, if anyone asks, you had it yourself."

Clutching the child to her humongous boobs, she bobbed her head. "My baby," she said, tears rolling down her fat cheeks.

The kid screamed. The brat didn't know how lucky he was to have a mother who loved him, even if she hadn't birthed him.

Frowning, Kevin slipped onto his couch and passed his fingers over the rim of the whiskey bottle. If only he'd had a mother to come home to.

Then he shrugged. Maybe the kid wasn't so lucky. He didn't have a daddy. It was a given that Miranda's old man would rot in prison. Hey, you take what you can get.

Enough sentimental hogwash. Tonight was a night for celebration. He savored the moment he'd first seen and heard of the impact of his actions.

The camera had switched from the court to the sight of Danny Callaway being led from the stadium by the team's physician and two cops.

From the broadcast booth, the announcer, Frank Monson, groped for words to explain what he was witnessing. "Danny Callaway, the Irish Michael Jordan, just played the best game of his life. He should be on cloud nine, but what's the matter with him? He looks like he's going to an execution."

The camera panned in on Callaway. The star's face was etched in agony. His deep blue eyes brimmed with pain. That oh-so-pretty mouth quivered while its owner fought for control. The cameraman, as if embarrassed, abruptly switched to the basketball court where bedlam ruled. Security couldn't restrain the mob.

"Look at this crowd! Could be our boy, Danny, is in fear for his life. I don't blame him. Folks, look what's happening. A person could get trampled to death."

Monson's laugh broke off abruptly. "This just in. A breaking story with shocking news. We're taking you live to the Sauganash section of Chicago. What's happening, Jay?"

"In the background you see all that's left of the once magnificent residence of basketball great, Danny Callaway. Seconds after the game you've just witnessed, in which Danny clinched the championship, a violent explosion rocked his home, knocking out windows in homes a mile away. Only moments ago, Chicago firemen gained access to the building. They carried out what appear to be the remains of Danny Callaway's wife, Cathy, as well as a security guard. It's uncertain whether Callaway's newborn, Sean, is still alive, but from the force of the explosion there's little hope for his survival."

Jay Gromley continued. "This event is tragic indeed. As you can see, an army of investigators has arrived on the scene. We'll advise you of any further developments. Now back to you, Frank."

In a solemn voice, Monson intoned, "This demonstrates all too well the fickleness of fate. Just a few minutes ago, Danny Callaway clinched the championship game, putting him on top of the world. On the heels of such a great victory, he's suffered a devastating loss. That'll make it doubly hard to recover. If you're listening, Danny, our hearts go out to you."

At that point Kevin had snorted in disbelief. What bull. *Who're you kidding, Monson?* he thought. *You media guys thrive on misery. You're almost as happy as I am. You pretend it's the end of the world, but you're really gloating over the ratings.*

Yes, he'd always savor the moments when he'd first witnessed Callaway's payback. The fullness of victory was sweet.

He still couldn't get over it. Hours after the deed was done, Kevin still felt like hugging himself and dancing around the room. Today was the golden day of days. The crowning moment. Callaway was getting his. Danny boy, how do you feel right now? Maybe kind of sick? Like a knife's twisted in your gut? And your bright beautiful world—has it grown dim, like a cold dark prison?

Kevin swigged the whiskey, ignoring the burning sensation, as his thoughts brewed.

Callaway, I hope you writhe in pain the rest of your miserable existence. You deserve to suffer. Because of you, I spent nine long years in prison. When the judge read the sentence, I saw the look in your eyes. You wanted me to rot.

Now, I've issued you your own death sentence; a living hell. Every miserable moment for the rest of your life you'll picture your loving wife and precious kid blown to smithereens. You'll never know the brat's still alive. That'll be my own little secret.

Kevin smiled to himself, then frowned as the familiar hatred consumed him. *Hey, Callaway, was it worth pointing the finger at me? Would you have kept that fucking mouth shut if you'd known this would happen?*

His mind spun. As the rabid thoughts crossed his brain, he decided it wasn't enough for Callaway to suffer. It would be better to witness it firsthand. He must drink wholly of the warlock's brew to be fully sated. He had a good mind to get up right now, drive over to the bomb site and wait for Callaway to show up.

When he did, Kevin could walk up to him and say, "Hey sap, remember me? I'm Kevin Green. You know, the guy whose life you destroyed." He'd point to the rubble. "See this. It's your fault. Now, what do you have to say for yourself?"

Man, he'd like to do that, but it would be insane. He muttered in frustration.

The ten o'clock evening news was jam-packed with the Callaway story. Kevin listened in satisfaction.

"Folks, in the midst of such calamity, we finally have good news to report."

Kevin leaned forward on the couch. *Good news, huh, that's impossible*, he thought. *They couldn't know I took out the kid.*

"A second guard from Alert Advantage has been found alive under some rubble. He tells reporters he'd been patrolling the grounds out back of the residence when the force of the explosion hit him and he blacked out. The doctors say he's suffered a slight concussion and is expected to live."

The bottle slipped from Kevin's hand onto the floor. What was the guy talking about? He'd checked the roster. Only Todd Weathersby was listed. Had Callaway ordered another guard at the last minute? Shades of Stone Branton's predicament sprang to mind. He stifled a sliver of fear. The guard couldn't have seen anything. There was no possible way Ed could be linked to the crime. There was nothing to worry about.

The peal of the phone made him jump. Who the hell was that?

Holding the bottle with one hand, he grabbed the receiver with the other.

"You know Dick George, that personnel guy at Alert Advantage?" Brad asked him.

Kevin's heart beat fast. "What of him?" he squeaked out.

"Well, you see, he's kind of bent out of shape. The heat's all over him. His ass is in the wringer and he wants some answers. He says you installed the system at the Callaway place. Listen, I know about your grudge. Tell me you didn't do anything crazy," Brad said.

The wires hummed with tension. Kevin searched for an answer. Hell, he should have known Brad would be suspicious. Kevin's hatred of Callaway had been a major topic in prison. Should he come clean?

"Shit, Brad, you know me better than that. I'm not crazy enough to wreck a good thing. I did my usual job on the security system, that's all. No more, no less." He hoped he sounded convincing.

"Okay, buddy. Sorry to bug you. When I think about going back to prison, I kind of lose it. None of us can afford scrutiny."

"Yeah, I know. I sure as hell wouldn't set you up for a fall. Have a little faith." Had he poured it on too thick? He better shut up or Brad would catch on.

"Sorry. I guess I'm edgy. Things were going along too well. One wrong move could blow it all."

"Hey, I understand. Listen, I've got to go. I mean, really. I feel a crap coming on. See you later, Brad, okay?"

That was one way to get him off the line. Who could argue with nature?

He didn't have time for such petty stuff like weaklings worrying about getting caught. He had a victory to celebrate. Shit, he was missing the action on TV.

Chapter Twenty-Three
Danny

DANNY PUT HIS arm around Dora's shoulders as they entered her parents' home. Its silent emptiness reproached him for harboring lustful thoughts about Dora, instead of grieving for his wife and child. He pulled his arm away.

What was going on in his head? All of a sudden he couldn't think straight. Maybe it was the drugs Doc Halman had given him.

He sank down onto the couch. Dora joined him. From the corner of his eye, he snuck a glance at her. A solitary lamp illuminated her face, casting an earthy glow across her features. Despite himself, something stirred deep within him. It was disgustingly out of place. He shut his eyes, feeling as if he'd sinned. His wife was dead. He'd never see her again. How could he want her sister?

Today was the best and the worst day of his life. He'd had it all for one brief moment. In the next, his world had collapsed. Now he felt as if he'd fallen into a dark well. Like fingers slipping on smooth bricks, his searching thoughts couldn't grasp at certainty.

Cameos flashed through his consciousness: Cathy's sparkling curls, her tinkling laugh, the day at the flower shop when they'd made love on the floor. His cheeks grew wet as he remembered the sight of Sean in the hospital bed, nuzzled at his mother's breast. He pressed his lids tight, fruitlessly trying to hold back the tears. His baby hadn't had a chance.

More pictures flashed through his mind. He couldn't halt their progression. The last time he'd seen his sweetheart, she'd looked like an angel, with the sunlight glittering off her strawberry curls. An angel. That's what he'd always thought of her. The analogy sent a shiver down his spine.

In the midst of the throbbing pain, he struggled to find meaning, but couldn't. If someone were to be taken, it should have been him. He was the sinner who'd plotted for years to kill another man.

Cathy's body had exploded. In the blink of an eye, she'd been catapulted from this world to the next. Had she known she was dying? He hoped not. He couldn't bear the thought of Cathy in pain.

Still, no evidence of Sean had been found. In the back of his mind, a tiny ray of hope still glimmered. Maybe his baby had survived. Perhaps someone had taken Sean out of the house before the blast. If so, where was he?

Danny shook his head, realizing his mind had reverted back to that day when he'd hoped in vain for his sister to reappear. Now, like then, he found it hard to grasp the finality of death.

His wife and child were gone. He must accept that fact and go on. A clamp closed around his heart and he felt suffocated.

Trying to get his bearings, he glanced around the tastefully appointed living room. He'd almost forgotten where he was

Absently he noted Cathy's sister still sitting beside him, staring ahead, also lost in misery.

Their eyes connected and she seemed to come out a trance. "I better try again for my parents." Her breath caught in a sob. "I don't want them to hear about it on the radio first."

Danny shuddered. His heart went out to Dora, who was facing a difficult task. He'd offer to break the news, but he knew her parents would rather hear it from their own flesh and blood.

The phone rang on the coffee table. Dora's hand shook as she reached to pick it up. She took a deep breath. "Mom. I was just trying to call. I wanted to tell you myself. No, there's no mistake. It was Cathy and the baby."

Fresh tears flowed down Dora's face. Danny pictured Nancy McGuire sobbing on the other end of the line.

Dora swallowed and continued. "I'm in shock. I still can't believe it. Yes, I've got Danny here with me right now. He has nowhere to go and he looks exhausted."

What did it matter where he went? He didn't care about the loss of his home. That was easily replaced. His family was another matter. Cathy and Sean could never come back. Now he had no one. Maybe he should book a room at a hotel. He shouldn't be alone with Dora. It didn't seem right.

Part of him wanted to be alone. Another part was afraid of what he might do. He didn't have much to live for. He could easily end it all.

Dora made no attempt to wipe the tears from her face as she quietly replaced the receiver on the cradle. Her suit was wrinkled. Her hair was tangled. Her mascara was smudged. Her lips trembled.

Danny's heart went out to her. He wasn't the only one suffering. It was selfish to think of himself. For both of their sakes, he better spend the night.

She turned to him. "Mom and Dad can't make it back until

tomorrow night. Can we set up the service for Thursday?"

"I'll try."

On one of the few occasions he and Cathy had brought up the subject of death, she'd asked to be cremated. She'd only wanted a memorial mass, no wake. He'd said the same. His eyes filled again. He strove for control, but failed, burying his head in his hands.

Dora placed her hand on his back. "Danny, if it helps any, I know that Cathy loved you more than anything. She was very proud of you. You were her life."

It was sweet of Dora to try to lighten his burden despite her grief. Somehow, just hearing her speak of Cathy helped. It made Danny feel as if his wife were still alive. Strange, how he'd always thought of himself as the strong one in his relationship with Cathy. As he listened to Dora's soothing words, he felt like a child. This woman was his only buoy left on a stormy sea. He clung to the comfort she dispensed.

His hand throbbed. The medication must be wearing off. He clutched it with the other.

She took his hand in hers. "Danny, what's wrong with your hand?"

"When I found out about Cathy and Sean, I kind of lost it."

"Oh, Danny."

She put her arm across his shoulders. His eyes filled.

He had no idea how it happened. One moment they were consoling each other. The next, he was touching her warm skin. He needed someone to be close to him. Dora understood. Without question he accepted her willingness. She was here and very much alive, a means of forgetting his troubles.

He stared into the glowing amber eyes which held the secrets of the world. His fingers reached under her blouse, touching her soft skin, as if to confirm that she was real. She sat still, as with great deliberation he opened the buttons of her blouse, then pulled the sleeves off her limp arms.

Her skin shone golden in the lamplight, making him catch his breath. She was beautiful and perfect. Dora stood up and slowly unzipped her skirt. It rustled to the floor. The blood rushed to Danny's face as he tugged off his clothes, his eyes fastened on the golden goddess in front of him. Right now she was his whole world, all he had left.

"Dora, help me," he groaned.

"Yes, Danny."

With trembling lips, he tasted the salt on her cheeks. He pressed his tongue into her warm mouth. His hands continued their exploration. He felt a shiver run through her, quickly answered by his own as he fingered the peaks of her full breasts. That was not enough. He lowered Dora onto the couch, feeling her hot breath on his chest.

Her fingers dug into his back as he plunged into her warm, welcoming wetness. With ruthless thoroughness he lost himself in her slippery smoothness, sinking deeper and deeper into her folds. Almost fiercely, Dora clung to him as he drove himself down. She responded measure for measure. His eyes saw black, then red as he was lost in a dizzying paroxysm. She pushed him further until more spasms shook him, then her.

When it was over, he lay limp beside her, listening to her uneven breathing. All about them, the house was still, as still as death.

What had he done?

His mind recoiled and he felt like screaming. He couldn't believe his wife hadn't even been buried and he'd had sex with her sister. How could he have done such a thing? From wherever Cathy was, could she tell?

Without a word, he reached for his clothes, keeping his eyes averted from Dora. At a weak moment, he'd taken advantage of Cathy's sister. The thought made him sick. He was a terrible person.

He heard the sound of a zipper snagging on cloth, then sobbing. *Dora, what have I done to you? Weren't things bad enough?* he thought, but couldn't say out loud.

Finally he heard her murmur, "I'll get the spare room ready."

He couldn't hear her footsteps on the carpet, but he knew the exact moment when she'd left. The room felt empty without her, though he still smelled her scent. He knew he should wash it off, yet it somehow comforted him.

He groaned. His mind had to be twisted. The best thing to do would be to get up, walk out the front door and get as far away from Dora as possible.

Somehow he couldn't. His limbs wouldn't move, as he fought to keep his eyelids open. His life was a giant mess and he couldn't function. He just wanted out.

Her resigned voice interrupted his thoughts. "Okay, Danny, you can sleep in the second room down the hall."

The soft words sent goose bumps up and down his skin. He rose and stumbled past her to the bedroom. He had no energy left to remove his clothes, so he just sank onto the soft down comforter. Before oblivion claimed him, he had one fleeting thought. He never wanted to see Dora again.

DANNY COULDN'T FACE Dora, so he left early the next morning to make the funeral arrangements. After he'd finished the hurtful task, he flagged a waiting cab. He thought maybe he should book a hotel room. Then he remembered. Ted and Nancy were coming home tonight. He had to be there for them and try to ease their burden.

When he got back, the McGuires' front door was unlocked. Dora was gone. The phone was ringing.

"Danny, I'm glad I tracked you down. I just got word. I'm sorry, man. As soon as I heard, I booked an early flight back." Tony's sympathetic voice brought fresh tears to Danny's eyes. His friends had loved Cathy and they'd taken Sean to their hearts.

Tony was the first of many callers. Danny's throat grew hoarse from fielding questions, yet it was comforting to know his wife had been loved. She'd brought light and beauty into many people's lives as well as his own.

By seven o'clock Ted and Nancy arrived. Dora was still gone. Silently he embraced them. Dropping his suitcase, Ted strode to the fireplace mantle and picked up the picture of the smiling bride and groom.

"I can't believe she's gone," he said, staring at the snapshot.

With a sick heart, Danny silently watched.

Nancy McGuire joined her husband. Ted gazed at his wife with tear-filled eyes. "Our sweetheart didn't deserve this. There wasn't a mean bone in her body. And the poor baby. He never stood a chance."

Danny stood silently, feeling awkward. Should he leave them in private?

Nancy glanced at Danny, then composed her face. "From the looks of you, you haven't eaten."

Despite his protests, Nancy pulled off her coat, then set off to the kitchen. He understood what she was doing. She'd keep occupied until she couldn't think. He'd done it himself before, but it didn't work this time. His world had been yanked apart once too often. Keeping busy would not set things right this time.

They silently sat around the kitchen table. Danny picked up his fork and tried to do justice to Nancy's efforts, but before long, he gave up. He settled for sipping the coffee, though its warmth did little to permeate the chill.

Dora entered. A spasm of indigestion shook Danny.

"I'm sorry. Excuse me," he said, pushing back his chair and

escaping to the guest bedroom.

His presence at the McGuires' home wasn't doing any good. Each time he looked at Ted or Nancy, it reminded him that he'd betrayed Cathy.

He couldn't impose on them any longer, especially with this guilt tearing him apart. He had to get away.

Early the next morning he called and booked a room at the Palmer House in downtown Chicago. After leaving a note saying where he'd be, he slipped out the back door.

As soon as he entered his hotel room, he closed the drapes. In the darkened room, he mourned the wonderful, beautiful creature he'd married and the child he'd lost before getting to know.

That night Tony called again, asking if Danny needed anything. He looked down at his wrinkled jeans and shirt, the only clothes he had left. "Could you do me a favor and pick up a suit? I don't feel like going out."

Tony stopped by a few hours later with the necessary articles of clothing. He offered to stay, but Danny almost pushed him out the door. He wasn't fit company for anyone, even close friends.

ON THURSDAY, THE memorial service was jammed with friends, relatives, reporters and fans. Some were sincere, while others just stared at Danny in his grief. The cameras zoomed in, even up to the doors of the chapel, cold-bloodedly catching his every expression.

They didn't matter. Nothing did. He had a good mind to teach all of them a lesson and quit basketball.

He placed a pink rose on the coffin. As Nancy and Ted followed suit, Danny blinked back sudden tears. Cathy had loved flowers so much.

Finally, the service was over. Only Danny and the McGuires remained in the chapel.

Nancy gazed at him kindly. "Danny, you're welcome to stay with us. Won't you reconsider?"

He swallowed past a huge lump in his throat. What Nancy suggested was out of the question. He couldn't look at his wife's mother without thinking of Cathy. They shared too many physical characteristics and mannerisms.

Also, he couldn't risk exposure to Dora. If this sweet woman in front of him knew what he'd done, she'd spit in his face.

"Nancy, I appreciate your offer, but it's time I sort things out. I'll stay at the Palmer House for a while."

Ted grasped him by the shoulders. “Are you sure, Danny? Why don’t you come back with us?”

Danny shook his head, avoiding Ted’s eyes.

The only person who didn’t extend an invitation was Dora. With lips pressed tight and eyes flashing with waiting tears, she held her post in back of her parents. He dare not go to her. If he did, he might throw his arms around her and not let go.

He made a hasty escape outside. After he’d stepped into Tony’s waiting Mustang and sank onto the front seat, he closed his eyes. Instead of seeing Cathy and Sean, he couldn’t shut out the vision of Dora. He felt her pain. He remembered her smell.

Chapter Twenty-Four
Kevin

KEVIN YAWNED AND stuck another hot dog in the microwave. He could have called in sick today, but someone might remember later. Almost too exhausted to eat, he raised the bun to his mouth. His lethargy was not surprising since he'd spent the entire night before watching television, then worked all day on an alarm system at Brown Elementary. He'd probably screwed that up.

The doorbell rang. His mind flashed back. Were the police here? Should he dash down the fire escape?

"Who's there?" he called, ready to bolt.

"It's Brad."

The tone gave nothing away, yet Kevin knew his friend could be more of a threat than the law. His fingers picked at the doorknob, as if it were hot toast. Summoning courage, he grabbed and turned it.

"Hi, how're you doing?" he asked.

With blank, inscrutable features, Brad stepped inside. In the lengthening silence, Kevin's nerves jangled.

His friend let out a sigh. "Hey, we go back a long time, don't we?"

Kevin nodded, wondering where the conversation was headed.

"I have to say, in a way I don't blame you. I know about the hell you went through. And you did get a golden opportunity."

"But, I didn't—"

"Hey, spare me the lies. This is Brad you're talking to, not some schmuck. I got another call from Dick George. The cops came back. It seems that, after the firemen pulled out Todd Weathersby from the carnage, the surviving guard, Jim Jordan, did a little chirping. Jim had an interesting chat with Todd shortly before his demise. Todd happened to mention to him that Ed Anderson paid a little visit to the Callaway home that day, though his work was completed months ago."

"He couldn't have seen me."

"So you were there."

"Yeah, I had some adjustments to make. I got them done while Todd was on break."

"Hey, didn't I say no lies?" Brad's voice rose. "Kevin, I'm one disappointed guy. I trusted you and you let me down big time."

Kevin had to make him understand. "Hey, buddy, I'm sorry. I had to, can't you see? A chance like that happens once in a lifetime. Don't worry...you're in the clear. No one can pin anything on you."

Brad's cold eyes bore into Kevin's. "Cut the crap. You know better. Hey, jerk, you screwed me and I won't forget it. And I'm not the only one. When word hits the street, lots of unhappy campers will be ready to tear you a new ass. We had a good gig going and you blew it. My advice is watch your back. You're not the only one who enjoys getting even."

Without a backward glance, Brad stormed out.

"Shit," Kevin said, aiming a kick at the door. "Ouch." His ankle bone connected. He ignored the shooting waves of pain. It was the least of his problems.

He was in a jam. If only Todd hadn't opened his fucking diarrhea mouth. The guy was trouble even from the grave. Man, he better think this out. If only he'd had more sleep. He'd barely gotten through the day in one piece.

Knowing Brad, this was not an idle threat. Ex-cons could hold massive grudges, especially when faced with the possibility of being sent back to prison. He was lucky Brad had warned him. For whatever reason, Brad still considered himself a friend.

Kevin knew when to take a hint. His friend was saying, "Get the hell out. Disappear before it's too late."

Glancing anxiously around the apartment, he wondered what he could bring with him. This would hurt. He'd enjoyed two successful years in this pad. He'd bought a suede couch and recliner, a fifty-two inch television set, a kick-ass stereo, and all kinds of good stuff.

He could buy more. It was no time to get soppy. He better move, and move fast. Someone might already be watching from outside, ready to strike. Kevin fought the urge to glance out the window.

Damn, he had to get some shuteye first. He stretched out on his bed and tried not to think. There must be some time left or his friend wouldn't have come over to warn him.

His mind whirled. Lying awake, he went through a mental checklist of what he needed to do. Tomorrow he'd search for a cheap furnished apartment. He'd use the spare ID he'd bought from Max Gonzalez. He'd make sure he didn't get tailed, then inconspicuously drop off his favorite clothes and a few items at the new place. Then he'd lay low. He'd get a job when the heat died down. If he were fortunate, no one would find him. Maybe, in time, they'd even forget.

Some things never changed. He'd always been a loser. He hadn't even had time to celebrate before he'd been dumped on. This was too much.

Well, to hell with everybody. He searched for a comfortable position and concentrated on drifting off.

Someone pounded on the door. It had to be the police. Crooks didn't knock. How had they discovered him so fast? In slow motion, Kevin swung the door open. He found himself face-to-face with Officer Dugan, who was holding up Kevin's old gym shoe.

"Do you see that blood?" Dugan asked, jamming the dirty sole under Kevin's nose. "How dare you kill an innocent woman? What kind of animal are you?"

Dugan threw the shoe across the room, then produced a pinch collar and clamped it around Kevin's throat. It was attached to a leash which Dugan jerked. "Bad dog. You must be punished. I'm locking you up."

The collar was too tight. Kevin was choking. He had to get it off. He reached to grab it. It didn't feel like a collar, just the sheet all wound up. With shaking fingers, he pushed it away.

Man, that was spooky.

He'd been so happy. Why couldn't it have lasted? That visit from Brad had set him off, transporting his subconscious mind to a place he didn't want to go. He'd purposely ignored the victims. They were pawns in his game of revenge, not real people.

He pictured Cathy propped up in the giant four-poster bed with sunlight sparkling off her fiery ringlets. He remembered how sweetly she'd smiled at him, so genuinely grateful he'd delivered the pretty package.

His stomach contracted. Had he made a mistake? Should he have offed Callaway instead? Why had he taken the coward's way out?

It was too late. The deed was done.

He stumbled into the kitchen. With unsteady hands he reached into the cupboard, pushing aside cans of spaghetti and beef stew, withdrawing a fifth of Jim Beam. He gulped the fiery liquid straight from the bottle. It burned his gut going down.

He tasted acid and recognized it for what it was: raw fear. He'd struck down his enemy the coward's way. Now he must face the enemy within.

Chapter Twenty-Five
Danny

WITH A CONSCIOUS EFFORT, Danny eliminated Dora from his thoughts. She was an aberration, another spot on his not-so-clean conscience.

He missed Cathy daily, especially the sharing. There were all sorts of things he wanted to tell her, but never could.

Then the dreams began. He drifted off to a place where Cathy's tinkling laugh rang out. They were alone in the flower shop, where they sank to the floor amidst the fragrance of roses and he buried himself inside of her. Though the shades were drawn, somehow her strawberry curls caught the sunlight, flashing into his eyes, making them tear.

He awoke to find himself sobbing and reached for the comfort of her arms. Reality slapped him. Cathy would never come back. Neither would Sean. He'd never know his little boy. Nothing was left of him after the fiery cremation.

Danny barely ate, but when his body insisted, he rang for room service. Through an empty week, he drifted, wallowing in self-pity, not bathing or shaving.

A strident buzz jarred him from his semi-awake state, making him frown. He'd given a strict "Do Not Disturb" order at the front desk. The intruder jammed on the bell. Another second of the racket and Danny's head would explode. He stumbled into jeans and swung open the door.

An olive-skinned, pockmarked man held up a shiny badge. "I'm Detective Nicholas DeVino. You're Danny Callaway, right?"

He nodded.

"I need to speak to you."

Numbly Danny ushered him in. Shades of other police visits surfaced, making him shudder. What else could go wrong?

The officer studied the room. Danny could read the man's mind. He had to wonder how one person could create such a mess. Hell, it was simple when nothing mattered. Danny pushed a greasy lock of hair away from his eyes. He kicked a pair of sneakers to the side and beckoned to the couch.

The policeman gingerly sat down, then began. "Our bomb squad recovered some peculiar evidence on your property. First of all, have you heard of Ed Anderson?"

"Sure. He set up our security system."

"Did you ever meet him?"

"No. I was on the road when he came. Cathy let him in. What does he have to do with this?"

"Well, it appears this Anderson fellow visited your home the day of the blast."

Danny frowned, trying to remember. "Oh, that's right. Someone else mentioned he was there. It slipped my mind."

"Mr. Callaway, do you know anything about a package delivered to your wife that day?"

Danny frowned. Dora had mentioned something about a package when she'd picked him up at the airport, but he hadn't paid attention to it. He'd had more important things to think about, such as the death of his wife and child. "I heard one of the guards dropped it off, saying it was a present from me, but there was some kind of mistake. I never thought of a gift for her. I should have."

Detective DeVino gave him a measured look. "It wasn't a present. It was a bomb."

Blood surged through Danny's head. His ears rang. "A bomb," he whispered.

He should have guessed. With everything else going on, he hadn't made the connection. Danny stared at the officer, as if it were he holding the explosive. This was too much. Why would anyone bomb his house? He'd assumed the explosion was from a gas leak or an electrical malfunction, not something sinister.

He had to think. Maybe the bomb was for him. Had a deranged fan sought revenge? Cathy had wanted him to give up basketball. Perhaps his obsession with the sport had sealed her fate. God, he hoped not. How could anyone be so perverted as to take a sport that seriously?

The silence lengthened. Detective DeVino cleared his throat. "The signs are obvious. There was a huge crater in the area of the master bedroom. After we sifted through the soil samples and ran an acetone test, it verified RDX footprints. That's a common explosive in package bombs."

Danny listened without comment. His life had turned into a bad action flick.

"Our guys combed the scene. We discovered portions of a blasting cap. From every indication, the explosion was cold-blooded murder."

"I don't understand. No one hated Cathy or Sean. Maybe the

bomb was meant for me and the timing got screwed up."

The officer shook his head. "I don't think so. Everything appears to have been planned. The offender familiarized himself with the security system, then set off the remote. What he didn't count on was the extra guard who went out back. That lucky slob was Jim Jordan."

"How do you know this?"

"Jim came to after being knocked out by the explosion. It shook him up enough to make him confess he and Todd had met for some smoke breaks earlier on. During one of them, Todd happened to mention how your wife was excited about a package Ed Anderson delivered right after half-time."

Danny's heart pounded hard.

"Officer, have you spoken to Anderson?"

The man shook his head. "He's disappeared. Not only that. We checked the Alert Advantage payroll records. It turns out his social security number belongs to a dead man. The personnel manager also owns a fishy ID and is a known felon who served time at Heartland Penitentiary."

Danny's mind snapped to attention. Heartland. Could this be connected to Kevin Green? Was he paranoid to think so? Heartland was a huge facility. It didn't mean every prisoner knew each other. Still, what if? A wild scenario played through his mind, flashing ice water though his veins. Could it be that, while he'd complacently enjoyed the good life, what he'd thought of as his past enemy had plotted revenge? Had Kevin still not forgiven him, but instead orchestrated a grand finale?

No, it didn't make sense. Kevin hadn't killed Mary Alice. Larry Murphy had done that and was rotting in jail with a life sentence.

Still, what if?

After the judge had issued the verdict, Kevin's eyes had turned murderous. Also, when Danny had visited him in jail, he'd refused any peace offerings. Kevin had to know Danny would suffer more from the loss of his wife and child than a direct hit against himself. Still, could anyone be so heartless?

Well, Kevin had spent nine long years in the company of murderers and felons, long enough to harden the most innocent soul. Long enough to learn dangerous tricks from the pros.

He could have done it. He had a motive. It fit too well.

Kevin Green had to be Ed Anderson. A resolve tightened in Danny's chest. If that was true, Kevin would receive no mercy.

How could he make sure? Well, that's what the police were for.

"Officer, are there any leads on this Anderson guy?"

The man shook his head.

"We haven't rounded up any valid prints, but we're trying. He had to have slipped up somewhere."

"I'd appreciate your keeping me informed."

"Of course, Mr. Callaway."

Chapter Twenty-Six
Kevin

KEVIN GLANCED INTO the refrigerator and shook his head. What he craved was a juicy T-bone, but what stared back at him was a half-finished package of bologna. That did it. To hell with risks. He needed a job.

It was bad enough he'd had to transfer a meager portion of his belongings to this scrappy, pint-sized dump, which could only be reached by entering a urine-soaked hallway and climbing endless flights of rotting stairs.

The kitchenette, bedroom and living room were so close to each other the roaches and mice darted back and forth from the sink to the mattress, accounting for the rustling he heard at night.

He'd bought a nine-inch black-and-white set at a resale shop. Watching the tiny screen was the only thing that kept him sane. That is, until last week, when it had also betrayed him by flashing his release picture and a sketch of his Ed Anderson disguise. The cops had made the connection. A fragment of the silver-and-gold bow he'd taken such pains in tying had retained his fingerprint.

He'd never go back to prison. Immediately after seeing himself on the news, he'd dyed his hair black and pasted on a fake mustache. Matching black-framed non-prescription glasses shielded his eyes. The sketches on television didn't even look like him now. Still, cops and crooks were wise to disguises and tricks.

He sighed. Being careful was a pain and awfully lonely. Even in prison he'd had his mates to talk to, and once in a while, his old man. Now he had no one. If he tried to reach Derek, either side would nab him.

Shit, right now he'd settle for talking to the second Mrs. Green. The times he'd met her she'd seemed sympathetic and friendly, making him feel warm inside. He wished she'd have been his mother. How soppy. The solitary life was getting to him. He ought to be planning, not bellyaching. It was Thursday. Rent was due Monday. He had to get some bread.

The next morning, a gnawing hunger made him grab his grubbiest jeans and tear the sleeve off his flannel shirt. Using his last five quarters as fare, he hopped the bus. He got off outside the Madison Street Metra station. That's where the bums hung out. With sad faces and plastic cups, they moaned and sang ditties to passersby. Some even played crude instruments like plastic buckets. And for doing that, they got money tax-free. People were suckers.

When he stepped onto the bridge, he felt self-conscious and nervous. Would one of his pursuers discover him?

His stomach growled, reminding him of why he'd come. With eyes downcast and holding out his cup, he put on a hopeless face.

After a few minutes, he was rewarded with a clink, then another. One generous soul donated a ten spot, which Kevin immediately pocketed.

After an hour his legs grew tired, so he sat down and huddled on the side of the bridge, leaving his cup extended. That drew an even greater response since people thought he was sick and felt sorry for him.

When dusk fell, Kevin trudged home and spread out his haul, a whole ninety-eight dollars. Not bad for a first day. Better than most jobs.

The following morning he parked himself at the same spot, but those who'd been generous before passed him by. After a slow time of it, he moved a few blocks down. He had to keep switching to find fresh victims.

For a few weeks, he was satisfied. Then the constant contact with down-and-outers wore thin. He could do better.

Chapter Twenty-Seven
Danny

ANOTHER WEEK PASSED before Danny heard from the detective, this time by phone.

"Mr. Callaway, we got our prints. They're Kevin Green's. We've issued an arrest warrant."

Danny's heart stopped. Through the roaring in his ears, he barely heard DeVino's next words.

"We've got our motive. This Green's held a grudge against you all these years. Listen, if he should contact you, don't try to handle it yourself. We've got a dangerous man on our hands. It might be a good idea to hire some security guards."

With nerveless fingers, Danny replaced the receiver. His worst fears were realized. Though Kevin Green had been the instrument, Danny had ultimately caused Cathy's and Sean's deaths. If he hadn't have been so selfish, they'd still be alive. From the start, he should have given Cathy up. She'd never been meant for him.

Guilt overwhelmed him, making his head pound. He'd destroyed a beautiful human being. Also, he'd killed his own child just as surely as if he'd set the bomb himself. He should have known better. He'd longed for a beautiful world, a happy life, but wanting it couldn't make it happen. Ignoring evil didn't erase it.

Danny sunk his head into his hands. Crushed with remorse, he couldn't move.

As darkness fell, he sought relief. Hey, he was a weak, worthless person, so he decided he may as well act the part. This hotel had been so honored by his presence that they'd provided him with a well-stocked bar. He'd ignored it before, but now it would serve to drive away the pain.

Blindly he reached for a bottle. He gulped down the liquid, ignoring the burn. He drank more. No matter how much he swallowed, the thirst consumed him. The Jack Daniels was almost gone before it dawned on him. He had a mission. Why was he wasting time? He needed to get out and find Kevin. He grabbed another bottle for the road.

He'd not hired the security guards the detective had suggested because a face-to-face encounter with Kevin would suit him just fine. Too bad his gun had been blown away in the explosion. He'd have to get another.

Ignoring his spinning head, Danny stumbled into the night. Monroe Street was lit not only by street lamps, but also by blinding headlights, which all seemed to be aimed at his eyes.

His enemy could be lurking around any corner. It was up to Danny to discover where. He headed east toward Michigan Avenue and the lakefront. It was as good a direction as any. The lake breeze blew briskly, making him shiver. With trembling fingers, he twisted the cap off the bottle, then gulped down another swallow. The whiskey warmed him some, yet now he had other problems. The sky and ground wanted to meld together. He'd have to ignore that.

Before long the crashing of the waves grew louder. Mesmerized, he followed the sound. As he moved in the direction of the beckoning wetness, his feet sank into the sand. He could easily disappear into the darkness and the pain would end. No one would be the wiser. No one would care.

Wait a minute...didn't he have something to do first? Why couldn't he remember? Suddenly everything blurred. He slid down onto the sand's cool softness.

DANNY AWAKENED WITH gritty eyes and grainy shoes. A fragment of memory surfaced. Like a glass shard, it punctured his heart. Cathy and Sean were dead. It had really happened He ached so badly he could barely breathe.

He must set things right. Kevin must pay.

Balancing precariously on one foot, then the other, he tried to empty the sand from his shoes. It obstinately stuck to his socks, so he gave up.

His mouth felt cottony. A merciless thirst consumed him. He reached for the whisky and finished it off, then threw the bottle into the lake. Years from now someone might find it and wonder how it had gotten there.

He turned away, intent on completing his task. Stumbling, his body wavered weakly, yet his will remained strong. He forged ahead, only to discover he was traveling in circles.

He couldn't think straight. His head vibrated so much he couldn't tell where he was going. He decided to head away from the lake, down Madison Street and toward the train station where the bums and the homeless hung out. That would be a perfect place for someone as lowly as Kevin Green. He congratulated himself on being clever enough to figure that out.

He trudged on and on, not knowing where he was or how long he'd walked. His stinging eyes barely made out a sign on the corner of Wabash and Madison. Surprisingly, he hadn't gone far, though it seemed as if he had. The sun was hot, yet he continued on.

It wasn't easy, but he made it to State and Madison. It was a start, but not his destination. He must keep going. He took another step, but his legs crumpled beneath him. His forehead slammed onto the cement.

The next thing Danny knew, he was lying face down on the ground. His head clanged. A rancid odor of perspiration clung to him, making him nauseous. From a distance, he heard a young boy's wondering voice. "Daddy, look. That man's sleeping on the sidewalk."

"That's just a bum. Don't pay any attention."

Was the man talking about him? He wasn't a bum. He was a basketball star who had lots of money. He had to let him know.

"Would you like an autograph?" he mumbled.

They looked at him strangely. He couldn't blame them. For all they knew, he may as well be a bum.

Again the welcoming pain gripped him. He deserved to be punished. Flat on the ground was exactly where he belonged. His thoughtlessness had caused the death of his wife and child. He was no better than dirt.

Chapter Twenty-Eight
Kevin

WHAT A HOOT. The wasted bastard across the street was a dead ringer for Callaway. Yeah, if Callaway were a bum, Kevin Green was a millionaire.

No, the Great One had won the championship and was rolling in dough. Callaway was not out begging on the streets, that's for sure.

Kevin glowered from the opposite corner. Shit, he'd never erase the jerk from his mind. He could never forgive the bastard for fingering him. Heartland and his present predicament were all Callaway's fault.

The more he thought of it, the more he realized what a mistake he'd made. He should have offed Callaway, not the wife.

Hell, he could still do it. In fact, he would. After the heat died down, people would forget what had happened. All he had to do was wait and play his cards right. Acting the bum grated, but he'd stick it out long enough to get some moolah together. Then he'd strike.

He was as fit as he'd ever been and could easily outmuscle a basketball player.

When his revenge was complete, he'd not be hallucinating make-believe Callaways, that's for sure.

Chapter Twenty-Nine
Danny

"DANNY, ARE YOU all right?" a woman's voice asked. It sounded familiar, almost like Cathy's. Was he dead or had his wife returned to life? He tried to move, but couldn't. "Danny, can you hear me?"

She bent so close he could smell her perfume—a scent which had driven him over the edge. This was not Cathy. He lay helpless, again in her power. What would she do to him?

Footsteps approached.

"I've found him," her voice called out to the new arrival.

Someone tried to move him.

"Answer me, Danny boy. Can you hear me?" Tony's voice floated up. "Hey, man, just nod if you understand. That's all I ask."

Okay, he could do that. Cautiously, Danny moved his head, but a gong clanged inside.

"Okay, he's still with us. Dora, stay here. I'll get the car."

Dora sat beside Danny, holding his head in her lap, brushing her soft fingers through his hair. He sighed at the soothing feeling. He'd missed the touch of a woman, especially this one. He shouldn't allow her to do this, but it felt wonderful. He'd been so alone. Each soft stroke dulled the roaring pain.

Then he was lifted up and carried. He found himself resting in the back seat of a car, with his aching head cuddled in Dora's lap. He wanted to stay there forever. Dora was strong. He needed her.

There had always been a link between them. Out of respect for Cathy, he'd denied it. Now he hadn't the strength to fight it. One fact was painfully clear. Cathy would never come back. Whatever he and Dora did couldn't harm her.

He managed to push open his weighted eyelids. A blurry vision with dark, flowing hair greeted him. Golden eyes delved into his soul as competent, tanned arms nestled him.

"Dora," he whispered.

He'd startled her. A flicker of something like fear crossed her face before she composed it. Her fingers clenched and unclenched. That's when it hit him, though he'd almost guessed it before. He saw everything with blinding clarity, perhaps because his defenses were completely stripped. He knew why he'd shied from her.

Dora loved him. The realization stabbed him. He'd taken advantage of her. She'd given her all to him and he'd thrown it back in her face. She'd sought comfort in her time of need and he'd rejected her, yet she hadn't given up on him. Had he unwittingly put her through torture? How long had she suffered while he and Cathy had paraded their love in front of her? She didn't deserve that. He'd give anything to wipe the pain from her eyes.

His lips had trouble forming the words, but he forced them out. "I'm sorry," he gasped.

She looked down at him, a tender smile illuminating her features. Her fingers brushed a strand of hair from his forehead. "It's all right, Danny. Don't worry. Everything will be all right."

He wanted to ask her how that could be. Nothing was right. Cathy and the baby were dead. It was all his fault. Also, he'd hurt Dora. He'd taken too much from her and given nothing in return. How could everything be all right?

Her fingers massaged his forehead, calming his tense muscles. Her touch was soothing. He couldn't think of anything else except the gentle pressure of her fingertips. Blessed relief flowed through him.

DANNY AWAKENED TO find himself lying on an incredibly soft mattress. It had to be goose down. The room was dark, yet he knew where he was from the lingering scent in the air. He was at Dora's condo.

He must have been asleep for a while. Except for the foul taste in his mouth, he almost felt human. Snippets of memory returned, carrying with them a sense of shame. Had he gotten so drunk he'd wandered around the lakefront and onto State and Madison? Had he passed out right on the sidewalk? He let out a groan of embarrassment.

Dora immediately appeared beside the bed, asking, "Danny, are you all right?"

This time he could answer coherently. "Yes, Dora, considering the circumstances."

She pressed her hand into his. "I know, Danny. I understand. None of us will ever be the same. Still, we have to go on. That's all we can do. We can't give up. Cathy wouldn't want it that way. She loved us, you know."

He understood what she was driving at. Cathy had always been unselfish. She'd loved them both. She'd have insisted they live fully. She'd never have wanted them to suffer from misguided loyalty. In his heart, he'd realized that all along, but he'd still been afraid. He didn't feel right about loving Dora. His love for Cathy was too fresh, the pain of separation too strong. It was too soon.

"Dora, how did you find me? What made you look?"

"Detective DeVino called and said Ed Anderson was Kevin Green. I knew you'd take the news to heart." She stopped and swallowed hard. "I remembered our talk before you married Cathy."

As she continued, an almost desperate look crossed her face. "I had to be sure you were all right. I drove to the Palmer House. When I got there, your door was open. The place was ransacked. A whiskey bottle lay on the floor. I was afraid, so I called Tony. We scoured the area, hoping you hadn't gone far."

He frowned, looking across at her. "I'm sorry you had to go through all that trouble. I don't know what got into me. I guess I'm not much of a drinker."

"It's all right, Danny. I understand." Her eyes held a wealth of unspoken knowledge, as if she knew him better than he knew himself.

"I guess the news was just too much. I couldn't handle it. I had this overpowering sense of guilt. I still feel it. If I hadn't married Cathy, she'd still be alive. I'll have to live with that knowledge the rest of my life."

A look of pain crossed Dora's face. "Danny, I know how you feel. Remember, I could've stopped you. You told me about Kevin. I was stupid, too. I thought if you ignored Kevin, he'd not be a threat. That means I'm also to blame."

He squeezed her hand tightly. "No, Dora, don't. You had nothing to do with it. None of this is your fault. I know you loved Cathy. You'd never have hurt her. You only wanted her to be happy."

"What about you Danny? You loved Cathy, too. Why torture yourself? You didn't set the bomb. It's not your fault, either."

He went silent, mulling over her words. Some of it made sense, yet he couldn't stop blaming himself. Perhaps it was survivor's guilt. In time maybe the feeling would fade, but for now it didn't seem likely. Through it all, no matter what else was true, one thing remained unchanged. Kevin Green must pay.

Danny realized he'd been going about his mission wrong. In a deadly contest, it was important for a contestant to stay at his peak and keep a clear head. To do otherwise invited defeat. A sodden drunk was an easy mark.

Danny looked deep into Dora's eyes. Their amber glow flashed like the sun on a hot summer day. She was breathtakingly beautiful.

Some day he might love her as much as Cathy, maybe more. Maybe he already did. It was too early to tell.

He couldn't in good conscience involve her. He'd made that mistake before, with disastrous consequences. This time he'd stand strong. That meant separating himself from Dora when he needed her the most. He already felt the hurt, but it had to be done. Kevin must never learn of Danny's new discovery. That would draw Dora into danger.

Right now he had a job to do. He'd finish this mess once and for all. "Dora, I thank you for your kindness, but I have to get going," he said, resolve strengthening him.

The light faded from her eyes. With a pang, Danny realized he'd hurt her again. She wanted him to stay, yet he'd shunned her by his eagerness to leave. Well, she'd be better off without him. She'd discover that.

She sighed. "Okay, Danny. I'll get your clothes from the dryer. They should be ready by now."

He listened to the sound of her firm footsteps marching across the hardwood floor. He ached to call her back, to beg her to climb into bed with him. He felt the heat of her body warming him.

Instead of Dora, he settled for the poor substitute of clothes warm from the dryer.

A FEW DAYS LATER, Tony and Ritchie stopped by his hotel room.

Ritchie let out a whistle. "Danny, it looks like a bomb went off here." He paused, eyes wide in horror. "Shit, I didn't mean to say that."

Danny tried to put him at ease. "Yeah, well, I could call a cleaning service, but that would be too cruel. I'll get it straightened out eventually." He ran his fingers through his newly washed hair. "I've gone through hell lately."

Ritchie patted him on the back. "I know, buddy. What happened to Cathy and the baby makes me sick. It's still hard to believe."

Tony echoed his sentiments. "Danny, man, you look a lot better than the last time I saw you. Just remember, we're your buddies. You mean the world to us. We don't want to lose you."

Danny's eyes filled. His friends' words made him feel ashamed. He'd thought he meant nothing to anyone. He hadn't considered his best friends, and that was wrong. He should be grateful he had two outstanding buddies, and also a woman who cared a lot about him. He was not alone.

"Thanks, you guys. You're choking me up."

They had no idea of the wealth of emotions rushing through him. Only someone who'd been through hellfire and back could understand. He swallowed a lump in his throat. It was time to stop being a coward and live life. He had to make the effort.

He broached a tentative suggestion. "Want to go out for tacos, guys? That is, if the wives don't mind."

"No, they're only too eager to get rid of us," Tony said, laughing. "In fact, Tracy ordered me not to come home until I put a smile on your face. I told her that might take a while."

"Marilyn gave the same order."

"Okay, then prepare to spend eternity with me," Danny said, the corners of his mouth twitching.

After dinner, Danny felt better. He hadn't realized how much he needed his friends. With their help, he'd rise above what had happened. He wouldn't give in to self-pity.

He would not allow Kevin to defeat him. When it was time, he'd hunt down the bastard and give him his due. For now, he'd concentrate on survival. He'd go back to basketball. As before, it would sustain him. Also, it would keep him in shape for his mission.

That reminded him. Already a stack of envelopes loomed in one corner of the hotel room, reaching from the floor to almost the ceiling. Knowing they'd remind him of his loss, he'd avoided them. He shouldn't. The cards and letters were from people who cared. He grabbed a handful and sat down at the table to read. The first was from a woman whose husband of fifty years had passed on. It read, *Take courage, Danny. You're not alone. I'll pray for you.*

The woman's unselfishness touched him, making him feel ashamed. How much greater was her pain compared to his? She'd bonded with her man for so long she'd probably had little recollection of being without him, yet she'd had the heart to sympathize with Danny. He had a lot to learn from people like her.

He opened another envelope. A ten-year-old's mother had died, yet he cared enough to console his basketball idol. Courage came in all sizes. He put that letter aside. He'd surprise the boy by sending him basketball tickets.

Danny delved into more envelopes, empathizing with the plights of the writers, sharing their miseries. In a way it made him depressed, but more than anything, it was therapeutic. As the woman in the first letter had written, he was not alone. Others fought misery day after day, but would not give up. Could he, a healthy, virile male, do less?

That made him remember. When he'd been laid up before, he'd

become aware of others who'd fought infirmities. He'd vowed to help. Now was the time. His actions could work both ways. By assisting them, he'd find a way to channel his grief.

He'd always donated to charities, but had shied away from public displays. An urge swelled inside him to do more. He'd been blessed with talent. He was well known. He shouldn't be so self-absorbed. He'd share his gifts, not only financially, but personally. He'd visit children's hospitals. He'd promote charities. He'd make public service announcements and commercials and do anything it took. From now on, the focus would not be on him, but on others. It was time to acknowledge the rest of the world.

He longed to share his insights with one particular fan, but she was off-limits. The fact he was strong enough to think of her needs and not of his own made him wonder. Did he love Dora that much, or was he wiser than before?

Chapter Thirty
Kevin

IN DES PLAINES, a crazed biker mowed down a man. At a south suburban bank, a group of masked robbers shot a teller and made off with the money. With each new crime, others followed. After five months, Kevin's actions had faded into insignificance and his face was no longer on the news. Even without his disguise, he didn't warrant a second glance from the average citizen.

But what about the ex-cons? Were they still on the lookout? He wished he knew.

Nicky Montgomery, a short, black bum in a dirty tank top, stumbled up to Kevin one afternoon, invading his bridge territory. The mini-twerp with huge, gutsy balls delved into Kevin's cup, withdrawing half the coins.

"Hey, prick what're you doing?" Kevin yelled.

In a deceptively soft voice, Little Nicky said, "Kevin, my man, if I were you, I wouldn't draw attention. You're doing damn good. Don't blow your gig."

Kevin stared. "What did you call me?"

"Kevin. Kevin Green. That's your name, isn't it?"

Shit. They were wise. He glanced down the street. Where were they?

"They're not here yet. Listen, they won't be, if you play your cards right. All I'm asking for is a small piece of the action, that's all. My lips are sealed."

Sure, until Kevin felt the cold metal piercing his heart. He was doomed. He couldn't trust anyone, especially this little creep.

"I know what you're thinking, but listen, it works both ways. We can be friends. I could come in handy."

"How?"

"Oh, say, by throwing in a little info now and then, some juicy, little tidbits."

Did he have a choice? The weasel could turn Kevin in whenever he wanted, to the cops or the cons, with no skin off his back. Wishing he could pummel him, Kevin stared at the skinny bastard. He couldn't take the chance. It was no use. He sighed. "Okay, Little Nicky, I'm in."

That day he joined the legions of others who paid for Nicky's services. The guy worked both sides, storing tons of information in his pint-sized brain, dancing a dangerous tightrope. Power made him tick.

"Remember, Roscoe the Poacher?" Nicky asked him on one occasion.

Kevin shook his head.

"Well, old Roscoe was a dumb bunny who tried to make a go of it on his own, thinking he didn't need Little Nicky."

With fascinated loathing, Kevin listened.

"Well, Roscoe got what he deserved. The cops just happened to find an empty beer can with Roscoe's fingerprints after the heist at the Glencoe mansion. I myself offered that beer to Roscoe before the job. Like a poor slob, he guzzled it down. I then conveniently planted it and dropped a hint to the pigs. Now dumb Roscoe's in the slammer. It serves him right."

"What about when he gets out?"

"Hell, I've got friends. One wrong move and Roscoe's dead meat."

That story was Little Nicky's warning to Kevin not to get smart. It worked. Kevin had enough problems without borrowing more. Anyway, Nicky proved useful, keeping him informed of the whereabouts of the "Heartland Grads."

That's how Kevin learned they'd hit on a new scheme that had become more lucrative than the security scam. They'd gone technical and latched onto Internet gambling. The gang was making killings and its members were sitting pretty. Kevin had to be far from their minds. In fact, they should be grateful. If it weren't for him, they never would have ridden the wave of the future.

Even Dick George, the personnel manager from Alert Advantage, had escaped conviction. The investigation of the Callaway bombing had come to a halt. Without Kevin, there was no case. The cops couldn't prove a thing.

That was useful to know. He was sick of being a bum. He'd look around, get the lay of the land, then make his move.

Before Kevin could make up his mind what to do, basketball season started. Against his will, he was drawn to his tiny television set to watch the Cyclones' opener. The spotlight shone brightly on Callaway's familiar figure as he strutted onto the court. The gullible crowd stood up and awarded him a standing ovation.

Fuming, Kevin paced the confines of his dinky apartment. A normal person would still be wasted in a drunk tank or at least drugged up, but not the unsinkable Danny Callaway. No, there was the hero, larger than life, prancing around the court and slam-dunking basketballs for all the world to see. Was he invincible?

Kevin cringed as Callaway's three-pointer clinched a hard-won victory. Gritting his teeth, he threw the remote control against the wall. It should have been him batheing in glory. He had the height. He had the talent. Instead, he struggled to make ends meet, even begged off the streets, while Callaway, acting high and mighty, graced the world with his presence. Something had to be done, this time for good.

It got worse. Newspaper articles again appeared and not just in the sports section. They touted Callaway as a generous superhero.

The Mr. I'm-So-Perfect-I-Even-Visit-Hospitals Callaway was spreading goodwill everywhere, smiling from atop bus posters where he balanced sick kids on his knees and pleaded for donations. Nowhere in the world was safe from the prick's presence. Each sighting tied a fresh knot in Kevin's stomach. He chugged antacids to no avail. Callaway was destroying him.

Just as he'd sunken to his lowest level, it happened. Kevin opened the *Chicago Tribune* to a full-page, color ad of Callaway hyping evening appearances at Marshall Field and Company's Walnut Room.

For fifty dollars apiece, loyal fans could reserve numbers in line to get their pictures taken beside the great MVP Callaway, under the famed Christmas tree in the Walnut Room between eight and ten-thirty p.m. the week of December 16. During those hours, the rest of Marshall Field's would be closed, except for the candy concession where customers could purchase the ever popular *Frango* mints. All proceeds from the pictures and candy were targeted for Children's Memorial Hospital.

He had to hand it to Callaway. With the big tree being so popular at Christmas, the lines for the Walnut Room were humongous. Now the select would be guaranteed entry to see their idol, view the tree, and feel saintly to boot.

As if by fate, another ad directly underneath caught his eye. To gear up for the holiday rush, Marshall Field's was offering full and part-time temporary jobs. Kevin's heart raced. Could he get in? He'd be a fool to pass up the opportunity.

The next morning he approached Nicky, who, for a price, obliged him with a new ID. After dyeing his hair and adding a few touches, Kevin glanced at the results, almost not recognizing himself as the reserved dude with the clipped chestnut locks and thin mustache.

Then he was off. Dressed in his one good suit, he stepped into the elevator on the ground floor of Marshall Field's and alighted on the ninth floor. He opened the door marked Human Resources Department. There he was directed to a wooden desk where the personnel manager, Gertrude Winston, a graying, homely creature, presided.

Could she resist him? Of course not. With no hesitation, she handed Kevin an application.

He filled it out as Godfrey Gordon, a poor bloke who'd worked ten years at a now-defunct grocery store in the small town of Irma, Wisconsin. Assuming a groveling eager-to-please expression, Kevin handed the form back to the woman.

"Mr. Gordon, do you have any references?" she asked.

That was the tricky part. In a soft respectful voice, Kevin regretfully informed her that his past employer had expired.

"My, that's a shame." She pursed her lips, then brightened. "I know, what about personal references?"

This time Nicky proved of help. The little twerp had a special cell phone number for just such contingencies. Let's see, what was his alias? Oh, yeah, Nicholas Richardson.

"Well, there is someone I've known for years who'd give me a good recommendation. I'd be glad to give you his name and number."

"That's fine, Mr. Gordon. I'll get back to you."

BY THE END of the week, Kevin aka Godfrey received his work summons. On the following Monday he reported to Ms. Winston.

"Congratulations, Mr. Gordon. We're most happy to utilize your services."

She pointed to a bald, butler-type guy. "This is Morris Bentley. I'll leave you in his capable hands."

Bentley promptly whisked Kevin away to an elevator. As it descended, the orientation began. "Mr. Gordon, let's go over the fundamentals."

Though he groaned inside, Kevin tried to look respectful. Normally he'd steer clear of a stuffed shirt like Bentley, but for now he'd put up with anyone, even this blue-blooded schmuck.

"Do you hear me, Mr. Gordon?"

For a moment Kevin had forgotten his new identity. He politely nodded, doing his best to imitate Bentley's mannerisms.

"I cannot stress nearly enough that, at Marshall Field and Company, the customer is always right. We treat our clientele with the utmost dignity, from the down-and-out spinster to the most influential man-about-town. Nothing is too good for them. Also, they never make mistakes. If there is anyone at fault, you must assume the blame, even if it's uncalled for."

Kevin tried not to look skeptical. He hated being taken advantage of, but he'd comply. He'd hold onto this job if it killed him. "I understand, Mr. Bentley. You can be assured I will perform no action that will blemish the store's reputation."

As they alighted, a thin smile tugged at Bentley's lips. Kevin knew he had uttered the magic words. Hell, he was turning into an Academy Award actor.

Bentley led him to a small area at the back of the store, far from the customers, where Kevin was to receive instructions on running the cash register. At first he was confused, but soon learned there were no secrets. Even a kid could understand that the lighted display indicated how much change a customer got.

After another day of training, Bentley pronounced, "I believe you're ready. Let's see, your application indicates you'd prefer the candy department. Is that right? Wouldn't you rather sell wallets or ties? Those positions pay more."

A surge of alarm hit Kevin, making his ears burn. He had to work in candy.

"I'd feel more comfortable with the candy," he said. "In fact I'm willing to put in overtime. I hear you've got a promotion coming up with the basketball player, Danny Callaway. I'd be glad to stay late and work that as well."

"Well, Mr. Gordon, I appreciate your enthusiasm. For now, I'll assign you to the candy station, and we'll see how it works out. If you do well, you'll be awarded the shift during the promotion."

This guy was a pushover. Kevin hid a smirk.

He quickened his steps to catch up with Bentley, who was already marching across the marble floor.

At the center of the cosmetics department, Bentley abruptly halted. Kevin almost knocked into him.

"Look up, Mr. Gordon. Here you see the six thousand-square foot Tiffany Dome, designed by Louis Comfort Tiffany himself. This mosaic masterpiece was crafted from one point six million pieces of Favrile glass."

Kevin tried to look impressed, though he held little appreciation for the iridescent blue and gold glass. What hogwash. Sure it was pretty, but not real. The treasures here were part of a fantasy world people wished existed. Outside, in the real world, people smoked dope, coped to make ends meet, and stabbed each other. Their houses were cramped and dirty, far from pretty.

As they approached the atrium area, Bentley insisted on throwing out more data about how the space was originally an alley called Holden Court before the renovation in 1992 joined the two Marshall Field's buildings together.

"One more item I'm sure you'd be most interested in," Bentley interjected.

Oh, brother, not more, thought Kevin.

"This marvelous Victorian fountain was originally designed by the famous architect, Daniel Burnhan, the gentleman responsible for the original layout of the city of Chicago."

Kevin didn't give a damn. The dripping water only made him want to pee.

They descended the escalator. He finally was allowed to enter the candy alcove, where Bentley introduced him to an African American named Randall Danders, who was a seasoned employee.

"Carry on, Danders," Bentley said, before exiting.

Determined to make a good impression, Kevin listened intently to his instructor, who filled him in on the intricacies of working the scale, as well as the prices and sizes of the *Frango* offerings.

Kevin was exactly where he wanted to be, right near the escalators and elevators. He'd make friends with the guards and get a look at the security system.

It worked out well. He even had some free time. On some of his breaks, he took the escalator to the first floor where he sat and gazed at the flowing water of the fountain. It had a mesmerizing effect. The shoppers also seemed drawn to the famous fountain and stopped to rest alongside it. Some threw in coins and made wishes. He wondered what they wished for, especially those who looked too rich to need anything.

After a week of dispensing candy to pleased customers, who walked away smiling and carrying their trademarked, multi-striped green bags, Kevin considered himself a pro.

Another customer approached the candy counter. Smiling, he snapped to attention, while inside, he snarled. He must come off as a model employee, although his previously unused facial muscles hurt from so much smiling.

By the end of Kevin's second week, Bentley stopped with a progress report. "Mr. Gordon, I hear you're doing extremely well. Mr. Danders has received nothing but compliments on your behavior. Everyone agrees you're most charming and helpful. One dear lady remarked how you went out of your way to ensure additional containers were delivered to her. Now that's the kind of service we're noted for.

"You're doing so well, I think it's time for you to be on your own. You should be very proud of yourself. We just might be able to use you after the Christmas rush, if you so desire."

Over my dead body, Kevin thought. This little venture was wearing mighty thin. He was tired of being ultra pleasant to little, old ladies who dickered over the kind of itty bitty candies they wanted to buy.

"Thank you, Mr. Bentley," Kevin murmured. "You've been most kind. I strive to do my best."

He had another ace in his hole, a way to pour it on thick. He'd overheard one of his co-workers talking about the candy. Now he could display his knowledge. "I must say, Mr. Bentley, these *Frango* mints intrigue me. The candies are out of this world. No wonder over a million pounds are sold each year to six continents."

The man's eyes lit up. "Splendid, Mr. Gordon. I applaud your interest and diligence. You'll make a fine addition to our permanent staff."

It didn't take much to make this dolt happy. Would Bentley be as thrilled if he learned what Godfrey Gordon really had up his sleeves?

The time was drawing near for Callaway's appearance. Soon the masquerade would end. Before that, there was still a small matter to arrange.

"By the way, Mr. Bentley, I was thinking about that promotion. Wouldn't it be a wonderful gesture if Fields provided, gratis to Danny Callaway, the MVP, his choice of candy the last night? I'd be most delighted to be of service to him."

"My, my, Mr. Gordon, I must say you do come up with some splendid suggestions. That would be a fine touch indeed, a marvelous parting surprise for our guest."

A surprise indeed, Kevin thought.

"Sir, could you please get me three pounds of original *Frango* mints?" a wavering voice piped in. "I mustn't forget my Bingo friends. This will make a lovely gift, don't you think?"

Kevin gritted his teeth and hastened to follow the biddy's bidding. It wouldn't be long. He could do it. He'd smile and act polite, though he'd like nothing more than to grab her by the ears, drag her up the escalator and smash her skull against the cast iron fountain.

Chapter Thirty-One
Danny

DANNY'S FINGER HESITATED on the doorbell. The McGuires had invited him over for Thanksgiving. He'd run out of excuses to decline. Though it was already a year-and-a-half since he'd lost Cathy and the baby, he still didn't feel right about being around her family.

The door swung open.

"How are you, Danny?" Ted asked, reaching out his hand.

"Okay, I guess."

What other response could he give? Should he say what he really felt? *I'm miserable. I can't sleep. I still miss Cathy and Sean.*

Ted took his son-in-law's coat just as Nancy appeared. When she looked at Danny, her eyes filled with tears. She blinked rapidly. "Happy Thanksgiving," she said, kissing him on the check, then turning her head. "I'll go and check the turkey."

With a muffled sob, she fled. Maybe he shouldn't have come. His presence was too much of a reminder.

Ted stood there with the coat in his hands. "I'll just put this away," he said awkwardly. "Danny, why don't you join Dora in the family room?"

Things were not off to a good start. This holiday would be difficult. Everyone still suffered. No one had forgotten.

Well, what did he expect? In a way, it was comforting to know he wasn't alone. Perhaps by banding together they'd gain strength. He wondered if Dora fared any better than the others.

He bit his lip at the thought of seeing her again. They hadn't parted on the best of terms, and it was his fault. He had much atoning to do. Bracing himself for a confrontation, he stepped into the family room. She sat quietly on the leather couch and staring somberly into the fireplace.

"How are you, Dora?" he asked, slipping down beside her.

The crackle of the logs was the only sound in the room. The silence lengthened.

Finally, she said, "I'm getting by."

He couldn't fault Dora for the terse answer. He was lucky she even spoke to him after the way he'd treated her. Sneaking a glance at her hooded features, he watched the firelight flicker across her face, making its planes look more mysterious, her amber eyes more golden. She shone like a goddess, though her lips were tightly drawn.

He remembered another time when those lips had opened wide with passion. Thinking of that night was dangerous. He dare not tell Dora he cared. By making that sacrifice, he'd provide the ultimate proof of his love.

Love? Yes, it was true. He'd always loved her. Not as a substitute for Cathy, but as a special, unique being unto herself.

Deep inside her was a core of strength, barely concealed beneath her obvious femininity. That force drew Danny to her, though it would scare off many men. At the moment, his entire body felt attuned to her. He luxuriated in her alluring scent. It filled his waiting nostrils, unnerving his resolve. His ears strained for the tones of her soft, assured voice. His arms braced to hold her.

Dinner was called.

They sat beside each other. Each time she passed him a dish, her tapered fingers lingered on his a bit longer than necessary. With each contact, voltage singed his arm. Those fingers had touched him before, had soothed and done more. They'd made him feel things he shouldn't. Remembering made his face grow hot.

Apparently her parents didn't notice, which was just as well. They'd never understand. How could they, when he didn't understand it himself?

Ted sat at the head of the table, putting on a brave front, steering the conversation to a safe and happy course. "I'm proud of our Dora. She had quite a number of offers, yet she set up her shingle with her old dad. She's doing quite well for herself I might add." His eyes lit with pride.

Danny also felt proud, but for another reason. Dora was kind, a trait that made her all the more lovable. She'd held the power to strike out on her own, yet she'd not wielded it.

She was a confident woman, capable of making her own decisions. Her only failing might be her feelings for Danny. That is, if she still cared.

Without thinking, Danny threw her a tender look. He immediately regretted it. He shouldn't offer her hope.

Her brows knit in puzzlement. Uncertainty clouded her features. Understandably, his mixed signals threw her off.

With heart hammering, he turned from the hopeful face. He wanted her, God help him, yet he must be strong and resist.

Nancy broke into his thoughts. "Danny, I read that, in a few weeks, you'll be donating your services at Marshall Field's for Children's Memorial."

"Well, I like to do my part, Nancy. Those children need all the help they can get."

He tried not to think of one particular child whom he missed terribly. Sean was gone, though Danny still found it hard to accept. His child's life had been cut too short. They'd never even gotten to know each other. At least by helping other children, he could prolong their lives, assuring their parents wouldn't miss the experience of seeing them grow up.

Nancy McGuire's face assumed a wistful expression. "I remember the first time we took Cathy and Dora to the Walnut Room. They looked up at the big tree with such shiny, bright eyes. And then, you should have seen their expressions when the waitress set down those cute, little ice cream snowmen with the coconut on top." Her voice shook. "It seems like only yesterday."

"We did have some wonderful times, Mom," Dora said, reaching across the table and pressing her mother's hand into hers. "We need to remember the good. That's how Cathy would've wanted it."

"I know, dear," Nancy said. "Sometimes it's awfully hard."

Silence descended. For a brief period they'd been able to forget.

Ted voiced his emotions aloud. "I try to go on. I have the best wife I could ever deserve and the most wonderful daughter." He glanced at Danny. "And also a great son-in-law. Even so, every time I start to feel happy, I get scared. I remember what's happened. It grabs me by the throat. I think of Cathy and my grandson. I can't be happy, no matter how hard I try."

Ted collapsed, putting his head in his hands. Giant sobs racked his shoulders. Nancy pushed back her chair and rushed to his side. Their brave attempt to celebrate the holiday had failed.

This was a private moment. Danny wondered if he should leave.

"They should be alone. Why don't we go into the other room?" Dora whispered.

They retired to the family room where they sat on the couch again and stared at the fire. Danny shuddered, picturing the flames licking his wife and child.

A small movement beside him brought him to. Thank God, Dora had survived. He remembered how happy he'd been when he'd heard the news. He still couldn't get over the scare. He slowly turned and looked deep into her eyes. Right now he'd like to crush her against him and never let go.

She looked back at him with hope, then seemed to gather herself together. "Danny, this is taking my last ounce of courage, but I've got to say it. Since that first day when Cathy brought you home to dinner, I've loved you. Even if it had been possible, I'd never have separated the two of you, no matter how much I wanted you. I loved my sister. Even now, if somehow I could bring her back and never have you, I'd do it."

Dora's eyes filled. She fought to control a quaver in her voice. Danny's heart went out to her.

"We know that could never be," he said.

She swallowed and continued on, despite his interruption. "Losing Cathy and the baby made me realize just how precious and short life is. No matter how much we try to fool ourselves, no one is guaranteed tomorrow. At this point, with everything horrible that's happened, I need something good in my life. You're that something, that someone I need. Am I wrong to bring this up? Could you ever feel something for me, even a little?"

He stared at Dora proudly. It had cost her a lot to say that. He wanted her so fiercely it hurt.

With unwavering eyes, Dora bravely faced him. Those amber pools drew him in, tempting him to forget his vow. Her pull on him was tremendous. God help him, he was weakening. When he'd been away from her, he'd thought he could resist. Face to face was a different matter.

"Yes, Dora, I could and I do feel a great deal for you."

To confirm his statement, he slid his hand into her long, soft hair. He drew his mouth toward her parted lips, then hungrily pressed his own lips to them. A flash-fire roared through him.

He'd had her before. He remembered everything about her—her warmth, her touch and her smell.

A strangled moan escaped her. It reminded him of pain. That awakened him. She mustn't get hurt. He had to show reason.

Dropping his hand from her hair, he pulled away.

"I'm sorry, Dora. I still have dangerous business to attend to. It wouldn't be fair to make you wait."

Disappointment, swiftly followed by comprehension, flickered in her eyes. "Danny, no, you still can't be thinking of..."

"Yes, Dora, I am. Not one of us is safe until that bastard's destroyed."

"Don't go after him. You could get killed. Leave it to the police."

Danny emitted a short laugh. "The cops can't help. Notice how effectively they've apprehended him. Unless he's finished off, there's no reason to believe I—or anyone I love—will be safe. Weren't Cathy and the baby enough? What if he returns for more?"

She silently gazed back. He didn't like scaring her, but he had to.

"And what about you, Dora? If he discovered I love you, would you be gone, too? Well, I don't care to find that out."

She took a deep breath and looked him squarely in the eyes. "If I said I wouldn't love you for pursuing this, would you stop?"

It made him sick to think he could be throwing her love away, but he had no choice. "Dora, don't ask that. I don't want to refuse you. This is something I have to do. I must hunt Kevin down. I must destroy him like the animal he is. You can't stop me. No one can."

Dora sighed. "I knew the answer, but I had to try. Danny, I can't help you find Kevin, but I can do something better."

"What's that, Dora?"

"I'll pray for you," she said. "My prayer will be that you'll come back safely to me."

DANNY COULDN'T FORGET Dora's words. She loved him. That made him happy, yet sad. If Cathy hadn't died, he'd never have considered Dora, no matter how attracted to her he was. It wouldn't have been right.

It was difficult to acknowledge, but he must face it—Cathy and Sean belonged to another life. Still, he couldn't ignore they'd existed. They must not have died in vain. He would not let Kevin go free. Once that business was dealt with, Danny could try and reconstruct what he had left of his tangled life.

Dora had said she'd wait, but for how long? What if he spent the rest of his days hunting down Kevin Green? He'd had little success so far. He'd hired a private investigator, who'd secured an illegal wire tap on Derek Green's line, but the son never called. His quarry didn't use credit cards or frequent old hangouts. The only lead was that Kevin had once turned up on Madison Street, posing as a bum, but then had disappeared. With every false lead, Danny felt torn.

Finally, after a month's work, the private eye admitted defeat.

Now it was up to Danny to find Kevin, but he didn't know where to start. The man could be anywhere—down the block or out of the country.

He missed Cathy, yet more often than not, he found his thoughts straying to Dora's golden knowing eyes and lush body. She was very much alive. The temptation was great. He need only abandon his search, go to her and build a new life. Then he could be with her, inside her. At the thought, he broke into a sweat.

He knew such bliss would be short-lived and carry a heavy price. He dare not play with Dora's life. A wife and child in a thousand pieces were more than enough. Kevin must never find out about Dora.

So he continued his search alone. It hurt deeply, but he often revisited the explosion scene, hoping Kevin would someday show up. You'd think he'd be drawn there sooner or later. If so, Danny would be waiting, the cold steel of the automatic bulging in his pocket.

But, he didn't live in a vacuum. All around him, normal life had resumed. Danny pretended he was part of the real world. Doing charity work helped lighten his load.

A few weeks before Christmas, he stood, unrecognized and alone, blending in with the excited crowd staring at the window displays at Marshall Field's. As usual, the store had outdone itself. Figures from a fairytale land skated on make-believe ice under man-made snowflakes. Music rippled onto the sidewalk.

Next to him, a father hoisted his son atop his shoulders. The child pointed and laughed. Danny's eyes filled. That could have been him and Sean. He pressed his lids together tightly before opening them again and staring ahead. He had to quit thinking of himself. He had to focus elsewhere. Tonight, his goal was to make special youngsters happy—those who couldn't fend for themselves.

He glanced toward the corner. The green, weathered clock pointed at seven-thirty. It was time. He wended his way through the happy crowd and slipped over to the Washington Street entrance. At the door, he was greeted by an affable looking bald man, who held out his hand in greeting.

"I'm Morris Bentley. You must be Daniel Callaway. I must commend you, sir. This is a wonderful thing you're doing. The response is overwhelming. From the moment the publicity began, we've been bombarded with requests. Each and every reservation has been filled. The tickets could easily have run higher."

"Well, let's hope our efforts aren't wasted. If just one child recovers, it'll be worth it."

"You're very right, sir."

They stepped inside.

"By the way, what do you think of our humble quarters?" Bentley's arms encircled the broad expanse. His voice understandably invited praise.

While Danny assessed the high ceilinged store, memories rushed over him.

The man stood still, waiting for his reply.

Danny came to. "I've always held a great affection for Marshall Field and Company. It symbolizes what's best of Chicago," Danny assured him.

Mr. Bentley beamed. "We're honored you feel that way, sir."

They trekked across the magnificent marble floor, their footsteps muffled by the red carpeting running down its center. As they passed through a golden archway, Bentley gestured toward giant green vases adorned with red gleaming balls and dancing statues twirling along the side of the aisles.

"May I draw your attention, sir, to the fabulous Christmas decorations that our able craftsmen began designing over a year ago?"

Danny nodded in appreciation.

"Now, let's go a little out of our way," Bentley said. "We must visit the fountain." Passing the service desk, they proceeded into the atrium, the home of the Burnham fountain.

Danny gazed upwards in awe at the Romanesque columns ending in gilded edges. Two balconies with gold railings stood in front of huge lighted windows. The place resembled a palace.

Danny threw a coin into the water for good luck. Heavens knows, he could use some.

His mind drifted. When he was young, his family couldn't afford to shop here. Still, they'd excitedly made annual trips around Christmas just to soak in the grandeur. Mom and Dad had always splurged on a box of *Frango* mints. He and his sister never waited until they got home, but devoured them as they sat across from each other on the subway.

"This is so good," he heard his sister say, as, with bright shining eyes, she savored each piece.

He sighed. That was long ago. Those days would never return.

"Well, it's time to get down to business," Bentley announced.

They made a U-turn to the elevator and proceeded up to the seventh floor. At the Walnut Room, Bentley introduced Danny to the photographer, Robert Langley, who was readying the lighting and equipment. The man fumbled, almost dropping his tripod.

Danny tried to put him at ease. "You know more about this than I do. I'll stand or sit or do whatever you want."

It still surprised him that he was a celebrity. He didn't feel like one. He was no better than anyone else. In many ways, he was worse.

He doubted if the nervous Mr. Langley held a hidden agenda in his heart. Also, only a select few could say they'd been responsible for the deaths of others—only people like Danny. He wouldn't think of that now. He was here to assist in a worthwhile cause and he'd make the most of it. Sick children counted on him.

He listened patiently as Bentley outlined the procedure. To be on the safe side, two guards would flank Danny and provide protection at all times. Since the store was officially closed, ticket bearers would be greeted at the designated door, then escorted up the solitary operating elevator. On the seventh floor, they'd receive further instructions.

Individual pictures cost fifty dollars. Families were allowed one group picture, but this privilege would carry the cost of fifty dollars per person.

The session would soon begin. From his position next to the big tree, Danny heard the sound of hushed, excited voices. He smiled as the enthusiasm of the fans rubbed off on him. The first in line advanced, nervously assessing their hero. He greeted everyone cordially and tried to put them at ease.

As he smilingly balanced children on his knee, a feeling of warmth stole over him. He found himself laughing. It was exhilarating to know he was making others happy, especially in such a festive location, beneath the famed forty-five foot tall Marshall Field's Christmas tree.

Tony and Tracy approached with little Angela, all decked out in a pink fluffy dress. Matching ribbons tied back her dark, curly locks.

"Danny boy, you fit in real well. Have you considered working for Field's?" Tony asked.

Danny laughed, taking the ribbing in stride. "You never know. I may need to. I'm keeping all options open."

Next came Ritchie's family. The blond-haired twin boys ran around in circles and almost darted off before Ritchie could catch up with them.

Mr. Langley's lips pursed. Danny felt sorry for him. He obviously found it difficult to deal with children. In his line of business, that wasn't good.

"Remember Uncle Danny? Okay, boys, just sit here for a few minutes until the picture's taken," Marilyn pleaded.

Langley ran his fingers through his frazzled hair several times before he finally managed to get off his shot. "Mrs. Corcoran, your picture will be ready before Christmas."

With an innocent smile, Ritchie turned toward his friend. "Now

I'll have proof I knew the famous Danny Callaway. My future grandchildren will be mighty impressed."

"What are you talking about? You've got millions of pictures of me," Danny reminded him with a mock shove. "Seriously though, the hospital is grateful for your donation."

Ritchie face sobered. "I thank God I've got two healthy children."

On cue, one twin tugged at his father's sleeve, while the other one whined. Which was Donald? Which Joseph? Danny still had trouble telling the boys apart. He'd have to spend more time with them.

"I better go. See you around," Ritchie said, hauling off his mischief-makers.

Countless others followed. The remaining hours flew by, as did the next three evenings.

On Friday night, Robert Langley sighed with relief as he disassembled his tripod.

"Well, that's a wrap," he said, wiping his brow with his handkerchief and gathering up the rest of his equipment.

Poor man, Danny thought. *If he isn't careful, he'll have a nervous breakdown.* Before Danny could blink, the photographer had disappeared.

For one last time, Danny glanced around the Walnut Room, taking in the myriad spotlights shining over the majestic, sparkling pine tree with its twelve thousand ornaments and fifteen thousand lights. The walnut paneling gleamed like new, while the carpeting beneath him was decorated with elegant fleur-de-lis.

The room was magnificent. He'd had a great time here forgetting himself in the satisfaction of doing good for others. For a short while, he'd succeeded in his goal and taken his mind off his problems.

Now came the letdown. Soon he'd trudge back to his lonely, undecorated hotel suite. He was alone and had nothing to celebrate. His eyelids grew heavy, maybe from his turn of thought. He'd make an early night of it. First, he had some goodbyes to say. He thanked the security guards for their help, then looked around for Bentley. Where had the man gone?

On cue, Mr. Bentley rounded the corner by the escalator and approached Danny. "Oh, Mr. Callaway..." Before Bentley could finish the sentence, the lights on the tree flickered. "We can't have this. What's going on?" Bentley asked, turning to the guards.

"I'm not sure, sir," one of them said.

They all conferred, engrossed in solving the mystery.

"I think I'll be on my way now," Danny said.

Mr. Bentley smiled absently. "Yes, all right Mr. Callaway. I want to thank you for your services. We appreciate everything you've done. Oh, and by the way, please stop at the lower level candy shop on the way out. Whatever you choose is on the house. Our man, Godfrey Gordon, will assist you."

"Thanks, I'll do that," Danny said, smiling.

He stepped onto the empty elevator. He had to hand it to Bentley. The man thought of everything. The candy was a nice gesture.

Anticipation of the treat made him hungry.

Chapter Thirty-Two
Danny and Kevin

DANNY STEPPED OFF the elevator onto the lower level of the store. A chocolate mint scent lured him in the direction of the alcove. As he drew near, he made out the distinctive green-wrapped *Frango* mint candy boxes on the shelves. The sight increased his appetite.

He stepped inside, but didn't get far before discovering something quaint, but nice. Plaster replicas of the Marshall Field's clocks sat on one of the shelves. Now that was ingenuous. He'd never noticed them before. Were they candy holders? Distracted, he picked one up and turned it around in his hand.

The next thing he knew, he heard a crack. The clock burst into tiny pieces and fell to the floor. Puzzled, he bent down to look. Something whizzed past his ear, then landed with a thwack on a nearby candy box, toppling it over.

He whirled. What was happening?

Quick comprehension dawned. He'd done target practice and knew the sounds. He was under attack.

He leaned to the side of the display, craning for a glimpse of the gunman. A chestnut haired, mustached man stood next to the scale with his arm upraised.

Who was it? Who would want to shoot him? There was but one person he could think of. From here it didn't look like Kevin, but Danny hadn't seen him in a while. He didn't have time to solve the puzzle as a bullet winged past.

How could he have guessed the showdown would be here of all places? He had no defense. His weapon lay in a sock drawer at the Palmer House.

"Callaway, you're dead meat."

The familiar voice sent chills up his spine and poured fire into his gut. He would not be a victim like the others. He turned, but his pursuer was close behind, blocking his exit. The only direction was up. Dodging bullets, Danny flung himself onto the escalator. He jumped up the stairs two at a time. What should he do? How could he escape?

If only he were prepared to face Kevin Green head on, but again his enemy had surprised him. He must think fast to gain the advantage.

What type of gun was Kevin using? Danny hadn't gotten a good look, but from a brief glimpse, it appeared to be a Magnum.

How many bullets were left? Five or six? He had no time for arithmetic while he was fleeing for his life. Another shot rang out. He twisted and stooped, almost falling off the escalator.

The situation was deadly and frustrating. He hated to run like a coward, but until the cartridge was spent, he had no choice. The problem was how to live that long. The thought lent him extra speed as he ascended up the escalator with Kevin steadily gaining.

Where were the security men? Were they still clustered around the precious tree? The lighting snafu had to be Kevin's doing—a simple matter for a proficient bomb-maker.

Another thought flashed through Danny's mind. Had Kevin tampered with the security system? Did the monitor reflect something that wasn't happening? You'd think by now someone would have noticed the commotion. Help should have arrived.

He was alone and would have to fight his own war. He couldn't give up. Innocent people had died. He had to make it stop. Kevin must be wiped out. If necessary, he'd go down himself in the process.

Another bullet flew by, singeing the back of Danny's hair. That was close. Where would the next one land? He dare not think of it. The cartridge had to run out soon.

He continued his climb, reaching the fourth floor landing. Finally he was blessed by a sweet sound. *Click.*

"You motherfucker," Kevin swore.

Good. Now Kevin had to stop and reload. That would take valuable time. For now, he was weaponless. It was Danny's chance. He swiped at Kevin's hand. The gun fell, clanking as it bounced down the stairs of the escalator.

Roaring, Kevin threw himself at Danny. Rolling, they rained blows on each other, then staggered upright.

Once again Danny gazed into the coldest green eyes he'd ever seen. Time flashed back. He was a young man standing in the courtroom, facing an evil monster, feeling afraid and mad. It was the same as then, yet importantly different. Years had passed. Now he was a grown man capable of destroying Kevin. That's what he'd vowed to do and he'd do it. The day of reckoning had come. Kevin would pay, but not for the original crime of which he'd not been guilty. Danny lashed out with his fist, connecting with Kevin's chin, knocking him sideways toward the marble floor.

Kevin proved surprisingly agile. Before hitting the landing, he rolled away, then lurched upright at Danny, knuckles boring into Danny's abdomen.

Danny's breath gave out and he gasped for air. Kevin moved in.

He had to do something, but it was hard when you couldn't breathe. Taking hasty gulps, Danny stumbled down the escalator with Kevin trailing behind. On the second floor, he jumped off and dashed to the right into men's sportswear. Sure enough, Kevin followed.

Grasping a zippered sweater jacket off a rack, Danny flung it over Kevin's head, then wrestled him to the floor. He jumped astride him, pounding Kevin's shoulders against the marble.

With almost superhuman strength, Kevin thrashed, managing to rip the jacket off his head and throw it over Danny's eyes instead. Danny couldn't see the knee that crashed into his groin, but he could sure feel it. This was what it meant to see stars.

"You bastard," he said, elbowing his enemy in the neck.

Kevin retaliated by kicking Danny's cheek. They exchanged blow for blow, with neither of them weakening. One, then the other, gained then lost the advantage, as they retraced their steps out of men's sportswear. Danny tripped and felt himself being pushed backward against the top bar of the escalator. Kevin's hands tightened over his throat. The world spun. He couldn't breathe, yet the hold on his throat tightened. Any minute he'd fall. Was this how it would end? Here of all places?

Through a red film he heard Kevin speak. "You fuckin' prick. You put me in prison and wrecked my life. Callaway, before you go, here's some tidbits to take to your grave. You know the auto accident Senior Day when your parents were killed? It was supposed to have been you, not them. My friend, Billy Holliday, drained the brake fluid from your car as a favor to me."

A feeling of unreality gripped Danny. A picture of Mary Alice in her prom dress flashed through his mind. His parents joined her, along with Cathy and Sean.

Kevin crowed. "You've lived on borrowed time ever since. Your number was up long ago, Danny boy. I'm just getting around to finishing the job."

Danny's mind reeled.

His enemy laughed. "What do you say to that?"

Kevin momentarily released his grip.

"You're not human," Danny croaked out, as hatred overwhelmed him.

"Thanks for the compliment. Oh, I've got more news for you."

Kevin grasped Danny's chin in his hand. With bright eyes glaring into Danny's, he said, "By the way, that kid of yours—the one you thought died in the explosion? Well, I gave him to the wife of a deserving crook. He'll be raised as a murderer's son. Pretty neat, huh?"

Joy, then despair filled Danny. The son he'd thought was dead was alive, yet he might not see him again. If so, Sean would be raised by the worst elements. At the prospect, adrenaline pumped through Danny. He had to fight for his son. He must survive and rescue him.

He pushed forward against Kevin with all his might, but Kevin returned the push.

Danny fell backwards, over the side of the escalator, crashing against the outer side of the balcony. As he fell into space, he groped for some kind of hold. His right hand miraculously closed over the lower ledge of the balcony. All the tireless basketball workouts stood him in good stead as he swung the left side of his body forward and grasped the ledge with his other hand as well.

He dangled, his legs slipping on the smooth column below. A thump told him Kevin had jumped onto the other side of the balcony. Danny had to do something and fast. Was it his imagination or did the water from the fountain below gurgle louder than before?

With all his might, he heaved upwards as if he were doing a chin-up. His wrists, biceps, all the way up his arms to his shoulders, as well as his back, felt the strain as he fought to raise himself. Sweat dripped down his cheeks, but he couldn't wipe it away.

His left knee slipped off the ledge, but his right one connected and he was able to pull the left up. On his knees, he teetered and reached for the rail. He breathed a sigh of relief as his fingers closed over the gold metal.

Before he could rise, a foot smashed his left hand off the rail. Kevin had climbed over the balcony rail to the outer ledge. Pain screeched up Danny's arm. He lost his hard-earned balance.

Again he swung, this time holding onto the bcttom of the rail with his right hand. The pressure of the ledge dug into his abdomen. A shadow from above moved closer. He had one hope left. As Kevin's foot descended, Danny chopped as hard as he could at Kevin's ankle with his free hand.

Kevin teetered, then lost his balance.

Danny ducked as Kevin cartwheeled over his head and plummeted past him.

"Nooooooo," Kevin bellowed.

Danny fought the urge to look down. In the background, he heard the sound of bone striking iron, followed by a splash.

The sounds, instead of making him happy, increased his terror. Would he be the next to crash into the elegant Victorian fountain? Desperately he swung the left side of his body back toward the railing and groped for it. His sweating fingers barely grasped the gold metal. His left foot almost slipped off the bottom, but somehow he steadied himself and got his other foot in place solidly on the outside ledge. When he'd caught his breath, he swung over the rail to the safe side.

Danny stood still, waiting for his equilibrium to return, trying to calm his racing heart. Thank God he'd made it. He felt like crying.

He couldn't dally around and feel sorry for himself. A voice told him to check on Kevin and find out if his enemy was really destroyed. He had to be sure. With quaking legs, he made his way down the escalator and stumbled off. As he stepped onto the main floor, he saw a body sprawled face up in the fountain.

With dreadful fascination, Danny moved closer to the rushing water. Kevin had to be dead, didn't he? Danny drew up to the fountain and stopped, blinking blood and sweat from his eyes as he gazed at the unmoving form. Surprisingly, Kevin's eyelids were open His eyes followed Danny's movements. It seemed impossible, yet the devil still lived.

Rage filled Danny. Kevin had almost killed him. His parents and wife, plus an innocent guard had been murdered. His baby was stolen. Through it all, the bastard had survived. Danny wouldn't allow it. Kevin deserved to die. With deadly intent, Danny gazed into the comprehending eyes of the man who would now be his victim. Kevin lay defenseless, awaiting the blow which would rock him into hell's eternity.

Danny's arm rose to administer Kevin's just punishment. As it descended, he heard a voice say, "'Do not avenge yourselves; leave that to God's wrath, for it is written: Vengeance is mine; I will repay, says the Lord... Do not be conquered by evil but conquer evil with good.'"

Torn, his eyes filled with tears. He'd sworn to God he'd abandon revenge, but under the circumstances, keeping that promise was asking too much.

He looked down at Kevin and saw himself lying there instead. Once upon a time, Kevin had been released from prison, healthy and whole. His entire life had stretched ahead of him to enjoy, yet the corruption of vengeance had eaten his soul and destroyed his happiness.

Did he want the same fate? If Danny struck that final blow, how could he live with himself? Would he be as evil as the monster before him? Guilt would eat at him constantly, eroding his joy. His father had told him as much after the trial, when he'd said, "Two wrongs don't make a right." Dad, in his wisdom, had realized the consequences of letting vengeance rule.

But what about the harm Kevin had done? Shouldn't he be punished for that?

Danny wavered, then lowered his arm. It wasn't for him to decide. Leave it to God and the judicial system.

Footsteps rushed across the marble floor. Uniformed men approached. Bentley anxiously peered at him. "My dear Mr. Callaway, are you all right?"

Danny stood there numbly as Bentley rambled on. "This is dreadful, most dreadful. The monitors were misaimed. When they were readjusted, we couldn't believe our eyes. Two of our security guards were knocked out on the lower level. Then I saw someone trying to kill you. I say, sir, are you positive you're all right?"

Danny took a shaky breath, then pointed at the fountain. "I think you should be more concerned about him."

Bentley switched his attention to the fountain's occupant. "My goodness, that's our Godfrey Gordon. I had no idea. He seemed such a pleasant chap."

Bentley gazed with distaste at the unmoving water-soaked figure, then shook his head. "Well, we'll have to get an ambulance to attend to Mr. Gordon. I think he may have hit his head. It's a wonder he's still alive." The look on Bentley's face indicated he wished otherwise.

"Yes, it's a wonder," Danny said.

Bentley couldn't guess how true that was.

Chapter Thirty-Three
Danny

AS DANNY STOOD by, the paramedics loaded Kevin onto an ambulance. When it pulled away, he heaved a sigh of relief. It was over. His enemy had been defeated.

He'd fought the toughest battle of his life and had emerged triumphant. He could have swiped Kevin into eternity, but had resisted. By facing temptation and conquering it, he'd regained his soul and recaptured his integrity. Now he was at peace with himself, knowing he'd done the right thing.

His whole life stretched ahead of him. He could do whatever he pleased. If he wished, he could play basketball, not as a crutch but out of enjoyment. Also, the path was clear for him to claim what was his. He'd witnessed too much evidence that life was fragile. From this day forward, he'd enjoy each moment to its fullest. It was time to get on with his life. He'd earned the right.

First, he'd find Sean no matter what. Then he'd ask Sean's godmother to marry him.

He pictured Dora's smiling face. He could smell her perfume. He had to be in love.

"DO YOU, DANNY Callaway, take this woman, Dora McGuire, to be your lawfully wedded wife, in sickness and in health?"

With heart swelling, Danny looked into the shining amber eyes of the golden goddess standing beside him. Dora, dear Dora. She was so right for him. Together, step by step they'd construct a new life, one of laughter and love. Of course, the past would always be a part of them and they'd never forget it. However, ahead of them beckoned a golden future. Picturing the evening to come, he kissed his beautiful bride. Tonight they'd make love with no regrets. Perhaps they'd even make a baby.

He glanced toward Nancy McGuire, who was holding onto a fidgeting Sean. Danny still couldn't get over the miracle that his son had been spared.

It had taken a week of questioning prisoners before Detective DeVino found his target. When asked about the whereabouts of Sean, lifer Anthony Edwards's eye had twitched. DeVino didn't give up. "If we find out you've lied, you'll get solitary."

Edwards cracked. "My boy was killed. My wife deserved another baby. Kevin said he'd give her one. He didn't say from where."

That's all DeVino had to hear. He pealed over in his squad car and rescued Sean from the tearful Miranda.

When Danny saw his child for the first time since that fateful weekend, tears streamed down his face. His son stood still, looking up at him curiously.

"Sean, it's Daddy," Danny said before gathering him up and hugging him close to his heart.

He'd forever be in the officer's debt. It was as if his son had been reborn. Sean was Cathy's gift to them. He and Dora would cherish the child who was conceived the afternoon in the flower shop.

Considering everything that had happened, the news of Danny and Dora's love for each other had not upset the elder McGuires. Practicality had prevailed. Life was as fragile as a bubble. Everyone agreed that Danny and Dora deserved happiness.

"I'm sure Cathy would've wanted it this way," Ted had said, swiping back a tear.

Danny glanced to the side of the altar where Tony and Ritchie, along with Dora's bridesmaids, Margaret Lynley and her daughter, Tory, beamed profusely.

As *Ode to Joy* played, Danny walked arm-in-arm with his new wife down the aisle.

Outside the church, Tony grasped his hand. "Hey, Danny, all the luck in the world, man. You've made a great choice. Dora, take care of my good friend," he ordered.

She nodded serenely.

Tracy reached up to kiss Danny, laughingly predicting, "You've met your match, Danny. Dora will keep you in line. She'll give back as much as she gets."

From the church, they tooted their way to a private luncheon reception. The three hours of celebration seemed a lifetime, he was that eager to get away. He hadn't made love to Dora since that horrible day of Cathy's murder, one that was forever etched in his memory.

This time their union must be perfect. He owed it to her. He had much to make up for. Gone were his vows of revenge. His new vow was to fill Dora's life with love. Luckily he had a week's hiatus from basketball. He and his bride, along with Sean, whom they couldn't bear to part with for even a few minutes, rode in a limousine to the airport where they boarded a plane to Florida.

Dora had said, "Let's just go somewhere warm, where we can lay in the sun...that is, when we're not inside doing other things."

She wasn't afraid to admit her desire for him. That was one of the thousand things he loved about her.

THE BABY WAS asleep. Dora disappeared into the bedroom to put on something special.

The vision that reappeared turned Danny rock hard. Sparkling straps and wispy scraps outlined glowing round curves. Dora was a model of golden perfection.

He gazed spellbound as she stepped up to him. She was beautiful and all woman. He stood paralyzed as her hands cupped his face.

"Danny, my love," she murmured.

Her hand slipped into his hair. Helplessness invaded him. He was completely in her power, as her deft fingers lovingly discarded his clothing. Danny stood before Dora, his need clearly exposed. He wasn't afraid to exhibit the evidence of his love. He trusted this woman with his life. With her there would never be secrets.

Her fingertips reached down to capture their prize. Sparks ignited, about to explode.

"Dora," he groaned. "What are you doing to me?"

She smiled back innocently. "Whatever you want," she said.

Chapter Thirty-Four
Kevin

ALL KEVIN COULD do was stare. Stare at the blank ceiling. Stare at the white linens. Stare at the open door he could never walk out of. There were no guards posted as was usually the case with murderers in prison hospitals. With him, they weren't necessary.

As a child, he'd seen scary pictures of hell with its red and yellow scorching flames. The artists were wrong. Hell was not fire and heat. Hell was boredom and helplessness. Hell was lying here day after day, unable to move, thinking, but not being able to talk.

In the background, the damn clock kept ticking. He wanted to crash it against the wall, but couldn't.

Hunger gnawed at him, though the feeding tube continuously nourished him. Paralyzed from the nose down, he'd never again chew a juicy steak or taste a gooey pizza.

No one knew he could think. This morning he'd overheard the morning crew exchange raunchy jokes as they went about their cleaning.

One of them had shown twisted compassion. "Hey, let's go outside. Why get the stiff all stiff?"

Smiling knowingly, the other had shaken his head. "Are you kidding? That poor bastard doesn't understand anything. He couldn't get a hard-on if he tried. Everything's gone but his eyes."

They were wrong. Dead wrong. God help him, he could think. That's all he could do. Day after day, night after night, he lay still with his mind racing. Rage, hurt and frustration consumed him. Worst of all was the loss of hope. Though he thirsted for revenge, it would never be. It had chewed and destroyed him, yet the overpowering need still remained.

He must face the truth. It was the end of the line for Kevin Green. For the rest of his days, he'd lie here at Heartland Hospital with muscles and bones wasting. He couldn't even get up to go to the john, but had to wear diapers and smell his own filth.

The doctor had said Kevin's brain stem was injured when he struck the fountain.

When it had happened, Kevin had felt a sharp pain, then nothing.

He'd thought he'd die. Unable to move, except for his eyes, he'd lain still, wondering when he'd fall into hell.

Then Callaway had appeared with his arm upraised, ready to administer the final blow. For some incomprehensible reason, the bastard had lowered his arm. In his supreme goodness, the Great Callaway had spared the lowly Kevin Green.

Callaway probably thought he'd done Kevin a favor The joke was on both of them. Callaway had unknowingly dealt the harshest punishment of all—a revenge worse than death.

The shadows were thickening. It must be evening. One of the jokesters from the morning crew poked his head in. "Hey, poor Joe, the Cyclones are playing tonight. I'll turn on the game for you."

Kevin's eyes filled with revulsion. He shut his lids tight so he wouldn't see the screen, but it didn't help. Frank Monson's words still bored into his brain.

"The Universal Center's come alive. Looks like another spectacular play by Danny Callaway."

Kevin winced. The torture would never end.

~ * ~

Morgan Mandel

Morgan Mandel lives in a suburb of Chicago and works by day as an administrative assistant at a Chicago Loop law firm. Her writing office consists of a seat on the Metra, where she weaves mysteries and romances on a notebook computer. At home, when she's not reading or writing, Morgan watches action flicks with her husband, Paul, and participates in local festivals. She also confesses to a weakness for nickel slot machines. You can learn more about Morgan by visiting her web site at www.morganmandel.com